P9-APM-300

ARNOLD

Matthew Arnold (1822–88) was the son of the famous Dr Thomas Arnold, headmaster of Rugby. After a fairly carefree time as a student at Oxford, where he graduated in 1844 with second class honours, he spent several years travelling and writing experimental verse. His first volume of poetry was published in 1849 and surprised his friends and family with its concern for moral issues. It was his third volume, *Poems: A New Edition*, published in 1853, that established his reputation; this volume contains the famous Preface in which he rejected Romantic subjectivism.

Matthew Arnold wrote most of his poetry before he was thirty-three and all of it before the age of forty-five. In 1851 he became an inspector of schools, a position which he held throughout his life except for a ten-year period (1857–67) as Professor of Poetry at Oxford. Towards the end of this tenure he turned to writing prose; his poetry has never ceased to be widely read and enjoyed, but his influence as a social and literary critic and as a controversial thinker on religious and educational issues has also been felt far into this century.

Arnold

Poems

—————◆—————

Selected by Kenneth Allott
Introduction by Jenni Calder

PENGUIN BOOKS

Penguin Books Ltd, Harmondsworth, Middlesex, England
Viking Penguin Inc., 40 West 23rd Street, New York, New York 10010, U.S.A.
Penguin Books Australia Ltd, Ringwood, Victoria, Australia
Penguin Books Canada Ltd, 2801 John Street, Markham, Ontario, Canada L3R 1B4
Penguin Books (N.Z.) Ltd, 182–190 Wairau Road, Auckland 10, New Zealand

This selection first published 1954
Reprinted with a new introduction 1985

Made and printed in Great Britain by
Cox and Wyman Ltd, Reading
Typeset in Monotype Bell
Introduction reset by Merrion Letters, London

CONTENTS

CONTENTS

CONTENTS

INTRODUCTION

MATTHEW ARNOLD was born in 1822, the son of Thomas Arnold, headmaster of Rugby. He made up for the somewhat constrained atmosphere of Rugby by his liveliness as an undergraduate at Oxford, where he gained a reputation for being a dilettante. He graduated in 1844, and the following year was elected to a fellowship at Oriel. After a period of travel and unsettled experiment he became an inspector of schools in 1851, which was his life's career, except for ten years as Professor of Poetry at Oxford (1857–67). His job, though often dull and pedestrian, brought direct experience of educational methods (not only in England but in France and other European countries to which he was sent on special missions) and this influenced his larger involvement with the quality of culture and the responsibility of the cultured. In 1883–4 he went on a lecture tour of America.

His first poems, which surprised his friends and family by their concern with moral issues, were published in 1849. It was a third volume, *Poems: A New Edition* (1853), that made his reputation. Arnold held that poetry should be 'a criticism of life', but his own poetry was withdrawn in tone, and it was perhaps this, and his parallel emphasis on the educational importance of criticism, that led him to turn to prose as a more efficient analytical instrument. He regarded the spiritual death of Victorian England with a mind that was critical but humanist and sympathetic. He was confident that culture, which he saw as classless and universal, was the power that could save modern society from materialism. 'Culture and Anarchy' (1869) and 'Friendship's Garland' (1871) were the crucial essays in this discussion. His uncompromising analysis is sharpened by an ironic sense of humour and a brilliantly apt use of reference and quotation. He characterizes the upper, middle and working classes as Barbarians, Philistines and Populace, and shows how each is inadequate in its consciousness of proper actions and attitudes. He calls for 'sweetness and light', humanist sensitivity combined with intellectual toughness, and although he condemns middle-class complacency he sees that class as being the most competent to guide the nation's progress.

Arnold was the first to emphasize, in *Essays in Criticism* (1st series, 1865, 2nd series, 1888), the poet's position in society rather than his position in the artistic world. He closely associated the function of religion with that of the poet and in 'Literature and Dogma' (1873) and 'God and the Bible' (1875) he attacked dogmatism and conventional orthodoxy. He considered that the Bible was important as poetry, as a means of combating spiritual paralysis. His own poetry expresses less aggressively his sense of a widening gulf between the possibilities of belief and the facts of the modern world, although it is coloured by didacticism. His rhythms are solemn and often lax, and his language restrained and reflective. His poetry was a means of relating in more personal terms his own responses to the society he examined so vigorously in prose. The dominant mood is elegiac, a controlled and pulsing melancholy. 'Dover Beach' (1867), in which private happiness is woven with the calm relentlessness of the natural world and the large confusions of humanity, is an eloquent expression of this. Two of Arnold's best-known poems, 'The Scholar-Gypsy' (1853), about a seventeenth-century student who leaves Oxford to live amongst gypsies, and 'Thyrsis' (1866), written in memory of his close friend Arthur Hugh Clough, are a characteristic blend of an introspective contemplation of the countryside, personal doubts and a transcendent sadness. In the former Arnold, as he did frequently, used the bones of a traditional story to carry his own speculations. He often slowed his poems down to a grave and composed conclusion, even in the case of his major narrative poem 'Sohrab and Rustum' (1853), but it is the doubts and quiet pain that linger. There is a contradiction between Arnold's belief that poetry should deal with 'human actions', that situations in which 'the suffering finds no vent in action' are inadmissible and his own brooding, elegiac verse, and this contradiction was another reason for his giving up poetry for critical prose.

Arnold's refusal to compromise his absolute values is both the strength and the weakness of his thought. Critically, this provided a relentless weapon, but it rendered his constructive proposals imprecise. The reasons for his faith in culture were not always presented with absolute logic and clarity. Nevertheless he produced what was perhaps the most articulate expression of the Victorian malaise, and in his investigation of the intimate relationship between the arts, criticism and society he broke new ground and provided an influence that has been felt far into this century.

JENNI CALDER

NOTE ON THE TEXT AND
SELECTION

THE text of the present selection follows that of the three-volume Library Edition of Arnold's *Poems* in the reprint of 1888, the last issue of his verse with which the poet had anything to do. The text of the critical prefaces is from *Irish Essays* (1882). To make the selection I have dropped the Rugby and Oxford prize-poems, 'Balder Dead', almost all the sonnets of *New Poems* (1867), 'Merope' and 'Westminster Abbey', those two monuments to frigidity, and some of the lyrics, but the best of Arnold is here.

The order of the poems is new. Both Quiller-Couch's chronological arrangement in the Oxford Standard Authors edition and Arnold's plan in the Library Edition, followed by the editors of the Oxford edition, have their advantages. But the first separates poems that belong together, for example, the lyrics in 'Switzerland' and 'Faded Leaves', and has other inconveniences; and the second involves playing Arnold's game of dismissing to 'Early Poems' work that dissatisfied him and labelling genuinely early work misleadingly. There is no section of 'Early Poems' in the present text, and to 'Empedocles on Etna', which stands first here, and the three main divisions – 'Narrative Poems', 'Lyric Poems', and 'Elegiac Poems' – I have added two shorter sections of 'Sonnets' and 'Love Poems'. Inside each section the order is the chronological order of first publication in a volume, and these dates have been given in the 'Contents'.

Several poems first appeared in periodicals. For the dates of these appearances and for a detailed picture of the rather confusing make-up of Arnold's successive volumes of poetry – with their withdrawals, restorations, and frequent changes of title and position – the reader should consult Thomas B. Smart's *Bibliography* (1892), reprinted in Vol. XV of the Edition de Luxe (1903–4) of Arnold's *Works*.

KENNETH ALLOTT

CHRONOLOGICAL TABLE OF MATTHEW ARNOLD'S LIFE AND CHIEF PUBLICATIONS

1822   Born at Laleham-on-Thames on 24 December.

1828   Father appointed Headmaster of Rugby School.

1834   Fox How, near Ambleside, becomes holiday-home of the Arnolds. Wordsworth a neighbour.

1836   At Winchester College. First attempts at verse about this time.

1837   Removed to be under his father at Rugby.

1840   Rugby prize-poem, 'Alaric at Rome'. Elected to open scholarship at Balliol College, Oxford.

1841   In residence at Oxford. Beginning of intimacy with Clough. Dr Arnold appointed Regius Professor of Modern History at Oxford.

1842   Death of Dr Arnold on 12 June.

1843   Newdigate prize-poem, 'Cromwell', published

1844   B.A. (Second Class).

1845   Temporary assistant-master at Rugby. Elected Fellow Oriel College, Oxford, on 28 March.

1846   Visit to George Sand at Nohant in July.

1847   Private secretary to Lord Lansdowne.

1848   Visit to Switzerland in September. 'Tomorrow I repass the Gemmi and get to Thun: linger one day at the Hotel Bellevue for the sake of the blue eyes of one of its inmates . . .'

1849   *The Strayed Reveller and Other Poems* (26 February). Again visits Switzerland in September. 'I wrote . . . from this place last year . . . I am here in a curious and not altogether comfortable state.'

1850   Death of Wordsworth on 23 April.

1851   Appointed Inspector of Schools in April. Marries Frances Lucy Wightman on 10 June.

1852   *Empedocles on Etna and Other Poems* (October).

1853   *Poems. A New Edition* (including 'Sohrab and Rustum', 'The Scholar-Gipsy' and the famous critical Preface).

1855   *Poems Second Series.*

1857   Elected Professor of Poetry at Oxford on 5 May.

1858   Settles at 2, Chester Square, London : '. . . it will be something to unpack one's portmanteau for the first time since I married . . .'

1859   Abroad for some months in France, Holland, and Switzerland as Foreign Assistant Commissioner to Education Commission. Meets Sainte-Beuve in Paris on 19 August.

1861   'On Translating Homer'. 'The Popular Education of France'. Death of Clough on 13 November.

1864   'A French Eton'.

1865   Abroad in France, Italy, Germany, and Switzerland as Foreign Assistant Commissioner to the Schools Enquiry Commission. *Essays in Criticism* (First Series).

1866   Living at West Humble, Dorking. 'Thyrsis' printed in *Macmillan's Magazine* (April).

1867   *New Poems.* 'On the Study of Celtic Literature'. Tenure of Chair of Poetry ends.

1868   Takes house at Harrow.

1869   Two-volume collected edition of *Poems.* 'Culture and Anarchy'.

1870   'St Paul and Protestantism'.

1871   'Friendship's Garland'

1873   Settles permanently at Cobham, Surrey. 'Literature and Dogma'.

1875   'God and the Bible'.

1877   *Last Essays on Church and Religion.*

1878   *Selected Poems* (Golden Treasury Series).

1879   *Mixed Essays.* Compiles and introduces selected *Poems of Wordsworth.*

1880   Compiles and introduces selected *Poetry of Byron.* Contributes 'The Study of Poetry' and essays on Gray and Keats to T. H. Ward's *The English Poets.*

1882   *Irish Essays.*

1883   Civil List Pension of £250 a year in 'public recogni-
tion of service to the poetry and literature of England'.
Visits U.S.A. in October for lecture-tour lasting until
March 1884.

1885   *Discourses in America.* Abroad in France, Switzerland
and Germany for Royal Commission on Education.
Three-volume collected edition of *Poems* (Library
Edition).

1886   Retirement from Inspectorship of Schools on 30 April.
Second visit to U.S.A.

1888   Death at Liverpool on 15 April. Burial at Laleham.
Posthumous publication of *Essays in Criticism* (Second
Series).

EMPEDOCLES ON ETNA

A DRAMATIC POEM

PERSONS

EMPEDOCLES.
PAUSANIAS, *a Physician.*
CALLICLES, *a young Harp-player.*

*The Scene of the Poem is on Mount Etna; at first in the forest region,
afterwards on the summit of the mountain.*

ACT I. SCENE I

Morning. A Pass in the forest region of Etna.

CALLICLES
(*Alone, resting on a rock by the path.*)

THE mules, I think, will not be here this hour;
They feel the cool wet turf under their feet
By the stream-side, after the dusty lanes
In which they have toil'd all night from Catana,
And scarcely will they budge a yard. O Pan,　　　　　5
How gracious is the mountain at this hour!
A thousand times have I been here alone,
Or with the revellers from the mountain-towns,
But never on so fair a morn; – the sun
Is shining on the brilliant mountain-crests,　　　　　10
And on the highest pines; but farther down,
Here in the valley, is in shade; the sward
Is dark, and on the stream the mist still hangs;
One sees one's footprints crush'd in the wet grass,
One's breath curls in the air; and on these pines　　　　　15
That climb from the stream's edge, the long grey tufts,
Which the goats love, are jewell'd thick with dew.
Here will I stay till the slow litter comes.

I have my harp too – that is well. – Apollo!
What mortal could be sick or sorry here?   20
I know not in what mind Empedocles,
Whose mules I follow'd, may be coming up,
But if, as most men say, he is half mad
With exile, and with brooding on his wrongs,
Pausanias, his sage friend, who mounts with him,   25
Could scarce have lighted on a lovelier cure.
The mules must be below, far down. I hear
Their tinkling bells, mix'd with the song of birds,
Rise faintly to me – now it stops! – Who's here?
Pausanias! and on foot? alone?

Pausanias

           And thou, then?   30
I left thee supping with Peisianax,
With thy head full of wine, and thy hair crown'd,
Touching thy harp as the whim came on thee,
And praised and spoil'd by master and by guests
Almost as much as the new dancing-girl.   35
Why hast thou follow'd us?

Callicles

           The night was hot,
And the feast past its prime; so we slipp'd out,
Some of us, to the portico to breathe; –
Peisianax, thou know'st, drinks late; – and then,
As I was lifting my soil'd garland off,   40
I saw the mules and litter in the court,
And in the litter sate Empedocles;
Thou, too, wast with him. Straightway I sped home;
I saddled my white mule, and all night long
Through the cool lovely country follow'd you,   45
Pass'd you a little since as morning dawn'd,
And have this hour sate by the torrent here,
Till the slow mules should climb in sight again.
And now?

Pausanias

And now, back to the town with speed!
Crouch in the wood first, till the mules have pass'd;　　50
They do but halt, they will be here anon.
Thou must be viewless to Empedocles;
Save mine, he must not meet a human eye.
One of his moods is on him that thou know'st;
I think, thou wouldst not vex him.

Callicles

No – and yet　　55
I would fain stay, and help thee tend him. Once
He knew me well, and would oft notice me;
And still, I know not how, he draws me to him,
And I could watch him with his proud sad face,
His flowing locks and gold-encircled brow　　60
And kingly gait, for ever; such a spell
In his severe looks, such a majesty
As drew of old the people after him,
In Agrigentum and Olympia,
When his star reign'd, before his banishment,　　65
Is potent still on me in his decline.
But oh! Pausanias, he is changed of late;
There is a settled trouble in his air
Admits no momentary brightening now,
And when he comes among his friends at feasts,　　70
'Tis as an orphan among prosperous boys.
Thou know'st of old he loved this harp of mine,
When first he sojourn'd with Peisianax;
He is now always moody, and I fear him;
But I would serve him, soothe him, if I could,　　75
Dared one but try.

Pausanias

Thou wast a kind child ever!
He loves thee, but he must not see thee now.
Thou hast indeed a rare touch on thy harp,
He loves that in thee, too; – there was a time

(But that is pass'd), he would have paid thy strain   80
With music to have drawn the stars from heaven.
He hath his harp and laurel with him still,
But he has laid the use of music by,
And all which might relax his settled gloom.
Yet thou may'st try thy playing, if thou wilt –   85
But thou must keep unseen; follow us on,
But at a distance! in these solitudes,
In this clear mountain-air, a voice will rise,
Though from afar, distinctly; it may soothe him.
Play when we halt, and, when the evening comes   90
And I must leave him (for his pleasure is
To be left musing these soft nights alone
In the high unfrequented mountain-spots),
Then watch him, for he ranges swift and far,
Sometimes to Etna's top, and to the cone;   95
But hide thee in the rocks a great way down,
And try thy noblest strains, my Callicles,
With the sweet night to help thy harmony!
Thou wilt earn my thanks sure, and perhaps his.

Callicles

More than a day and night, Pausanias,   100
Of this fair summer-weather, on these hills,
Would I bestow to help Empedocles.
That needs no thanks; one is far better here
Than in the broiling city in these heats.
But tell me, how hast thou persuaded him   105
In this his present fierce, man-hating mood,
To bring thee out with him alone on Etna?

Pausanias

Thou hast heard all men speaking of Pantheia,
The woman who at Agrigentum lay
Thirty long days in a cold trance of death,   110
And whom Empedocles call'd back to life.
Thou art too young to note it, but his power

Swells with the swelling evil of this time,
And holds men mute to see where it will rise.
He could stay swift diseases in old days, 115
Chain madmen by the music of his lyre,
Cleanse to sweet airs the breath of poisonous streams,
And in the mountain-chinks inter the winds.
This he could do of old; but now, since all
Clouds and grows daily worse in Sicily, 120
Since broils tear us in twain, since this new swarm
Of sophists has got empire in our schools
Where he was paramount, since he is banish'd
And lives a lonely man in triple gloom –
He grasps the very reins of life and death. 125
I ask'd him of Pantheia yesterday,
When we were gather'd with Peisianax,
And he made answer, I should come at night
On Etna here, and be alone with him,
And he would tell me, as his old, tried friend, 130
Who still was faithful, what might profit me;
That is, the secret of this miracle.

Callicles

Bah! Thou a doctor! Thou art superstitious.
Simple Pausanias, 'twas no miracle!
Pantheia, for I know her kinsmen well, 135
Was subject to these trances from a girl.
Empedocles would say so, did he deign;
But he still lets the people, whom he scorns,
Gape and cry *wizard* at him, if they list.
But thou, thou art no company for him! 140
Thou art as cross, as sour'd as himself!
Thou hast some wrong from thine own citizens,
And then thy friend is banish'd, and on that,
Straightway thou fallest to arraign the times,
As if the sky was impious not to fall. 145
The sophists are no enemies of his;
I hear, Gorgias, their chief, speaks nobly of him,

As of his gifted master, and once friend.
He is too scornful, too high-wrought, too bitter.
'Tis not the times, 'tis not the sophists vex him;   150
There is some root of suffering in himself,
Some secret and unfollow'd vein of woe,
Which makes the time look black and sad to him.
Pester him not in this his sombre mood
With questionings about an idle tale,   155
But lead him through the lovely mountain-paths,
And keep his mind from preying on itself,
And talk to him of things at hand and common,
Not miracles! thou art a learned man,
But credulous of fables as a girl.   160

Pausanias

And thou, a boy whose tongue outruns his knowledge,
And on whose lightness blame is thrown away.
Enough of this! I see the litter wind
Up by the torrent-side, under the pines.
I must rejoin Empedocles. Do thou   165
Crouch in the brushwood till the mules have pass'd;
Then play thy kind part well. Farewell till night!

SCENE II

*Noon. A Glen on the highest skirts of the woody region
of Etna.*

EMPEDOCLES. PAUSANIAS.

Pausanias

The noon is hot. When we have cross'd the stream,
We shall have left the woody tract, and come
Upon the open shoulder of the hill.
See how the giant spires of yellow bloom
Of the sun-loving gentian, in the heat,   5
Are shining on those naked slopes like flame!

Let us rest here; and now, Empedocles,
Pantheia's history!

[*A harp-note below is heard.*

Empedocles

   Hark! what sound was that
Rose from below? If it were possible,
And we were not so far from human haunt,   10
I should have said that some one touch'd a harp.
Hark! there again!

Pausanias

   'Tis the boy Callicles,
The sweetest harp-player in Catana.
He is for ever coming on these hills,
In summer, to all country-festivals,   15
With a gay revelling band; he breaks from them
Sometimes, and wanders far among the glens.
But heed him not, he will not mount to us;
I spoke with him this morning. Once more, therefore,
Instruct me of Pantheia's story, Master,   20
As I have pray'd thee.

Empedocles

   That? and to what end?

Pausanias

It is enough that all men speak of it.
But I will also say, that when the Gods
Visit us as they do with sign and plague,
To know those spells of thine which stay their hand   25
Were to live free from terror.

Empedocles

   Spells? Mistrust them!
Mind is the spell which governs earth and heaven.
Man has a mind with which to plan his safety;
Know that, and help thyself!

Pausanias

            But thine own words?
'The wit and counsel of man was never clear,   30
Troubles confound the little wit he has.'
Mind is a light which the Gods mock us with,
To lead those false who trust it.

                    [*The harp sounds again.*

Empedocles

            Hist! once more!
Listen, Pausanias! – Ay, 'tis Callicles;
I know these notes among a thousand. Hark!   35

Callicles

(*Sings unseen, from below*)

The track winds down to the clear stream,
To cross the sparkling shallows; there
The cattle love to gather, on their way
To the high mountain-pastures, and to stay,
Till the rough cow-herds drive them past,   40
Knee-deep in the cool ford; for 'tis the last
Of all the woody, high, well-water'd dells
On Etna; and the beam
Of noon is broken there by chestnut-boughs
Down its steep verdant sides; the air   45
Is freshen'd by the leaping stream, which throws
Eternal showers of spray on the moss'd roots
Of trees, and veins of turf, and long dark shoots
Of ivy-plants, and fragrant hanging bells
Of hyacinths, and on late anemones,   50
That muffle its wet banks; but glade,
And stream, and sward, and chestnut-trees,
End here; Etna beyond, in the broad glare
Of the hot noon, without a shade,

Slope behind slope, up to the peak, lies bare;   55
The peak, round which the white clouds play.

  In such a glen, on such a day,
  On Pelion, on the grassy ground,
  Chiron, the aged Centaur lay,
  The young Achilles standing by.   60
  The Centaur taught him to explore
  The mountains; where the glens are dry
  And the tired Centaurs come to rest,
  And where the soaking springs abound
  And the straight ashes grow for spears,   65
  And where the hill-goats come to feed,
  And the sea-eagles build their nest.
  He show'd him Phthia far away,
  And said: O boy, I taught this lore
  To Peleus, in long distant years!   70
  He told him of the Gods, the stars,
  The tides; – and then of mortal wars,
  And of the life which heroes lead
  Before they reach the Elysian place
  And rest in the immortal mead;   75
  And all the wisdom of his race.

The music below ceases, and EMPEDOCLES *speaks, accompany-
  ing himself in a solemn manner on his harp.*

    The out-spread world to span
    A cord the Gods first slung,
    And then the soul of man
    There, like a mirror, hung,   80
And bade the winds through space impel the gusty toy.

    Hither and thither spins
    The wind-borne, mirroring soul,
    A thousand glimpses wins,
    And never sees a whole;   85
Looks once, and drives elsewhere, and leaves its last
  employ.

The Gods laugh in their sleeve
To watch man doubt and fear,
Who knows not what to believe
Since he sees nothing clear,   90
And dares stamp nothing false where he finds nothing sure.

Is this, Pausanias, so?
And can our souls not strive,
But with the winds must go,
And hurry where they drive?   95
Is fate indeed so strong, man's strength indeed so poor?

I will not judge. That man,
Howbeit, I judge as lost,
Whose mind allows a plan,
Which would degrade it most;   100
And he treats doubt the best who tries to see least ill.

Be not, then, fear's blind slave!
Thou art my friend; to thee,
All knowledge that I have,
All skill I wield, are free.   105
Ask not the latest news of the last miracle,

Ask not what days and nights
In trance Pantheia lay,
But ask how thou such sights
May'st see without dismay;   110
Ask what most helps when known, thou son of Anchitus!

What? hate, and awe, and shame
Fill thee to see our time;
Thou feelest thy soul's frame
Shaken and out of chime?   115
What? life and chance go hard with thee too, as with us;

Thy citizens, 'tis said,
Envy thee and oppress,
Thy goodness no men aid,
All strive to make it less;   120
Tyranny, pride, and lust, fill Sicily's abodes;

Heaven is with earth at strife,
Signs make thy soul afraid,
The dead return to life,
Rivers are dried, winds stay'd;   125
Scarce can one think in calm, so threatening are the Gods;

And we feel, day and night,
The burden of ourselves —
Well, then, the wiser wight
In his own bosom delves,   130
And asks what ails him so, and gets what cure he can.

The sophist sneers: Fool, take
Thy pleasure, right or wrong.
The pious wail: Forsake
A world these sophists throng.   135
Be neither saint nor sophist-led, but be a man!

These hundred doctors try
To preach thee to their school.
We have the truth! they cry;
And yet their oracle,   140
Trumpet it as they will, is but the same as thine.

Once read thy own breast right,
And thou hast done with fears;
Man gets no other light,
Search he a thousand years.   145
Sink in thyself! there ask what ails thee, at that shrine!

What makes thee struggle and rave?
Why are men ill at ease? —
'Tis that the lot they have
Fails their own will to please;   150
For man would make no murmuring, were his will obey'd.

And why is it, that still
Man with his lot thus fights? —
'Tis that he makes this *will*
The measure of his *rights*,   155
And believes Nature outraged if his will's gainsaid.

Couldst thou, Pausanias, learn
How deep a fault is this;
Couldst thou but once discern
Thou hast no *right* to bliss,   160
No title from the Gods to welfare and repose;

Then thou wouldst look less mazed
Whene'er of bliss debarr'd,
Nor think the Gods were crazed
When thy own lot went hard.   165
But we are all the same — the fools of our own woes!

For, from the first faint morn
Of life, the thirst for bliss
Deep in man's heart is born;
And, sceptic as he is,   170
He fails not to judge clear if this be quench'd or no.

Nor is the thirst to blame.
Man errs not that he deems
His welfare his true aim,
He errs because he dreams   175
The world does but exist that welfare to bestow.

We mortals are no kings
For each of whom to sway
A new-made world up-springs,
Meant merely for his play;   180
No, we are strangers here; the world is from of old.

In vain our pent wills fret,
And would the world subdue.
Limits we did not set
Condition all we do;   185
Born into life we are, and life must be our mould.

Born into life! — man grows
Forth from his parents' stem,
And blends their bloods, as those
Of theirs are blent in them;   190
So each new man strikes root into a far fore-time.

Born into life! – we bring
A bias with us here,
And, when here, each new thing
Affects us we come near;   195
To tunes we did not call our being must keep chime.

Born into life! – in vain,
Opinions, those or these,
Unalter'd to retain
The obstinate mind decrees;   200
Experience, like a sea, soaks all-effacing in.

Born into life! – who lists
May what is false hold dear,
And for himself make mists
Through which to see less clear;   205
The world is what it is, for all our dust and din.

Born into life! – 'tis we,
And not the world, are new;
Our cry for bliss, our plea,
Others have urged it too –   210
Our wants have all been felt, our errors made before.

No eye could be too sound
To observe a world so vast,
No patience too profound
To sort what's here amass'd;   215
How man may here best live no care too great to explore.

But we – as some rude guest
Would change, where'er he roam,
The manners there profess'd
To those he brings from home –   220
We mark not the world's course, but would have *it* take *ours*.

The world's course proves the terms
On which man wins content;
Reason the proof confirms –
We spurn it, and invent   225
A false course for the world, and for ourselves, false powers

Riches we wish to get,
Yet remain spendthrifts still;
We would have health, and yet
Still use our bodies ill;   230
Bafflers of our own prayers, from youth to life's last scenes.

We would have inward peace,
Yet will not look within;
We would have misery cease,
Yet will not cease from sin;   235
We want all pleasant ends, but will use no harsh means;

We do not what we ought,
What we ought not, we do,
And lean upon the thought
That chance will bring us through;   240
But our own acts, for good or ill, are mightier powers.

Yet, even when man forsakes
All sin, – is just, is pure,
Abandons all which makes
His welfare insecure, –   245
Other existences there are, that clash with ours.

Like us, the lightning-fires
Love to have scope and play;
The stream, like us, desires
An unimpeded way;   250
Like us, the Libyan wind delights to roam at large.

Streams will not curb their pride
The just man not to entomb,
Nor lightnings go aside
To give his virtues room;   255
Nor is that wind less rough which blows a good man's barge.

Nature, with equal mind,
Sees all her sons at play;
Sees man control the wind,
The wind sweep man away;   260
Allows the proudly-riding and the foundering bark.

And, lastly, though of ours
No weakness spoil our lot,
Though the non-human powers
Of Nature harm us not,   265
The ill deeds of other men make often *our* life dark.

What were the wise man's plan? –
Through this sharp, toil-set life,
To work as best he can,
And win what's won by strife. –   270
But we an easier way to cheat our pains have found.

Scratch'd by a fall, with moans
As children of weak age
Lend life to the dumb stones
Whereon to vent their rage,   275
And bend their little fists, and rate the senseless ground:

So, loath to suffer mute,
We, peopling the void air,
Make Gods to whom to impute
The ills we ought to bear;   280
With God and Fate to rail at, suffering easily.

Yet grant – as sense long miss'd
Things that are now perceived,
And much may still exist
Which is not yet believed –   285
Grant that the world were full of Gods we cannot see;

All things the world which fill
Of but one stuff are spun,
That we who rail are still,
With what we rail at, one;   290
One with the o'erlabour'd Power that through the
        breadth and length

Of earth, and air, and sea,
In men, and plants, and stones,
Hath toil perpetually,
And travails, pants, and moans;   295
Fain would do all things well, but sometimes fails in strength.

And patiently exact
This universal God
Alike to any act
Proceeds at any nod,   300
And quietly declaims the cursings of himself.

This is not what man hates,
Yet he can curse but this.
Harsh Gods and hostile Fates
Are dreams! this only *is* –   305
Is everywhere; sustains the wise, the foolish elf.

Nor only, in the intent
To attach blame elsewhere,
Do we at will invent
Stern Powers who make their care   310
To embitter human life, malignant Deities;

But, next, we would reverse
The scheme ourselves have spun,
And what we made to curse
We now would lean upon,   315
And feign kind Gods who perfect what man vainly tries.

Look, the world tempts our eye,
And we would know it all!
We map the starry sky,
We mine this earthen ball,   320
We measure the sea-tides, we number the sea-sands;

We scrutinize the dates
Of long-past human things,
The bounds of effaced states,
The lines of deceased kings;   325
We search out dead men's words, and works of dead
    men's hands;

We shut our eyes, and muse
How our own minds are made,
What springs of thought they use,
How righten'd, how betray'd –   330
And spend our wit to name what most employ unnamed.

But still, as we proceed
The mass swells more and more
Of volumes yet to read,
Of secrets yet to explore.   335
Our hair grows grey, our eyes are dimm'd, our heat is tamed:

We rest our faculties,
And thus address the Gods:
'True science if there is,
It stays in your abodes!   340
Man's measures cannot mete the immeasurable All.

'You only can take in
The world's immense design.
Our desperate search was sin,
Which henceforth we resign,   345
Sure only that your mind sees all things which befall.'

Fools! That in man's brief term
He cannot all things view,
Affords no ground to affirm
That there are Gods who do;   350
Nor does being weary prove that he has where to rest.

Again. – Our youthful blood
Claims rapture as its right;
The world, a rolling flood
Of newness and delight,   355
Draws in the enamour'd gazer to its shining breast;

Pleasure, to our hot grasp,
Gives flowers after flowers;
With passionate warmth we clasp
Hand after hand in ours;   360
Now do we soon perceive how fast our youth is spent.

At once our eyes grow clear!
We see, in blank dismay,
Year posting after year,
Sense after sense decay;   365
Our shivering heart is mined by secret discontent;

Yet still, in spite of truth,
In spite of hopes entomb'd,
That longing of our youth
Burns ever unconsumed,   370
Still hungrier for delight as delights grow more rare.

We pause; we hush our heart,
And thus address the Gods:
'The world hath fail'd to impart
The joy our youth forebodes,   375
Fail'd to fill up the void which in our breasts we bear.

'Changeful till now, we still
Look'd on to something new;
Let us, with changeless will,
Henceforth look on to you,   380
To find with you the joy we in vain here require!'

Fools! That so often here
Happiness mock'd our prayer,
I think, might make us fear
A like event elsewhere;   385
Make us, not fly to dreams, but moderate desire.

And yet, for those who know
Themselves, who wisely take
Their way through life, and bow
To what they cannot break,   390
Why should I say that life need yield but *moderate* bliss?

Shall we, with temper spoil'd,
Health sapp'd by living ill,
And judgement all embroil'd
By sadness and self-will   395
Shall *we* judge what for man is not true bliss or is?

Is it so small a thing
To have enjoy'd the sun,
To have lived light in the spring,
To·have loved, to have thought, to have done;   400
To have advanced true friends, and beat down baffling foes –

That we must feign a bliss
Of doubtful future date,
And, while we dream on this,
Lose all our present state,   405
And relegate to worlds yet distant our repose?

Not much, I know, you prize
What pleasures may be had,
Who look on life with eyes
Estranged, like mine, and sad;   410
And yet the village-churl feels the truth more than you,

Who's loath to leave this life
Which to him little yields –
His hard-task'd sunburnt wife,
His often-labour'd fields,   415
The boors with whom he talk'd, the country-spots he knew.

But thou, because thou hear'st
Men scoff at Heaven and Fate,
Because the Gods thou fear'st
Fail to make blest thy state,   420
Tremblest, and wilt not dare to trust the joys there are!

I say: Fear not! Life still
Leaves human effort scope.
But, since life teems with ill,
Nurse no extravagant hope;   425
Because thou must not dream, thou need'st not then despair!

*A long pause. At the end of it the notes of a harp below are
again heard, and* CALLICLES *sings:* –

Far, far from here,
The Adriatic breaks in a warm bay
Among the green Illyrian hills; and there
The sunshine in the happy glens is fair,   430
And by the sea, and in the brakes.

The grass is cool, the sea-side air
Buoyant and fresh, the mountain flowers
More virginal and sweet than ours.
And there, they say, two bright and aged snakes,   435
Who once were Cadmus and Harmonia,
Bask in the glens or on the warm sea-shore,
In breathless quiet, after all their ills;
Nor do they see their country, nor the place
Where the Sphinx lived among the frowning hills,   440
Nor the unhappy palace of their race,
Nor Thebes, nor the Ismenus, any more.

There those two live, far in the Illyrian brakes!
They had stay'd long enough to see,
In Thebes, the billow of calamity   445
Over their own dear children roll'd,
Curse upon curse, pang upon pang,
For years, they sitting helpless in their home,
A grey old man and woman; yet of old
The Gods had to their marriage come,   450
And at the banquet all the Muses sang.

Therefore they did not end their days
In sight of blood; but were rapt, far away,
To where the west-wind plays,
And murmurs of the Adriatic come   455
To those untrodden mountain-lawns; and there
Placed safely in changed forms, the pair
Wholly forget their first sad life, and home,
And all that Theban woe, and stray
For ever through the glens, placid and dumb.   460

Empedocles

That was my harp-player again! – where is he?
Down by the stream?

Pausanias

Yes, Master, in the wood.

Empedocles

He ever loved the Theban story well!
But the day wears. Go now, Pausanias,
For I must be alone. Leave me one mule;   465
Take down with thee the rest to Catana.
And for young Callicles, thank him from me;
Tell him, I never fail'd to love his lyre –
But he must follow me no more to-night.

Pausanias

Thou wilt return to-morrow to the city?   470

Empedocles

Either to-morrow or some other day,
In the sure revolutions of the world,
Good friend, I shall revisit Catana.
I have seen many cities in my time,
Till mine eyes ache with the long spectacle,   475
And I shall doubtless see them all again;
Thou know'st me for a wanderer from of old.
Meanwhile, stay me not now. Farewell, Pausanias!

> *He departs on his way up the mountain.*

Pausanias (alone)

I dare not urge him further – he must go;
But he is strangely wrought! – I will speed back   480
And bring Peisianax to him from the city;
His counsel could once soothe him. But, Apollo!
How his brow lighten'd as the music rose!
Callicles must wait here, and play to him;
I saw him through the chestnuts far below,   485
Just since, down at the stream. – Ho! Callicles!

> *He descends, calling.*

ACT II

Evening. The Summit of Etna.

EMPEDOCLES

Alone! –
On this charr'd, blacken'd, melancholy waste,
Crown'd by the awful peak, Etna's great mouth.
Round which the sullen vapour rolls – alone!
Pausanias is far hence, and that is well,   5
For I must henceforth speak no more with man.
He hath his lesson too, and that debt's paid;
And the good, learned, friendly, quiet man
May bravelier front his life, and in himself
Find henceforth energy and heart. But I –   10
The weary man, the banish'd citizen,
Whose banishment is not his greatest ill,
Whose weariness no energy can reach,
And for whose hurt courage is not the cure –
What should I do with life and living more?   15

No, thou art come too late, Empedocles!
And the world hath the day, and must break thee,
Not thou the world. With men thou canst not live,
Their thoughts, their ways, their wishes, are not thine;
And being lonely thou art miserable,   20
For something has impair'd thy spirit's strength,
And dried its self-sufficing fount of joy.
Thou canst not live with men nor with thyself –
O sage! O sage! – Take then the one way left;
And turn thee to the elements, thy friends,   25
Thy well-tried friends, thy willing ministers,
And say: Ye helpers, hear Empedocles,
Who asks this final service at your hands!
Before the sophist-brood hath overlaid
The last spark of man's consciousness with words –   30
Ere quite the being of man, ere quite the world

Be disarray'd of their divinity —
Before the soul lose all her solemn joys,
And awe be dead, and hope impossible,
And the soul's deep eternal night come on —   35
Receive me, hide me, quench me, take me home!

> *He advances to the edge of the crater. Smoke and fire break*
> *forth with a loud noise, and* CALLICLES *is heard below*
> *singing:* —

The lyre's voice is lovely everywhere;
In the court of Gods, in the city of men,
And in the lonely rock-strewn mountain-glen,
In the still mountain air.   40

Only to Typho it sounds hatefully;
To Typho only, the rebel o'erthrown,
Through whose heart Etna drives her roots of stone
To imbed them in the sea.

Wherefore dost thou groan so loud?   45
Wherefore do thy nostrils flash,
Through the dark night, suddenly,
Typho, such red jets of flame? —
Is thy tortured heart still proud?
Is thy fire-scathed arm still rash?   50
Still alert thy stone-crush'd frame?
Doth thy fierce soul still deplore
Thine ancient rout by the Cilician hills,
And that curst treachery on the Mount of Gore?
Do thy bloodshot eyes still weep   55
The fight which crown'd thine ills,
Thy last mischance on this Sicilian deep?
Hast thou sworn, in thy sad lair,
Where erst the strong sea-currents suck'd thee down,
Never to cease to writhe, and try to rest,   60
Letting the sea-stream wander through thy hair?
That thy groans, like thunder prest,
Begin to roll, and almost drown
The sweet notes whose lulling spell

Gods and the race of mortals love so well,   65
When through thy caves thou hearest music swell?

But an awful pleasure bland
Spreading o'er the Thunderer's face,
When the sound climbs near his seat,
The Olympian council sees;   70
As he lets his lax right hand,
Which the lightnings doth embrace,
Sink upon his mighty knees.
And the eagle, at the beck
Of the appeasing, gracious harmony,   75
Droops all his sheeny, brown, deep-feather'd neck,
Nestling nearer to Jove's feet;
While o'er his sovran eye
The curtains of the blue films slowly meet
And the white Olympus-peaks   80
Rosily brighten, and the soothed Gods smile
At one another from their golden chairs,
And no one round the charmed circle speaks.
Only the loved Hebe bears
The cup about, whose draughts beguile   85
Pain and care, with a dark store
Of fresh-pull'd violets wreathed and nodding o'er;
And her flush'd feet glow on the marble floor.

Empedocles

He fables, yet speaks truth!
The brave, impetuous heart yields everywhere   90
To the subtle, contriving head;
Great qualities are trodden down,
And littleness united
Is become invincible.

These rumblings are not Typho's groans, I know!   95
These angry smoke-bursts
Are not the passionate breath
Of the mountain-crush'd, tortured, intractable Titan king –

But over all the world
What suffering is there not seen   100
Of plainness oppress'd by cunning,
As the well-counsell'd Zeus oppress'd
That self-helping son of earth!
What anguish of greatness,
Rail'd and hunted from the world,   105
Because its simplicity rebukes
This envious, miserable age!

I am weary of it.
– Lie there, ye ensigns
Of my unloved preëminence   110
In an age like this!
Among a people of children,
Who throng'd me in their cities,
Who worshipp'd me in their houses,
And ask'd, not wisdom,   115
But drugs to charm with,
But spells to mutter –
All the fool's-armoury of magic! – Lie there,
My golden circlet,
My purple robe!   120

Callicles (from below).

As the sky-brightening south-wind clears the day,
And makes the mass'd clouds roll,
The music of the lyre blows away
The clouds which wrap the soul.

Oh! that Fate had let me see   125
That triumph of the sweet persuasive lyre,
That famous, final victory,
When jealous Pan with Marsyas did conspire;

When, from far Parnassus' side,
Young Apollo, all the pride   130
Of the Phrygian flutes to tame,

To the Phrygian highlands came;
Where the long green reed-beds sway
In the rippled waters grey
Of that solitary lake   135
Where Maeander's springs are born;
Whence the ridged pine-wooded roots
Of Messogis westward break,
Mounting westward, high and higher.
There was held the famous strife;   140
There the Phrygian brought his flutes,
And Apollo brought his lyre;
And, when now the westering sun
Touch'd the hills, the strife was done,
And the attentive Muses said: 145
'Marsyas, thou art vanquished!'
Then Apollo's minister
Hang'd upon a branching fir
Marsyas, that unhappy Faun,
And began to whet his knife.   150
But the Maenads, who were there,
Left their friend, and with robes flowing
In the wind, and loose dark hair
O'er their polish'd bosoms blowing,
Each her ribbon'd tambourine   155
Flinging on the mountain-sod,
With a lovely frighten'd mien
Came about the youthful God.
But he turn'd his beauteous face
Haughtily another way,   160
From the grassy sun-warm'd place
Where in proud repose he lay,
With one arm over his head,
Watching how the whetting sped.

  But aloof, on the lake-strand,   165
Did the young Olympus stand,

Weeping at his master's end;
For the Faun had been his friend.
For he taught him how to sing,
And he taught him flute-playing.   170
Many a morning had they gone
To the glimmering mountain-lakes,
And had torn up by the roots
The tall crested water-reeds
With long plumes and soft brown seeds,   175
And had carved them into flutes,
Sitting on a tabled stone
Where the shoreward ripple breaks.
And he taught him how to please
The red-snooded Phrygian girls,   180
Whom the summer evening sees
Flashing in the dance's whirls
Underneath the starlit trees
In the mountain-villages.
Therefore now Olympus stands,   185
At his master's piteous cries
Pressing fast with both his hands
His white garment to his eyes,
Not to see Apollo's scorn; –
Ah, poor Faun, poor Faun! ah, poor Faun!   190

Empedocles

And lie thou there,
My laurel bough!
Scornful Apollo's ensign, lie thou there!
Though thou hast been my shade in the world's heat –
Though I have loved thee, lived in honouring thee –   195
Yet lie thou there,
My laurel bough!

I am weary of thee.
I am weary of the solitude.

Where he who bears thee must abide –   200
Of the rocks of Parnassus,
Of the gorge of Delphi,
Of the moonlit peaks, and the caves.
Thou guardest them, Apollo!
Over the grave of the slain Pytho,   205
Though young, intolerably severe!
Thou keepest aloof the profane,
But the solitude oppresses thy votary!
The jars of men reach him not in thy valley –
But can life reach him?   210
Thou fencest him from the multitude –
Who will fence him from himself?
He hears nothing but the cry of the torrents,
And the beating of his own heart.
The air is thin, the veins swell,   215
The temples tighten and throb there –
Air! air!

Take thy bough, set me free from my solitude;
I have been enough alone!

Where shall thy votary fly then? back to men? –   220
But they will gladly welcome him once more,
And help him to unbend his too tense thought,
And rid him of the presence of himself,
And keep their friendly chatter at his ear,
And haunt him, till the absence from himself,   225
That other torment, grow unbearable;
And he will fly to solitude again,
And he will find its air too keen for him,
And so change back; and many thousand times
Be miserably bandied to and fro   230
Like a sea-wave, betwixt the world and thee,
Thou young, implacable God! and only death
Can cut his oscillations short, and so
Bring him to poise. There is no other way.

And yet what days were those, Parmenides!   235
When we were young, when we could number friends
In all the Italian cities like ourselves,
When with elated hearts we join'd your train,
Ye Sun-born Virgins! on the road of truth.
Then we could still enjoy, then neither thought   240
Nor outward things were closed and dead to us;
But we received the shock of mighty thoughts
On simple minds with a pure natural joy;
And if the sacred load oppress'd our brain,
We had the power to feel the pressure eased,   245
The brow unbound, the thoughts flow free again,
In the delightful commerce of the world.
We had not lost our balance then, nor grown
Thought's slaves, and dead to every natural joy.
The smallest thing could give us pleasure then –   250
The sports of the country-people,
A flute-note from the woods,
Sunset over the sea;
Seed-time and harvest,
The reapers in the corn,   255
The vinedresser in his vineyard,
The village-girl at her wheel.

Fulness of life and power of feeling, ye
Are for the happy, for the souls at ease,
Who dwell on a firm basis of content!   260
But he, who has outlived his prosperous days –
But he, whose youth fell on a different world
From that on which his exiled age is thrown –
Whose mind was fed on other food, was train'd
By other rules than are in vogue to-day –   265
Whose habit of thought is fix'd, who will not change,
But, in a world he loves not, must subsist
In ceaseless opposition, be the guard
Of his own breast, fetter'd to what he guards,
That the world win no mastery over him –   270
Who has no friend, no fellow left, not one;

Who has no minute's breathing space allow'd
To nurse his dwindling faculty of joy –
Joy and the outward world must die to him,
As they are dead to me.   275

> *A long pause, during which* EMPEDOCLES *remains motion-
> less, plunged in thought. The night deepens. He moves
> forward and gazes round him, and proceeds:* –

And you, ye stars,
Who slowly begin to marshal,
As of old, in the fields of heaven,
Your distant, melancholy lines !
Have you, too, survived yourselves?   280
Are you, too, what I fear to become?
You, too, once lived;
You, too, moved joyfully
Among august companions,
In an older world, peopled by Gods,   285
In a mightier order,
The radiant, rejoicing, intelligent Sons of Heaven.
But now, ye kindle
Your lonely, cold-shining lights,
Unwilling lingerers   290
In the heavenly wilderness,
For a younger, ignoble world;
And renew, by necessity,
Night after night your courses,
In echoing, unnear'd silence,   295
Above a race you know not –
Uncaring and undelighted,
Without friend and without home;
Weary like us, though not
Weary with our weariness.   300

No, no, ye stars ! there is no death with you,
No languor, no decay ! languor and death,
They are with me, not you ! ye are alive –
Ye, and the pure dark ether where ye ride

Brilliant above me! And thou, fiery world, 305
That sapp'st the vitals of this terrible mount
Upon whose charr'd and quaking crust I stand –
Thou, too, brimmest with life! – the sea of cloud,
That heaves its white and billowy vapours up
To moat this isle of ashes from the world, 310
Lives; and that other fainter sea, far down,
O'er whose lit floor a road of moonbeams leads
To Etna's Liparëan sister-fires
And the long dusky line of Italy –
That mild and luminous floor of waters lives, 315
With held-in joy swelling its heart; I only,
Whose spring of hope is dried, whose spirit has fail'd,
I, who have not, like these, in solitude
Maintain'd courage and force, and in myself
Nursed an immortal vigour – I alone 320
Am dead to life and joy, therefore I read
In all things my own deadness.

A long silence. He continues: –

Oh, that I could glow like this mountain!
Oh, that my heart bounded with the swell of the sea!
Oh, that my soul were full of light as the stars! 325
Oh, that it brooded over the world like the air!

But no, this heart will glow no more; thou art
A living man no more, Empedocles!
Nothing but a devouring flame of thought –
But a naked, eternally restless mind! 330

After a pause: –

To the elements it came from
Everything will return –
Our bodies to earth,
Our blood to water,
Heat to fire, 335
Breath to air.
They were well born, they will be well entomb'd –
But mind? . . .

And we might gladly share the fruitful stir
Down in our mother earth's miraculous womb;   340
Well would it be
With what roll'd of us in the stormy main;
We might have joy, blent with the all-bathing air,
Or with the nimble, radiant life of fire.

But mind, but thought —   345
If these have been the master part of us —
Where will *they* find their parent element?
What will receive *them*, who will call *them* home?
But we shall still be in them, and they in us,
And we shall be the strangers of the world,   350
And they will be our lords, as they are now;
And keep us prisoners of our consciousness,
And never let us clasp and feel the All
But through their forms, and modes, and stifling veils.
And we shall be unsatisfied as now;   355
And we shall feel the agony of thirst,
The ineffable longing for the life of life
Baffled for ever; and still thought and mind
Will hurry us with them on their homeless march,
Over the unallied unopening earth,   360
Over the unrecognizing sea; while air
Will blow us fiercely back to sea and earth,
And fire repel us from its living waves.
And then we shall unwillingly return
Back to this meadow of calamity,   365
This uncongenial place, this human life;
And in our individual human state
Go through the sad probation all again,
To see if we will poise our life at last,
To see if we will now at last be true   370
To our own only true, deep-buried selves,
Being one with which we are one with the whole world;
Or whether we will once more fall away
Into some bondage of the flesh or mind,
Some slough of sense, or some fantastic maze   375

Forged by the imperious lonely thinking-power.
And each succeeding age in which we are born
Will have more peril for us than the last;
Will goad our senses with a sharper spur,
Will fret our minds to an intenser play,   380
Will make ourselves harder to be discern'd.
And we shall struggle awhile, gasp and rebel –
And we shall fly for refuge to past times,
Their soul of unworn youth, their breath of greatness;
And the reality will pluck us back,   385
Knead us in its hot hand, and change our nature
And we shall feel our powers of effort flag,
And rally them for one last fight – and fail;
And we shall sink in the impossible strife,
And be astray for ever.

             Slave of sense   390
I have in no wise been; – but slave of thought? . . .
And who can say: I have been always free,
Lived ever in the light of my own soul? –
I cannot; I have lived in wrath and gloom,
Fierce, disputatious, ever at war with man,   395
Far from my own soul, far from warmth and light.
But I have not grown easy in these bonds –
But I have not denied what bonds these were.
Yea, I take myself to witness,
That I have loved no darkness,   400
Sophisticated no truth,
Nursed no delusion,
Allow'd no fear!

  And therefore, O ye elements! I know –
Ye know it too – it hath been granted me   405
Not to die wholly, not to be all enslaved.
I feel it in this hour. The numbing cloud
Mounts off my soul; I feel it, I breathe free.

Is it but for a moment?
– Ah, boil up, ye vapours!   410
Leap and roar, thou sea of fire!

My soul glows to meet you.
Ere it flag, ere the mists
Of despondency and gloom
Rush over it again,   415
Receive me, save me !

[*He plunges into the crater.*

Callicles

(*from below*).

Through the black, rushing smoke-bursts,
Thick breaks the red flame ;
All Etna heaves fiercely
Her forest-clothed frame.   420

Not here, O Apollo !
Are haunts meet for thee.
But, where Helicon breaks down
In cliff to the sea,

Where the moon-silver'd inlets   425
Send far their light voice
Up the still vale of Thisbe,
O speed, and rejoice !

On the sward at the cliff-top
Lie strewn the white flocks,   430
On the cliff-side the pigeons
Roost deep in the rocks.

In the moonlight the shepherds,
Soft lull'd by the rills,
Lie wrapt in their blankets   435
Asleep on the hills.

– What forms are these coming
So white through the gloom ?
What garments out-glistening
The gold-flower'd broom ?   440

What sweet-breathing presence
Out-perfumes the thyme?
What voices enrapture
The night's balmy prime? –

'Tis Apollo comes leading   445
His choir, the Nine.
– The leader is fairest,
But all are divine.

They are lost in the hollows!
They stream up again!   450
What seeks on this mountain
The glorified train? –

They bathe on this mountain,
In the spring by their road;
Then on to Olympus,   455
Their endless abode.

– Whose praise do they mention?
Of what is it told? –
What will be for ever;
What was from of old.   460

First hymn they the Father
Of all things; and then,
The rest of immortals,
The action of men.

The day in his hotness,   465
The strife with the palm;
The night in her silence,
The stars in their calm.

NARRATIVE POEMS

THE FORSAKEN MERMAN

COME, dear children, let us away;
Down and away below!
Now my brothers call from the bay,
Now the great winds shoreward blow,
Now the salt tides seaward flow; 5
Now the wild white horses play,
Champ and chafe and toss in the spray.
Children dear, let us away!
This way, this way!

Call her once before you go – 10
Call once yet!
In a voice that she will know:
'Margaret! Margaret!'
Children's voices should be dear
(Call once more) to a mother's ear; 15
Children's voices, wild with pain –
Surely she will come again!
Call her once and come away;
This way, this way!
'Mother dear, we cannot stay! 20
The wild white horses foam and fret.'
Margaret! Margaret!

Come, dear children, come away down;
Call no more!
One last look at the white-wall'd town, 25
And the little grey church on the windy shore,
Then come down!
She will not come though you call all day;
Come away, come away!

Children dear, was it yesterday 30
We heard the sweet bells over the bay?
In the caverns where we lay,
Through the surf and through the swell,
The far-off sound of a silver bell?
Sand-strewn caverns, cool and deep, 35
Where the winds are all asleep;
Where the spent lights quiver and gleam,
Where the salt weed sways in the stream,
Where the sea-beasts, ranged all round,
Feed in the ooze of their pasture-ground; 40
Where the sea-snakes coil and twine,
Dry their mail and bask in the brine;
Where great whales come sailing by,
Sail and sail, with unshut eye,
Round the world for ever and aye? 45
When did music come this way?
Children dear, was it yesterday?

Children dear, was it yesterday
(Call yet once) that she went away?
Once she sate with you and me, 50
On a red gold throne in the heart of the sea,
And the youngest sate on her knee.
She comb'd its bright hair, and she tended it well,
When down swung the sound of a far-off bell.
She sigh'd, she look'd up through the clear green sea; 55
She said: 'I must go, for my kinsfolk pray
In the little grey church on the shore to-day.
'Twill be Easter-time in the world – ah me!
And I lose my poor soul, Merman! here with thee.'
I said: 'Go up, dear heart, through the waves; 60
Say thy prayer, and come back to the kind sea-caves!'
She smiled, she went up through the surf in the bay.
Children dear, was it yesterday?

Children dear, were we long alone?
'The sea grows stormy, the little ones moan;   65
Long prayers,' I said, 'in the world they say;
Come!' I said; and we rose through the surf in the bay.
We went up the beach, by the sandy down
Where the sea-stocks bloom, to the white-wall'd town;
Through the narrow paved streets, where all was still,   70
To the little grey church on the windy hill.
From the church came a murmur of folk at their
      prayers,
But we stood without in the cold blowing airs.
We climb'd on the graves, on the stones worn with
      rains,
And we gazed up the aisle through the small leaded panes. 75
She sate by the pillar; we saw her clear:
'Margaret, hist! come quick, we are here!
Dear heart,' I said, 'we are long alone;
The sea grows stormy, the little ones moan.'
But, ah, she gave me never a look,   80
For her eyes were seal'd to the holy book!
Loud prays the priest; shut stands the door.
Come away, children, call no more!
Come away, come down, call no more!

Down, down, down!   85
Down to the depths of the sea!
She sits at her wheel in the humming town,
Singing most joyfully.
Hark what she sings: 'O joy, O joy,
For the humming street, and the child with its toy!   90
For the priest, and the bell, and the holy well;
For the wheel where I spun,
And the blessed light of the sun!'
And so she sings her fill,
Singing most joyfully,   95
Till the spindle drops from her hand,
And the whizzing wheel stands still.
She steals to the window, and looks at the sand,

And over the sand at the sea;
And her eyes are set in a stare;   100
And anon there breaks a sigh,
And anon there drops a tear,
From a sorrow-clouded eye,
And a heart sorrow-laden,
A long, long sigh;   105
For the cold strange eyes of a little Mermaiden
And the gleam of her golden hair.

   Come away, away children;
Come children, come down!
The hoarse wind blows coldly;   110
Lights shine in the town.
She will start from her slumber
When gusts shake the door;
She will hear the winds howling,
Will hear the waves roar.   115
We shall see, while above us
The waves roar and whirl,
A ceiling of amber,
A pavement of pearl.
Singing: 'Here came a mortal,   120
But faithless was she!
And alone dwell for ever
The kings of the sea.'

But, children, at midnight,
When soft the winds blow,   125
When clear falls the moonlight,
When spring-tides are low;
When sweet airs come seaward
From heaths starr'd with broom,
And high rocks throw mildly   130
On the blanch'd sands a gloom;
Up the still, glistening beaches,
Up the creeks we will hie,
Over banks of bright seaweed
The ebb-tide leaves dry.   135

We will gaze, from the sand-hills,
At the white, sleeping town;
At the church on the hill-side –
And then come back down.
Singing: 'There dwells a loved one,   140
But cruel is she!
She left lonely for ever
The kings of the sea.'

THE SICK KING IN BOKHARA

Hussein

O MOST just Vizier, send away
The cloth-merchants, and let them be,
Them and their dues, this day! the King
Is ill at ease, and calls for thee.

The Vizier

O merchants, tarry yet a day   5
Here in Bokhara! but at noon,
To-morrow, come, and ye shall pay
Each fortieth web of cloth to me,
As the law is, and go your way.

O Hussein, lead me to the King!   10
Thou teller of sweet tales, thine own,
Ferdousi's, and the others', lead!
How is it with my lord?

Hussein

    Alone,
Ever since prayer-time, he doth wait,
O Vizier! without lying down,   15
In the great window of the gate,
Looking into the Registàn,
Where through the sellers' booths the slaves
Are this way bringing the dead man. –
O Vizier, here is the King's door!   20

The King

O Vizier, I may bury him?

The Vizier

O King, thou know'st, I have been sick
These many days, and heard no thing
(For Allah shut my ears and mind),
Not even what thou dost, O King!   25
Wherefore, that I may counsel thee,
Let Hussein, if thou wilt, make haste
To speak in order what hath chanced.

The King

O Vizier, be it as thou say'st!

Hussein

Three days since, at the time of prayer   30
A certain Moollah, with his robe
All rent, and dust upon his hair,
Watch'd my lord's coming forth, and push'd
The golden mace-bearers aside,
And fell at the King's feet, and cried: 35

'Justice, O King, and on myself!
On this great sinner, who did break
The law, and by the law must die!
Vengeance, O King!'

                    But the King spake:
'What fool is this, that hurts our ears   40
With folly? or what drunken slave?
My guards, what, prick him with your spears!
Prick me the fellow from the path!'
As the King said, so it was done,
And to the mosque my lord pass'd on.   45

But on the morrow, when the King
Went forth again, the holy book
Carried before him, as is right,
And through the square his way he took;

My man comes running, fleck'd with blood   50
From yesterday, and falling down
Cries out most earnestly: 'O King,
My lord, O King, do right, I pray!

'How canst thou, ere thou hear, discern
If I speak folly? but a king,   55
Whether a thing be great or small,
Like Allah, hears and judges all.

'Wherefore hear thou! Thou know'st, how fierce
In these last days the sun hath burn'd;
That the green water in the tanks   60
Is to a putrid puddle turn'd;
And the canal, which from the stream
Of Samarcand is brought this way,
Wastes, and runs thinner every day.

'Now I at nightfall had gone forth   65
Alone, and in a darksome place
Under some mulberry-trees I found
A little pool; and in short space,
With all the water that was there
I fill'd my pitcher, and stole home   70
Unseen; and having drink to spare,
I hid the can behind the door,
And went up on the roof to sleep.

'But in the night, which was with wind
And burning dust, again I creep   75
Down, having fever, for a drink.

'Now meanwhile had my brethren found
The water-pitcher, where it stood
Behind the door upon the ground,
And call'd my mother; and they all,   80
As they were thirsty, and the night
Most sultry, drain'd the pitcher there;
That they sate with it, in my sight,
Their lips still wet, when I came down.

'Now mark! I, being fever'd, sick   85
(Most unblest also), at that sight
Brake forth, and cursed them – dost thou
   hear? –
One was my mother — Now, do right!'

But my lord mused a space, and said:
'Send him away, Sirs, and make on!   90
It is some madman!' the King said.
As the King bade, so was it done.

The morrow, at the self-same hour,
In the King's path, behold, the man,
Not kneeling, sternly fix'd! he stood   95
Right opposite, and thus began,

Frowning grim down: 'Thou wicked King,
Most deaf where thou shouldst most give
   ear!
What, must I howl in the next world,
Because thou wilt not listen here?   100

'What, wilt thou pray, and get thee grace,
And all grace shall to me be grudged?
Nay but, I swear, from this thy path
I will not stir till I be judged!'

Then they who stood about the King   105
Drew close together and conferr'd;
Till that the King stood forth and said:
'Before the priests thou shalt be heard.'

But when the Ulemas were met,
And the thing heard, they doubted not;   110
But sentenced him, as the law is,
To die by stoning on the spot.

Now the King charged us secretly:
'Stoned must he be, the law stands so.
Yet, if he seek to fly, give way;   115
Hinder him not, but let him go.'

So saying, the King took a stone,
And cast it softly; — but the man,
With a great joy upon his face,
Kneel'd down, and cried not, neither ran.   120

So they, whose lot it was, cast stones,
That they flew thick and bruised him sore.
But he praised Allah with loud voice,
And remain'd kneeling as before.

My lord had cover'd up his face;   125
But when one told him, 'He is dead,'
Turning him quickly to go in,
'Bring thou to me his corpse,' he said.

And truly, while I speak, O King,
I hear the bearers on the stair;   130
Wilt thou they straightway bring him in?
— Ho! enter ye who tarry there!

The Vizier

O King, in this I praise thee not!
Now must I call thy grief not wise.
Is he thy friend, or of thy blood,   135
To find such favour in thine eyes?

Nay, were he thine own mother's son,
Still, thou art king, and the law stands.
It were not meet the balance swerved,
The sword were broken in thy hands.   140

But being nothing, as he is,
Why for no cause make sad thy face? —
Lo, I am old! three kings, ere thee,
Have I seen reigning in this place.

But who, through all this length of time,   145
Could bear the burden of his years,
If he for strangers pain'd his heart
Not less than those who merit tears?

Fathers we *must* have, wife and child,
And grievous is the grief for these;   150
This pain alone, which *must* be borne,
Makes the head white, and bows the knees.

But other loads than this his own
One man is not well made to bear.
Besides, to each are his own friends,   155
To mourn with him, and show him care.

Look, this is but one single place,
Though it be great; all the earth round,
If a man bear to have it so,
Things which might vex him shall be found.   160

Upon the Russian frontier, where
The watchers of two armies stand
Near one another, many a man,
Seeking a prey unto his hand,

Hath snatch'd a little fair-hair'd slave;   165
They snatch also, towards Mervè,
The Shiah dogs, who pasture sheep,
And up from thence to Orgunjè.

And these all, labouring for a lord,
Eat not the fruit of their own hands;   170
Which is the heaviest of all plagues,
To that man's mind, who understands.

The kaffirs also (whom God curse!)
Vex one another, night and day;
There are the lepers, and all sick;   175
There are the poor, who faint alway.

All these have sorrow, and keep still,
Whilst other men make cheer, and sing.
Wilt thou have pity on all these?
No, nor on this dead dog, O King!   180

The King

O Vizier, thou art old, I young!
Clear in these things I cannot see.
My head is burning, and a heat
Is in my skin which angers me.

But hear ye this, ye sons of men!   185
They that bear rule, and are obey'd,
Unto a rule more strong than theirs
Are in their turn obedient made.

In vain therefore, with wistful eyes
Gazing up hither, the poor man,   190
Who loiters by the high-heap'd booths,
Below there, in the Registàn,

Says: 'Happy he, who lodges there!
With silken raiment, store of rice,
And for this drought, all kinds of fruits,   195
Grape-syrup, squares of colour'd ice,

'With cherries serv'd in drifts of snow.'
In vain hath a king power to build
Houses, arcades, enamell'd mosques;
And to make orchard-closes, fill'd   200

With curious fruit-trees brought from far;
With cisterns for the winter-rain,
And, in the desert, spacious inns
In divers places – if that pain

Is not more lighten'd, which he feels,   205
If his will be not satisfied;
And that it be not, from all time
The law is planted, to abide.

Thou wast a sinner, thou poor man!
Thou wast athirst; and didst not see,   210
That, though we take what we desire,
We must not snatch it eagerly.

And I have meat and drink at will,
And rooms of treasures, not a few.
But I am sick, nor heed I these;   215
And what I would, I cannot do.

Even the great honour which I have,
When I am dead, will soon grow still;
So have I neither joy, nor fame.
But what I can do, that I will.   220

I have a fretted brick-work tomb
Upon a hill on the right hand,
Hard by a close of apricots,
Upon the road of Samarcand;

Thither, O Vizier, will I bear   225
This man my pity could not save,
And, plucking up the marble flags,
There lay his body in my grave.

Bring water, nard, and linen rolls!
Wash off all blood, set smooth each limb!   230
Then say: 'He was not wholly vile,
Because a king shall bury him.'

MYCERINUS

'NOT by the justice that my father spurn'd,
Not for the thousands whom my father slew,
Altars unfed and temples overturn'd,
Cold hearts and thankless tongues, where thanks are due;
Fell this dread voice from lips that cannot lie,   5
Stern sentence of the Powers of Destiny.

'I will unfold my sentence and my crime.
My crime – that, rapt in reverential awe,
I sate obedient, in the fiery prime
Of youth, self-govern'd, at the feet of Law;   10
Ennobling this dull pomp, the life of kings,
By contemplation of diviner things.

'My father loved injustice, and lived long;
Crown'd with gray hairs he died, and full of sway.
I loved the good he scorn'd, and hated wrong –   15
The Gods declare my recompence to-day.
I look'd for life more lasting, rule more high;
And when six years are measured, lo, I die!

'Yet surely, O my people, did I deem
Man's justice from the all-just Gods was given;   20
A light that from some upper fount did beam,
Some better archetype, whose seat was heaven;
A light that, shining from the blest abodes,
Did shadow somewhat of the life of Gods.

'Mere phantoms of man's self-tormenting heart,   25
Which on the sweets that woo it dares not feed!
Vain dreams, which quench our pleasures, then depart,
When the duped soul, self-master'd, claims its meed;
When, on the strenuous just man, Heaven bestows,
Crown of his struggling life, an unjust close!   30

'Seems it so light a thing, then, austere Powers,
To spurn man's common lure, life's pleasant things?
Seems there no joy in dances crown'd with flowers,
Love, free to range, and regal banquetings?
Bend ye on these, indeed, an unmoved eye,   35
Not Gods but ghosts, in frozen apathy?

'Or is it that some Force, too wise, too strong,
Even for yourselves to conquer or beguile,
Sweeps earth, and heaven, and men, and gods along,
Like the broad volume of the insurgent Nile?   40
And the great powers we serve, themselves may be
Slaves of a tyrannous necessity?

'Or in mid-heaven, perhaps, your golden cars,
Where earthly voice climbs never, wing their flight,
And in wild hunt, through mazy tracts of stars,   45
Sweep in the sounding stillness of the night?
Or in deaf ease, on thrones of dazzling sheen,
Drinking deep draughts of joy, ye dwell serene?

'Oh, wherefore cheat our youth, if thus it be,
Of one short joy, one lust, one pleasant dream   50
Stringing vain words of powers we cannot see,
Blind divinations of a will supreme;
Lost labour! when the circumambient gloom
But hides, if Gods, Gods careless of our doom?

'The rest I give to joy. Even while I speak,   55
My sand runs short; and – as yon star-shot ray,
Hemm'd by two banks of cloud, peers pale and weak,
Now, as the barrier closes, dies away –
Even so do past and future intertwine,
Blotting this six years' space, which yet is mine.   60

'Six years – six little years – six drops of time!
Yet suns shall rise, and many moons shall wane,
And old men die, and young men pass their prime,
And languid pleasure fade and flower again,
And the dull Gods behold, ere these are flown,   65
Revels more deep, joy keener than their own.

'Into the silence of the groves and woods
I will go forth; though something would I say –
Something – yet what, I know not; for the Gods
The doom they pass revoke not, nor delay;   70
And prayers, and gifts, and tears, are fruitless all,
And the night waxes, and the shadows fall.

'Ye men of Egypt, ye have heard your king!
I go, and I return not. But the will
Of the great Gods is plain; and ye must bring   75
Ill deeds, ill passions, zealous to fulfil
Their pleasure, to their feet; and reap their praise,
The praise of Gods, rich boon! and length of days.'

– So spake he, half in anger, half in scorn;
And one loud cry of grief and of amaze   80
Broke from his sorrowing people; so he spake,
And turning, left them there; and with brief pause,
Girt with a throng of revellers, bent his way
To the cool region of the groves he loved.
There by the river-banks he wander'd on,   85
From palm-grove on to palm-grove, happy trees,
Their smooth tops shining sunward, and beneath
Burying their unsunn'd stems in grass and flowers;
Where in one dream the feverish time of youth
Might fade in slumber, and the feet of joy   90
Might wander all day long and never tire.
Here came the king, holding high feast, at morn,
Rose-crown'd; and ever, when the sun went down,
A hundred lamps beam'd in the tranquil gloom,
From tree to tree all through the twinkling grove,   95
Revealing all the tumult of the feast –
Flush'd guests, and golden goblets foam'd with wine;
While the deep-burnish'd foliage overhead
Splinter'd the silver arrows of the moon.
  It may be that sometimes his wondering soul   100
From the loud joyful laughter of his lips
Might shrink half startled, like a guilty man
Who wrestles with his dream; as some pale shape

Gliding half hidden through the dusky stems,
Would thrust a hand before the lifted bowl,   105
Whispering: *A little space, and thou art mine!*
It may be on that joyless feast his eye
Dwelt with mere outward seeming; he, within,
Took measure of his soul, and knew its strength,
And by that silent knowledge, day by day,   110
Was calm'd, ennobled, comforted, sustain'd.
It may be; but not less his brow was smooth,
And his clear laugh fled ringing through the gloom,
And his mirth quail'd not at the mild reproof
Sigh'd out by winter's sad tranquillity;   115
Nor, pall'd with its own fulness, ebb'd and died
In the rich languor of long summer-days;
Nor wither'd when the palm-tree plumes, that roof'd
With their mild dark his grassy banquet-hall,
Bent to the cold winds of the showerless spring;   120
No, nor grew dark when autumn brought the clouds.
   So six long years he revell'd, night and day.
And when the mirth wax'd loudest, with dull sound
Sometimes from the grove's centre echoes came,
To tell his wondering people of their king;   125
In the still night, across the steaming flats,
Mix'd with the murmur of the moving Nile.

TRISTRAM AND ISEULT

I

TRISTRAM

Tristram

Is she not come? The messenger was sure.
Prop me upon the pillows once again –
Raise me, my page! this cannot long endure.
– Christ, what a night! how the sleet whips the pane!
What lights will those out to the northward be?   5

The Page

The lanterns of the fishing-boats at sea.

Tristram

Soft – who is that, stands by the dying fire?

The Page

Iseult.

Tristram

Ah! not the Iseult I desire.

*   *   *

What Knight is this so weak and pale,
Though the locks are yet brown on his noble head,   10
Propt on pillows in his bed,
Gazing seaward for the light
Of some ship that fights the gale
On this wild December night?
Over the sick man's feet is spread   15
A dark green forest-dress;
A gold harp leans against the bed,
Ruddy in the fire's light.
I know him by his harp of gold,

72

Famous in Arthur's court of old;   20
I know him by his forest-dress —
The peerless hunter, harper, knight,
Tristram of Lyoness.

What Lady is this, whose silk attire
Gleams so rich in the light of the fire?   25
The ringlets on her shoulders lying
In their flitting lustre vying
With the clasp of burnish'd gold
Which her heavy robe doth hold.
Her looks are mild, her fingers slight   30
As the driven snow are white;
But her cheeks are sunk and pale.
Is it that the bleak sea-gale
Beating from the Atlantic sea
On this coast of Brittany,   35
Nips too keenly the sweet flower?
Is it that a deep fatigue
Hath come on her, a chilly fear,
Passing all her youthful hour
Spinning with her maidens here,   40
Listlessly through the window-bars
Gazing seawards many a league,
From her lonely shore-built tower,
While the knights are at the wars?
Or, perhaps, has her young heart   45
Felt already some deeper smart,
Of those that in secret the heart-strings rive,
Leaving her sunk and pale, though fair?
Who is this snowdrop by the sea? —
I know her by her mildness rare,   50
Her snow-white hands, her golden hair;
I know her by her rich silk dress,
And her fragile loveliness —
The sweetest Christian soul alive,
Iseult of Brittany.   55
Iseult of Brittany? — but where

Is that other Iseult fair,
That proud, first Iseult, Cornwall's queen?
She, whom Tristram's ship of yore
From Ireland to Cornwall bore,   60
To Tyntagel, to the side
Of King Marc, to be his bride?
She who, as they voyaged, quaff'd
With Tristram that spiced magic draught,
Which since then for ever rolls   65
Through their blood, and binds their souls,
Working love, but working teen? –
There were two Iseults who did sway
Each her hour of Tristram's day;
But one possess'd his waning time,   70
The other his resplendent prime.
Behold her here, the patient flower,
Who possess'd his darker hour!
Iseult of the Snow-White Hand
Watches pale by Tristram's bed.   75
She is here who had his gloom,
Where art thou who hadst his bloom?
One such kiss as those of yore
Might thy dying knight restore!
Does the love-draught work no more?   80
Art thou cold, or false, or dead,
Iseult of Ireland?

        *   *   *

Loud howls the wind, sharp patters the rain,
And the knight sinks back on his pillows again.
He is weak with fever and pain,   85
And his spirit is not clear.
Hark! he mutters in his sleep,
As he wanders far from here,
Changes place and time of year,
And his closéd eye doth sweep   90
O'er some fair unwintry sea,
Not this fierce Atlantic deep,
While he mutters brokenly: –

Tristram

The calm sea shines, loose hang the vessel's sails;
Before us are the sweet green fields of Wales,   95
And overhead the cloudless sky of May. –
'Ah, would I were in those green fields at play,
Not pent on ship-board this delicious day!
Tristram, I pray thee, of thy courtesy,
Reach me my golden phial stands by thee,   100
But pledge me in it first for courtesy. –'
Ha! dost thou start? are thy lips blanch'd like mine?
Child, 'tis no true draught this, 'tis poison'd wine!
Iseult! . . .

*　　*　　*

Ah, sweet angels, let him dream!   105
Keep his eyelids! let him seem
Not this fever-wasted wight
Thinn'd and paled before his time,
But the brilliant youthful knight
In the glory of his prime,   110
Sitting in the gilded barge,
At thy side, thou lovely charge,
Bending gaily o'er thy hand,
Iseult of Ireland!
And she too, that princess fair,   115
If her bloom be now less rare,
Let her have her youth again –
Let her be as she was then!
Let her have her proud dark eyes,
And her petulant quick replies –   120
Let her sweep her dazzling hand
With its gesture of command,
And shake back her raven hair
With the old imperious air!
As of old, so let her be,   125
That first Iseult, princess bright,
Chatting with her youthful knight
As he steers her o'er the sea,

Quitting at her father's will
The green isle where she was bred, 130
And her bower in Ireland,
For the surge-beat Cornish strand;
Where the prince whom she must wed
Dwells on loud Tyntagel's hill,
High above the sounding sea. 135
And that potion rare her mother
Gave her, that her future lord,
Gave her, that King Marc and she,
Might drink it on their marriage-day,
And for ever love each other -- 140
Let her, as she sits on board,
Ah, sweet saints, unwittingly!
See it shine, and take it up,
And to Tristram laughing say:
'Sir Tristram, of thy courtesy, 145
Pledge me in my golden cup!'
Let them drink it -- let their hands
Tremble, and their cheeks be flame,
As they feel the fatal bands
Of a love they dare not name, 150
With a wild delicious pain,
Twine about their hearts again!
Let the early summer be
Once more round them, and the sea
Blue, and o'er its mirror kind 155
Let the breath of the May-wind,
Wandering through their drooping sails,
Die on the green fields of Wales!
Let a dream like this restore
What his eye must see no more! 160

Tristram

Chill blows the wind, the pleasaunce-walks are drear --
Madcap, what jest was this, to meet me here?
Were feet like those made for so wild a way?
The southern winter-parlour, by my fay,

Had been the likeliest trysting-place to-day!   165
'Tristram! – nay, nay – thou must not take my hand! –
Tristram! – sweet love! – we are betray'd – out-plann'd.
Fly – save thyself – save me! – I dare not stay.' –
One last kiss first! – "Tis vain – to horse – away!'

*   *   *

    Ah! sweet saints, his dream doth move   170
    Faster surely than it should,
    From the fever in his blood!
    All the spring-time of his love
    Is already gone and past,
    And instead thereof is seen   175
    Its winter, which endureth still –
    Tyntagel on its surge-beat hill,
    The pleasaunce-walks, the weeping queen,
    The flying leaves, the straining blast,
    And that long, wild kiss – their last.   180
    And this rough December-night,
    And his burning fever-pain,
    Mingle with his hurrying dream,
    Till they rule it, till he seem
    The press'd fugitive again,   185
    The love-desperate banish'd knight
    With a fire in his brain
    Flying o'er the stormy main.
    – Whither does he wander now?
    Haply in his dreams the wind   190
    Wafts him here, and lets him find
    The lovely orphan child again
    In her castle by the coast;
    The youngest, fairest chatelaine,
    Whom this realm of France can boast,   195
    Our snowdrop by the Atlantic sea,
    Iseult of Brittany.
    And – for through the haggard air,
    The stain'd arms, the matted hair
    Of that stranger-knight ill-starr'd,   200

There gleam'd something, which recall'd
The Tristram who in better days
Was Launcelot's guest at Joyous Gard —
Welcomed here, and here install'd,
Tended of his fever here,   205
Haply he seems again to move
His young guardian's heart with love;
In his exiled loneliness,
In his stately, deep distress,
Without a word, without a tear.   210
— Ah! 'tis well he should retrace
His tranquil life in this lone place;
His gentle bearing at the side
Of his timid youthful bride;
His long rambles by the shore   215
On winter-evenings, when the roar
Of the near waves came, sadly grand,
Through the dark, up the drown'd sand,
Or his endless reveries
In the woods, where the gleams play   220
On the grass under the trees,
Passing the long summer's day
Idle as a mossy stone
In the forest-depths alone,
The chase neglected, and his hound   225
Couch'd beside him on the ground.
— Ah! what trouble's on his brow?
Hither let him wander now;
Hither, to the quiet hours
Pass'd among these heaths of ours   230
By the grey Atlantic sea;
Hours, if not of ecstasy,
From violent anguish surely free!

Tristram

All red with blood the whirling river flows,
The wide plain rings, the dazed air throbs with blows.   235

78

Upon us are the chivalry of Rome –
Their spears are down, their steeds are bathed in foam.
'Up, Tristram, up,' men cry, 'thou moonstruck knight !
What foul fiend rides thee? On into the fight !'
– Above the din her voice is in my ears;   240
I see her form glide through the crossing spears. –
Iseult ! . . .

* * *

Ah! he wanders forth again;
We cannot keep him; now, as then,
There's a secret in his breast   245
Which will never let him rest.
These musing fits in the green wood
They cloud the brain, they dull the blood !
– His sword is sharp, his horse is good;
Beyond the mountains will he see   250
The famous towns of Italy,
And label with the blessed sign
The heathen Saxons on the Rhine.
At Arthur's side he fights once more
With the Roman Emperor.   255
There's many a gay knight where he goes
Will help him to forget his care;
The march, the leaguer, Heaven's blithe air,
The neighing steeds, the ringing blows –
Sick pining comes not where these are.   260
Ah ! what boots it, that the jest
Lightens every other brow,
What, that every other breast
Dances as the trumpets blow,
If one's own heart beats not light   265
On the waves of the toss'd fight,
If oneself cannot get free
From the clog of misery ?
Thy lovely youthful wife grows pale
Watching by the salt sea-tide   270
With her children at her side
For the gleam of thy white sail.

Home, Tristram, to thy halls again!
To our lonely sea complain,
To our forests tell thy pain!   275

Tristram

All round the forest sweeps off, black in shade,
But it is moonlight in the open glade;
And in the bottom of the glade shine clear
The forest-chapel and the fountain near.
— I think, I have a fever in my blood;   280
Come, let me leave the shadow of this wood,
Ride down, and bathe my hot brow in the flood.
— Mild shines the cold spring in the moon's clear light;
God! 'tis *her* face plays in the waters bright.
'Fair love,' she says, 'canst thou forget so soon,   285
At this soft hour, under this sweet moon?' —
Iseult! . . .

*   *   *

Ah, poor soul! if this be so,
Only death can balm thy woe.
The solitudes of the green wood   290
Had no medicine for thy mood;
The rushing battle clear'd thy blood
As little as did solitude.
— Ah! his eyelids slowly break
Their hot seals, and let him wake;   295
What new change shall we now see?
A happier? Worse it cannot be.

Tristram

Is my page here? Come, turn me to the fire!
Upon the window-panes the moon shines bright;
The wind is down — but she'll not come to-night.   300
Ah no! she is asleep in Cornwall now,
Far hence; her dreams are fair — smooth is her brow.
Of me she recks not, nor my vain desire.

– I have had dreams, I have had dreams, my page,
Would take a score years from a strong man's age; 305
And with a blood like mine, will leave, I fear,
Scant leisure for a second messenger.
– My princess, art thou there? Sweet, do not wait!
To bed, and sleep! my fever is gone by;
To-night my page shall keep me company. 310
Where do the children sleep? kiss them for me!
Poor child, thou art almost as pale as I;
This comes of nursing long and watching late.
To bed – good night!

*　　*　　*

 She left the gleam-lit fireplace, 315
She came to the bed-side;
She took his hands in hers – her tears
Down on his wasted fingers rain'd.
She raised her eyes upon his face –
Not with a look of wounded pride, 320
A look as if the heart complained –
Her look was like a sad embrace;
The gaze of one who can divine
A grief, and sympathise.
Sweet flower! thy children's eyes 325
Are not more innocent than thine.
 But they sleep in shelter'd rest,
Like helpless birds in the warm nest,
On the castle's southern side;
Where feebly comes the mournful roar 330
Of buffeting wind and surging tide
Through many a room and corridor.
– Full on their window the moon's ray
Makes their chamber as bright as day.
It shines upon the blank white walls, 335
And on the snowy pillow falls,
And on two angel-heads doth play
Turn'd to each other – the eyes closed,
The lashes on the cheeks reposed.

81

Round each sweet brow the cap close-set   340
Hardly lets peep the golden hair;
Through the soft-open'd lips the air
Scarcely moves the coverlet.
One little wandering arm is thrown
At random on the counterpane,   345
And often the fingers close in haste
As if their baby-owner chased
The butterflies again.
This stir they have, and this alone;
But else they are so still!   350
– Ah, tired madcaps! you lie still;
But were you at the window now,
To look forth on the fairy sight
Of your illumined haunts by night,
To see the park-glades where you play   355
Far lovelier than they are by day,
To see the sparkle on the eaves,
And upon every giant-bough
Of those old oaks, whose wet red leaves
Are jewell'd with bright drops of rain –   360
How would your voices run again!
And far beyond the sparkling trees
Of the castle-park one sees
The bare heaths spreading, clear as day,
Moor behind moor, far, far away,   365
Into the heart of Brittany.
And here and there, lock'd by the land,
Long inlets of smooth glittering sea,
And many a stretch of watery sand
All shining in the white moon-beams –   370
But you see fairer in your dreams!
What voices are these on the clear night-air?
What lights in the court – what steps on the stair?

Tristram

Thou art paler – but thy sweet charm, Iseult!   25
    Would not fade with the dull years away.
Ah, how fair thou standest in the moonlight!
    I forgive thee, Iseult! – thou wilt stay?

Iseult

Fear me not, I will be always with thee;
    I will watch thee, tend thee, soothe thy pain;   30
Sing thee tales of true, long-parted lovers,
    Join'd at evening of their days again.

Tristram

No, thou shalt not speak! I should be finding
    Something alter'd in thy courtly tone.
Sit – sit by me! I will think, we've lived so   35
    In the green wood, all our lives, alone.

Iseult

Alter'd, Tristram? Not in courts, believe me,
    Love like mine is alter'd in the breast;
Courtly life is light and cannot reach it –
    Ah! it lives, because so deep-suppress'd!   40

What, thou think'st men speak in courtly chambers
    Words by which the wretched are consoled?
What, thou think'st this aching brow was cooler,
    Circled, Tristram, by a band of gold?

Royal state with Marc, my deep-wrong'd husband –   45
    That was bliss to make my sorrows flee!
Silken courtiers whispering honied nothings –
    Those were friends to make me false to thee!

Ah, on which, if both our lots were balanced,
    Was indeed the heaviest burden thrown –   50
Thee, a pining exile in thy forest,
    Me, a smiling queen upon my throne?

II

ISEULT OF IRELAND

Tristram

RAISE the light, my page! that I may see her. –
  Thou art come at last, then, haughty Queen!
Long I've waited, long I've fought my fever;
  Late thou comest, cruel thou hast been.

Iseult

Blame me not, poor sufferer! that I tarried;   5
  Bound I was, I could not break the band.
Chide not with the past, but feel the present!
  I am here – we meet – I hold thy hand.

Tristram

Thou art come, indeed – thou hast rejoin'd me;
  Thou hast dared it – but too late to save.   10
Fear not now that men should tax thine honour!
  I am dying: build – (thou may'st) – my grave!

Iseult

Tristram, ah, for love of Heaven, speak kindly!
  What, I hear these bitter words from thee?
Sick with grief I am, and faint with travel –   15
  Take my hand – dear Tristram, look on me!

Tristram

I forgot, thou comest from thy voyage –
  Yes, the spray is on thy cloak and hair.
But thy dark eyes are not dimm'd, proud Iseult!
  And thy beauty never was more fair.   20

Iseult

Ah, harsh flatterer! let alone my beauty!
  I, like thee, have left my youth afar.
Take my hand, and touch these wasted fingers –
  See my cheek and lips, how white they are!

Vain and strange debate, where both have suffer'd,
 Both have pass'd a youth consumed and sad,
Both have brought their anxious day to evening,   55
 And have now short space for being glad!

Join'd we are henceforth; nor will thy people,
 Nor thy younger Iseult take it ill,
That a former rival shares her office,
 When she sees her humbled, pale, and still.   60

I, a faded watcher by thy pillow,
 I, a statue on thy chapel-floor,
Pour'd in prayer before the Virgin-Mother,
 Rouse no anger, make no rivals more.

She will cry: 'Is this the foe I dreaded?   65
 This his idol? this that royal bride?
Ah, an hour of health would purge his eyesight!
 Stay, pale queen! for ever by my side.'

Hush, no words! that smile, I see, forgives me.
 I am now thy nurse, I bid thee sleep.   70
Close thine eyes – this flooding moonlight blinds
   them! –
 Nay, all's well again! thou must not weep.

Tristram

I am happy! yet I feel, there's something
 Swells my heart, and takes my breath away.
Through a mist I see thee; near – come nearer!   75
 Bend – bend down! – I yet have much to say.

Iseult

Heaven! his head sinks back upon the pillow –
 Tristram! Tristram! let thy heart not fail!
Call on God and on the holy angels!
 What, love, courage! – Christ! he is so pale.   80

Tristram

Hush, 'tis vain, I feel my end approaching!
  This is what my mother said should be;
When the fierce pains took her in the forest,
  The deep draughts of death, in bearing me.

'Son,' she said, 'thy name shall be of sorrow;   85
  Tristram art thou call'd for my death's sake.'
So she said, and died in the drear forest.
  Grief since then his home with me doth make.

I am dying. – Start not, nor look wildly!
  Me, thy living friend, thou canst not save.   90
But, since living we were ununited,
  Go not far, O Iseult! from my grave.

Close mine eyes, then seek the princess Iseult;
  Speak her fair, she is of royal blood!
Say, I will'd so, that thou stay beside me –   95
  She will grant it; she is kind and good.

Now to sail the seas of death I leave thee –
  One last kiss upon the living shore!

Iseult

Tristram! – Tristram! – stay – receive me with thee!
  Iseult leaves thee, Tristram! never more.   100

*   *   *

You see them clear – the moon shines bright.
Slow, slow and softly, where she stood,
She sinks upon the ground; – her hood
Had fallen back; her arms outspread
Still hold her lover's hand; her head   105
Is bow'd, half-buried, on the bed.
O'er the blanch'd sheet her raven hair
Lies in disorder'd streams; and there,
Strung like white stars, the pearls still are,
And the golden bracelets, heavy and rare,   110
Flash on her white arms still.

The very same which yesternight
Flash'd in the silver sconces' light,
When the feast was gay and the laughter loud
In Tyntagel's palace proud.   115
But then they deck'd a restless ghost
With hot-flush'd cheeks and brilliant eyes,
And quivering lips on which the tide
Of courtly speech abruptly died,
And a glance which over the crowded floor,   120
The dancers, and the festive host,
Flew ever to the door.
That the knights eyed her in surprise,
And the dames whispered scoffingly:
'Her moods, good lack, they pass like showers!   125
But yesternight and she would be
As pale and still as wither'd flowers,
And now to-night she laughs and speaks
And has a colour in her cheeks;
Christ keep us from such fantasy!' –   130

Yes, now the longing is o'erpast,
Which, dogg'd by fear and fought by shame,
Shook her weak bosom day and night,
Consumed her beauty like a flame,
And dimm'd it like the desert-blast.   135
And though the bed-clothes hide her face,
Yet were it lifted to the light,
The sweet expression of her brow
Would charm the gazer, till his thought
Erased the ravages of time,   140
Fill'd up the hollow cheek, and brought
A freshness back as of her prime –
So healing is her quiet now.
So perfectly the lines express
A tranquil, settled loveliness,   145
Her younger rival's purest grace.

The air of the December-night
Steals coldly around the chamber bright,

Where those lifeless lovers be;
Swinging with it, in the light   150
Flaps the ghostlike tapestry.
And on the arras wrought you see
A stately Huntsman, clad in green,
And round him a fresh forest-scene.
On that clear forest-knoll he stays,   155
With his pack round him, and delays.
He stares and stares, with troubled face,
At this huge, gleam-lit fireplace,
At that bright, iron-figured door,
And those blown rushes on the floor.   160
He gazes down into the room
With heated cheeks and flurried air,
And to himself he seems to say:
'What place is this, and who are they?
Who is that kneeling Lady fair?   165
And on his pillows that pale Knight
Who seems of marble on a tomb?
How comes it here, this chamber bright,
Through whose mullion'd windows clear
The castle-court all wet with rain,   170
The drawbridge and the moat appear,
And then the beach, and, mark'd with spray,
The sunken reefs, and far away
The unquiet bright Atlantic plain?
— What, has some glamour made me sleep,   175
And sent me with my dogs to sweep,
By night, with boisterous bugle-peal,
Through some old, sea-side, knightly hall,
Not in the free green wood at all?
That Knight's asleep, and at her prayer   180
That Lady by the bed doth kneel —
Then hush, thou boisterous bugle-peal!'
— The wild boar rustles in his lair;
The fierce hounds snuff the tainted air;
But lord and hounds keep rooted there.   185

Cheer, cheer thy dogs into the brake,
O Hunter! and without a fear
Thy golden-tassell'd bugle blow,
And through the glades thy pastime take –
For thou wilt rouse no sleepers here!   190
For these thou seest are unmoved;
Cold, cold as those who lived and loved
A thousand years ago.

III

ISEULT OF BRITTANY

A YEAR had flown, and o'er the sea away,
In Cornwall, Tristram and Queen Iseult lay;
In King Marc's chapel, in Tyntagel old –
There in a ship they bore those lovers cold.

The young surviving Iseult, one bright day,   5
Had wander'd forth. Her children were at play
In a green circular hollow in the heath
Which borders the sea-shore – a country path
Creeps over it from the till'd fields behind.
The hollow's grassy banks are soft-inclined,   10
And to one standing on them, far and near
The lone unbroken view spreads bright and clear
Over the waste. This cirque of open ground
Is light and green; the heather, which all round
Creeps thickly, grows not here; but the pale grass   15
Is strewn with rocks, and many a shiver'd mass
Of vein'd white-gleaming quartz, and here and there
Dotted with holly-trees and juniper.
In the smooth centre of the opening stood
Three hollies side by side, and made a screen,   20
Warm with the winter-sun, of burnish'd green
With scarlet berries gemm'd, the fell-fare's food.

Under the glittering hollies Iseult stands,
Watching her children play; their little hands
Are busy gathering spars of quartz, and streams   25
Of stagshorn for their hats; anon, with screams
Of mad delight they drop their spoils, and bound
Among the holly-clumps and broken ground,
Racing full speed, and startling in their rush
The fell-fares and the speckled missel-thrush   30
Out of their glossy coverts; – but when now
Their cheeks were flush'd, and over each hot brow,
Under the feather'd hats of the sweet pair,
In blinding masses shower'd the golden hair –
Then Iseult call'd them to her, and the three   35
Cluster'd under the holly-screen, and she
Told them an old-world Breton history.

Warm in their mantles wrapt the three stood there,
Under the hollies, in the clear still air –
Mantles with those rich furs deep glistering   40
Which Venice ships do from swart Egypt bring.
Long they stay'd still – then, pacing at their ease,
Moved up and down under the glossy trees.
But still, as they pursued their warm dry road,
From Iseult's lips the unbroken story flow'd,   45
And still the children listen'd, their blue eyes
Fix'd on their mother's face in wide surprise;
Nor did their looks stray once to the sea-side,
Nor to the brown heaths round them, bright and wide,
Nor to the snow, which, though 't was all away   50
From the open heath, still by the hedgerows lay,
Nor to the shining sea-fowl, that with screams
Bore up from where the bright Atlantic gleams,
Swooping to landward; nor to where, quite clear,
The fell-fares settled on the thickets near.   55
And they would still have listen'd, till dark night
Came keen and chill down on the heather bright;
But, when the red glow on the sea grew cold,
And the grey turrets of the castle old

Look'd sternly through the frosty evening-air,　　　　60
Then Iseult took by the hand those children fair,
And brought her tale to an end, and found the path,
And led them home over the darkening heath.

And is she happy? Does she see unmoved
The days in which she might have lived and
　　loved　　　　65
Slip without bringing bliss slowly away,
One after one, to-morrow like to-day?
Joy has not found her yet, nor ever will –
Is it this thought which makes her mien so still,
Her features so fatigued, her eyes. though sweet,　　70
So sunk, so rarely lifted save to meet
Her children's? She moves slow; her voice alone
Hath yet an infantine and silver tone,
But even that comes languidly; in truth,
She seems one dying in a mask of youth.　　75
And now she will go home, and softly lay
Her laughing children in their beds, and play
Awhile with them before they sleep; and then
She'll light her silver lamp, which fishermen
Dragging their nets through the rough waves, afar,　　80
Along this iron coast, know like a star,
And take her broidery-frame, and there she'll sit
Hour after hour, her gold curls sweeping it;
Lifting her soft-bent head only to mind
Her children, or to listen to the wind.　　85
And when the clock peals midnight, she will move
Her work away, and let her fingers rove
Across the shaggy brows of Tristram's hound
Who lies, guarding her feet, along the ground;
Or else she will fall musing, her blue eyes　　90
Fixt, her slight hands clasp'd on her lap; then rise,
And at her prie-dieu kneel, until she have told
Her rosary-beads of ebony tipp'd with gold,
Then to her soft sleep – and to-morrow'll be
To-day's exact repeated effigy.　　95

Yes, it is lonely for her in her hall.
The children, and the grey-hair'd seneschal,
Her women, and Sir Tristram's aged hound,
Are there the sole companions to be found.
But these she loves; and noisier life than this   100
She would find ill to bear, weak as she is.
She has her children, too, and night and day
Is with them; and the wide heaths where they play,
The hollies, and the cliff, and the sea-shore,
The sand, the sea-birds, and the distant sails,   105
These are to her dear as to them; the tales
With which this day the children she beguiled
She gleaned from Breton grandames, when a child,
In every hut along this sea-coast wild.
She herself loves them still, and, when they are told,   110
Can forget all to hear them, as of old.

Dear saints, it is not sorrow, as I hear,
Not suffering, which shuts up eye and ear
To all that has delighted them before,
And lets us be what we were once no more.   115
No, we may suffer deeply, yet retain
Power to be moved and soothed, for all our pain,
By what of old pleased us, and will again.
No, 'tis the gradual furnace of the world,
In whose hot air our spirits are upcurl'd   120
Until they crumble, or else grow like steel –
Which kills in us the bloom, the youth, the spring –
Which leaves the fierce necessity to feel,
But takes away the power – this can avail,
By drying up our joy in everything,   125
To make our former pleasures all seem stale.
This, or some tyrannous single thought, some fit
Of passion, which subdues our souls to it,
Till for its sake alone we live and move –
Call it ambition, or remorse, or love –   130
This too can change us wholly, and make seem
All which we did before, shadow and dream.

And yet, I swear, it angers me to see
How this fool passion gulls men potently;
Being, in truth, but a diseased unrest,   135
And an unnatural overheat at best.
How they are full of languor and distress
Not having it; which when they do possess,
They straightway are burnt up with fume and care,
And spend their lives in posting here and there   140
Where this plague drives them; and have little ease,
Are furious with themselves, and hard to please.
Like that bald Caesar, the famed Roman wight,
Who wept at reading of a Grecian knight
Who made a name at younger years than he;   145
Or that renown'd mirror of chivalry,
Prince Alexander, Philip's peerless son,
Who carried the great war from Macedon
Into the Soudan's realm, and thundered on
To die at thirty-five in Babylon.   150

What tale did Iseult to the children say,
Under the hollies, that bright winter's day?

She told them of the fairy-haunted land
Away the other side of Brittany,
Beyond the heaths, edged by the lonely sea;   155
Of the deep forest-glades of Broce-liande,
Through whose green boughs the golden sunshine creeps,
Where Merlin by the enchanted thorn-tree sleeps.
For here he came with the fay Vivian,
One April, when the warm days first began.   160
He was on foot, and that false fay, his friend,
On her white palfrey; here he met his end,
In these lone sylvan glades, that April-day.
This tale of Merlin and the lovely fay
Was the one Iseult chose, and she brought clear   165
Before the children's fancy him and her.

Blowing between the stems, the forest-air
Had loosen'd the brown locks of Vivian's hair,

Which play'd on her flush'd cheek, and her blue eyes
Sparkled with mocking glee and exercise.   170
Her palfrey's flanks were mired and bathed in sweat,
For they had travell'd far and not stopp'd yet.
A brier in that tangled wilderness
Had scored her white right hand, which she allows
To rest ungloved on her green riding-dress;   175
The other warded off the drooping boughs.
But still she chatted on, with her blue eyes
Fix'd full on Merlin's face, her stately prize.
Her 'haviour had the morning's fresh clear grace,
The spirit of the woods was in her face.   180
She look'd so witching fair, that learned wight
Forgot his craft, and his best wits took flight;
And he grew fond, and eager to obey
His mistress, use her empire as she may.

They came to where the brushwood ceased, and day   185
Peer'd 'twixt the stems; and the ground broke
    away,
In a sloped sward down to a brawling brook;
And up as high as where they stood to look
On the brook's farther side was clear, but then
The underwood and trees began again.   190
This open glen was studded thick with thorns
Then white with blossom; and you saw the horns,
Through last year's fern, of the shy fallow-deer
Who come at noon down to the water here.
You saw the bright-eyed squirrels dart along   195
Under the thorns on the green sward; and strong
The blackbird whistled from the dingles near,
And the weird chipping of the woodpecker
Rang lonelily and sharp; the sky was fair,
And a fresh breath of spring stirr'd everywhere.   200
Merlin and Vivian stopp'd on the slope's brow,
To gaze on the light sea of leaf and bough
Which glistening plays all round them, lone and mild,
As if to itself the quiet forest smiled.

Upon the brow-top grew a thorn, and here   205
The grass was dry and moss'd, and you saw clear
Across the hollow; white anemones
Starr'd the cool turf, and clumps of primroses
Ran out from the dark underwood behind.
No fairer resting-place a man could find.   210
'Here let us halt,' said Merlin then; and she
Nodded, and tied her palfrey to a tree.

They sate them down together, and a sleep
Fell upon Merlin, more like death, so deep.
Her finger on her lips, then Vivian rose,   215
And from her brown-lock'd head the wimple throws,
And takes it in her hand, and waves it over
The blossom'd thorn-tree and her sleeping lover.
Nine times she waved the fluttering wimple round,
And made a little plot of magic ground.   220
And in that daisied circle, as men say,
Is Merlin prisoner till the judgement-day;
But she herself whither she will can rove –
For she was passing weary of his love.

SOHRAB AND RUSTUM

AN EPISODE

AND the first grey of morning fill'd the east,
And the fog rose out of the Oxus stream.
But all the Tartar camp along the stream
Was hush'd, and still the men were plunged in sleep;
Sohrab alone, he slept not; all night long   5
He had lain wakeful, tossing on his bed;
But when the grey dawn stole into his tent,
He rose, and clad himself, and girt his sword,
And took his horseman's cloak, and left his tent,
And went abroad into the cold wet fog,   10
Through the dim camp to Peran-Wisa's tent.
    Through the black Tartar tents he pass'd, which stood
Clustering like bee-hives on the low flat strand
Of Oxus, where the summer-floods o'erflow
When the sun melts the snows in high Pamere;   15
Through the black tents he pass'd, o'er that low strand,
And to a hillock came, a little back
From the stream's brink – the spot where first a boat,
Crossing the stream in summer, scrapes the land.
The men of former times had crown'd the top   20
With a clay fort; but that was fall'n, and now
The Tartars built there Peran-Wisa's tent,
A dome of laths, and o'er it felts were spread.
And Sohrab came there, and went in, and stood
Upon the thick piled carpets in the tent,   25
And found the old man sleeping on his bed
Of rugs and felts, and near him lay his arms.
And Peran-Wisa heard him, though the step
Was dull'd; for he slept light, an old man's sleep;
And he rose quickly on one arm, and said: –   30
    'Who art thou? for it is not yet clear dawn.
Speak! is there news, or any night alarm?'

96

But Sohrab came to the bedside, and said: —
'Thou know'st me, Peran-Wisa! it is I.
The sun is not yet risen, and the foe   35
Sleep; but I sleep not; all night long I lie
Tossing and wakeful, and I come to thee.
For so did King Afrasiab bid me seek
Thy counsel, and to heed thee as thy son,
In Samarcand, before the army march'd;   40
And I will tell thee what my heart desires.
Thou know'st if, since from Ader-baijan first
I came among the Tartars and bore arms,
I have still served Afrasiab well, and shown,
At my boy's years, the courage of a man.   45
This too thou know'st, that while I still bear on
The conquering Tartar ensigns through the world,
And beat the Persians back on every field,
I seek one man, one man, and one alone —
Rustum, my father; who I hoped should greet,   50
Should one day greet, upon some well-fought field,
His not unworthy, not inglorious son.
So I long hoped, but him I never find.
Come then, hear now, and grant me what I ask.
Let the two armies rest to-day; but I   55
Will challenge forth the bravest Persian lords
To meet me, man to man; if I prevail,
Rustum will surely hear it; if I fall —
Old man, the dead need no one, claim no kin.
Dim is the rumour of a common fight,   60
Where host meets host, and many names are sunk;
But of a single combat fame speaks clear.'
    He spoke; and Peran-Wisa took the hand
Of the young man in his, and sigh'd, and said: —
    'O Sohrab, an unquiet heart is thine!   65
Canst thou not rest among the Tartar chiefs,
And share the battle's common chance with us
Who love thee, but must press for ever first,
In single fight incurring single risk,
To find a father thou hast never seen?   70

That were far best, my son, to stay with us
Unmurmuring; in our tents, while it is war,
And when 'tis truce, then in Afrasiab's towns.
But, if this one desire indeed rules all,
To seek out Rustum – seek him not through fight!   75
Seek him in peace, and carry to his arms,
O Sohrab, carry an unwounded son!
But far hence seek him, for he is not here.
For now it is not as when I was young,
When Rustum was in front of every fray;   80
But now he keeps apart, and sits at home,
In Seistan, with Zal, his father old.
Whether that his own mighty strength at last
Feels the abhorr'd approaches of old age,
Or in some quarrel with the Persian King.   85
There go! – Thou wilt not? Yet my heart forebodes
Danger or death awaits thee on this field.
Fain would I know thee safe and well, though lost
To us; fain therefore send thee hence, in peace
To seek thy father, not seek single fights   90
In vain; – but who can keep the lion's cub
From ravening, and who govern Rustum's son?
Go, I will grant thee what thy heart desires.'

    So said he, and dropp'd Sohrab's hand, and left
His bed, and the warm rugs whereon he lay;   95
And o'er his chilly limbs his woollen coat
He pass'd, and tied his sandals on his feet,
And threw a white cloak round him, and he took
In his right hand a ruler's staff, no sword;
And on his head he set his sheep-skin cap,   100
Black, glossy, curl'd, the fleece of Kara-Kul;
And raised the curtain of his tent, and call'd
His herald to his side, and went abroad.

    The sun by this had risen, and clear'd the fog
From the broad Oxus and the glittering sands.   105
And from their tents the Tartar horsemen filed
Into the open plain; so Haman bade –
Haman, who next to Peran-Wisa ruled

The host, and still was in his lusty prime.
From their black tents, long files of horse, they stream'd; 110
As when some grey November morn the files,
In marching order spread, of long-neck'd cranes
Stream over Casbin and the southern slopes
Of Elburz, from the Aralian estuaries,
Or some frore Caspian reed-bed, southward bound   115
For the warm Persian sea-board – so they stream'd.
The Tartars of the Oxus, the King's guard,
First, with black sheep-skin caps and with long spears;
Large men, large steeds; who from Bokhara come
And Khiva, and ferment the milk of mares.   120
Next, the more temperate Toorkmuns of the south,
The Tukas, and the lances of Salore,
And those from Attruck and the Caspian sands;
Light men and on light steeds, who only drink
The acrid milk of camels, and their wells.   125
And then a swarm of wandering horse, who came
From far, and a more doubtful service own'd;
The Tartars of Ferghana, from the banks
Of the Jaxartes, men with scanty beards
And close-set skull-caps; and those wilder hordes   130
Who roam o'er Kipchak and the northern waste,
Kalmucks and unkempt Kuzzaks, tribes who stray
Nearest the Pole, and wandering Kirghizzes,
Who come on shaggy ponies from Pamere;
These all filed out from camp into the plain.   135
And on the other side the Persians form'd; –
First a light cloud of horse, Tartars they seem'd,
The Ilyats of Khorassan; and behind,
The royal troops of Persia, horse and foot,
Marshall'd battalions bright in burnish'd steel.   140
But Peran-Wisa with his herald came,
Threading the Tartar squadrons to the front,
And with his staff kept back the foremost ranks.
And when Ferood, who led the Persians, saw
That Peran-Wisa kept the Tartars back,   145
He took his spear, and to the front he came,

And check'd his ranks, and fix'd them where they
    stood.
And the old Tartar came upon the sand
Betwixt the silent hosts, and spake, and said: —
    'Ferood, and ye, Persians and Tartars, hear!   150
Let there be truce between the hosts to-day.
But choose a champion from the Persian lords
To fight our champion Sohrab, man to man.'
    As, in the country, on a morn in June,
When the dew glistens on the pearled ears,   155
A shiver runs through the deep corn for joy —
So, when they heard what Peran-Wisa said,
A thrill through all the Tartar squadrons ran
Of pride and hope for Sohrab, whom they loved.
    But as a troop of pedlars, from Cabool,   160
Cross underneath the Indian Caucasus,
That vast sky-neighbouring mountain of milk snow;
Crossing so high, that, as they mount, they pass
Long flocks of travelling birds dead on the snow,
Choked by the air, and scarce can they themselves   165
Slake their parch'd throats with sugar'd mulberries —
In single file they move, and stop their breath,
For fear they should dislodge the o'erhanging snows —
So the pale Persians held their breath with fear.
    And to Ferood his brother chiefs came up   170
To counsel; Gudurz and Zoarrah came,
And Feraburz, who ruled the Persian host
Second, and was the uncle of the King;
These came and counsell'd, and then Gudurz said: —
    'Ferood, shame bids us take their challenge up,   175
Yet champion have we none to match this youth.
He has the wild stag's foot, the lion's heart.
But Rustum came last night; aloof he sits
And sullen, and has pitch'd his tents apart.
Him will I seek, and carry to his ear   180
The Tartar challenge, and this young man's name.
Haply he will forget his wrath, and fight.
Stand forth the while, and take their challenge up.'

So spake he; and Ferood stood forth and cried: –
'Old man, be it agreed as thou hast said!   185
Let Sohrab arm, and we will find a man.'
    He spake: and Peran-Wisa turn'd, and strode
Back through the opening squadrons to his tent.
But through the anxious Persians Gudurz ran,
And cross'd the camp which lay behind, and reach'd,   190
Out on the sands beyond it, Rustum's tents.
Of scarlet cloth they were, and glittering gay,
Just pitch'd; the high pavilion in the midst
Was Rustum's, and his men lay camp'd around.
And Gudurz enter'd Rustum's tent, and found   195
Rustum; his morning meal was done, but still
The table stood before him, charged with food –
A side of roasted sheep, and cakes of bread,
And dark green melons; and there Rustum sate
Listless, and held a falcon on his wrist,   200
And play'd with it; but Gudurz came and stood
Before him; and he look'd, and saw him stand,
And with a cry sprang up and dropp'd the bird,
And greeted Gudurz with both hands, and said: –
    'Welcome! these eyes could see no better sight.   205
What news? but sit down first, and eat and drink.'
    But Gudurz stood in the tent-door, and said: –
'Not now! a time will come to eat and drink,
But not to-day; to-day has other needs.   .
The armies are drawn out, and stand at gaze;   210
For from the Tartars is a challenge brought
To pick a champion from the Persian lords
To fight their champion – and thou know'st his name –
Sohrab men call him, but his birth is hid.
O Rustum, like thy might is this young man's!   215
He has the wild stag's foot, the lion's heart;
And he is young, and Iran's chiefs are old,
Or else too weak; and all eyes turn to thee.
Come down and help us, Rustum, or we lose!'
    He spoke; but Rustum answer'd with a smile: –   220
'Go to! if Iran's chiefs are old, then I

Am older; if the young are weak, the King
Errs strangely; for the King, for Kai Khosroo,
Himself is young, and honours younger men,
And lets the aged moulder to their graves.   225
Rustum he loves no more, but loves the young –
The young may rise at Sohrab's vaunts, not I.
For what care I, though all speak Sohrab's fame?
For would that I myself had such a son,
And not that one slight helpless girl I have –   230
A son so famed, so brave, to send to war,
And I to tarry with the snow-hair'd Zal,
My father, whom the robber Afghans vex,
And clip his borders short, and drive his herds,
And he has none to guard his weak old age.   235
There would I go, and hang my armour up,
And with my great name fence that weak old man,
And spend the goodly treasures I have got,
And rest my age, and hear of Sohrab's fame,
And leave to death the hosts of thankless kings,   240
And with these slaughterous hands draw sword no more.'

    He spoke, and smiled; and Gudurz made reply: –
'What then, O Rustum, will men say to this,
When Sohrab dares our bravest forth, and seeks
Thee most of all, and thou, whom most he seeks,   245
Hidest thy face? Take heed lest men should say:
Like some old miser, Rustum hoards his fame,
And shuns to peril it with younger men.'

    And greatly moved, then Rustum made reply: –
'O Gudurz, wherefore dost thou say such words?   250
Thou knowest better words than this to say.
What is one more, one less, obscure or famed,
Valiant or craven, young or old, to me?
Are not they mortal, am not I myself?
But who for men of nought would do great deeds?   255
Come, thou shalt see how Rustum hoards his fame!
But I will fight unknown, and in plain arms;
Let not men say of Rustum, he was match'd
In single fight with any mortal man.'

He spoke, and frown'd; and Gudurz turn'd, and ran   260
Back quickly through the camp in fear and joy —
Fear at his wrath, but joy that Rustum came.
But Rustum strode to his tent-door, and call'd
His followers in, and bade them bring his arms,
And clad himself in steel; the arms he chose   265
Were plain, and on his shield was no device,
Only his helm was rich, inlaid with gold,
And, from the fluted spine atop, a plume
Of horsehair waved, a scarlet horsehair plume.
So arm'd, he issued forth; and Ruksh, his horse,   270
Follow'd him like a faithful hound at heel —
Ruksh, whose renown was noised through all the earth,
The horse, whom Rustum on a foray once
Did in Bokhara by the river find
A colt beneath its dam, and drove him home,   275
And rear'd him; a bright bay, with lofty crest,
Dight with a saddle-cloth of broider'd green
Crusted with gold, and on the ground were work'd
All beasts of chase, all beasts which hunters know.
So follow'd, Rustum left his tents, and cross'd   280
The camp, and to the Persian host appear'd.
And all the Persians knew him, and with shouts
Hail'd; but the Tartars knew not who he was.
And dear as the wet diver to the eyes
Of his pale wife who waits and weeps on shore,   285
By sandy Bahrein, in the Persian Gulf,
Plunging all day in the blue waves, at night,
Having made up his tale of precious pearls,
Rejoins her in their hut upon the sands —
So dear to the pale Persians Rustum came.   290

And Rustum to the Persian front advanced,
And Sohrab arm'd in Haman's tent, and came.
And as afield the reapers cut a swath
Down through the middle of a rich man's corn,
And on each side are squares of standing corn,   295
And in the midst a stubble, short and bare —
So on each side were squares of men, with spears

Bristling, and in the midst, the open sand.
And Rustum came upon the sand, and cast
His eyes toward the Tartar tents, and saw   300
Sohrab come forth, and eyed him as he came.
     As some rich woman, on a winter's morn,
Eyes through her silken curtains the poor drudge
Who with numb blacken'd fingers makes her fire –
At cock-crow, on a starlit winter's morn,   305
When the frost flowers the whiten'd window-panes –
And wonders how she lives, and what the thoughts
Of that poor drudge may be; so Rustum eyed
The unknown adventurous youth, who from afar
Came seeking Rustum, and defying forth   310
All the most valiant chiefs; long he perused
His spirited air, and wonder'd who he was.
For very young he seem'd, tenderly rear'd;
Like some young cypress, tall, and dark, and straight,
Which in a queen's secluded garden throws   315
Its slight dark shadow on the moonlit turf,
By midnight, to a bubbling fountain's sound –
So slender Sohrab seem'd, so softly rear'd.
And a deep pity enter'd Rustum's soul
As he beheld him coming; and he stood,   320
And beckon'd to him with his hand, and said: –
     'O thou young man, the air of Heaven is soft,
And warm, and pleasant; but the grave is cold!
Heaven's air is better than the cold dead grave.
Behold me! I am vast, and clad in iron,   325
And tried; and I have stood on many a field
Of blood, and I have fought with many a foe –
Never was that field lost, or that foe saved.
O Sohrab, wherefore wilt thou rush on death?
Be govern'd! quit the Tartar host, and come   330
To Iran, and be as my son to me,
And fight beneath my banner till I die!
There are no youths in Iran brave as thou.'
     So he spake, mildly; Sohrab heard his voice,
The mighty voice of Rustum, and he saw   335

His giant figure planted on the sand,
Sole, like some single tower, which a chief
Hath builded on the waste in former years
Against the robbers; and he saw that head,
Streak'd with its first grey hairs; — hope filled his soul, 340
And he ran forward and embraced his knees,
And clasp'd his hand within his own, and said: —
 'O, by thy father's head! by thine own soul!
Art thou not Rustum? speak! art thou not he?'
 But Rustum eyed askance the kneeling youth, 345
And turn'd away, and spake to his own soul: —
 'Ah me, I muse what this young fox may mean!
False, wily, boastful, are these Tartar boys.
For if I now confess this thing he asks,
And hide it not, but say: *Rustum is here!* 350
He will not yield indeed, nor quit our foes,
But he will find some pretext not to fight,
And praise my fame, and proffer courteous gifts,
A belt or sword perhaps, and go his way.
And on a feast-tide, in Afrasiab's hall, 355
In Samarcand, he will arise and cry:
"I challenged once, when the two armies camp'd
Beside the Oxus, all the Persian lords
To cope with me in single fight; but they
Shrank, only Rustum dared; then he and I 360
Changed gifts, and went on equal terms away."
So will he speak, perhaps, while men applaud;
Then were the chiefs of Iran shamed through me.'
 And then he turn'd, and sternly spake aloud: —
 'Rise! wherefore dost thou vainly question thus 365
Of Rustum? I am here, whom thou hast call'd
By challenge forth; make good thy vaunt, or yield!
Is it with Rustum only thou wouldst fight?
Rash boy, men look on Rustum's face and flee!
For well I know, that did great Rustum stand 370
Before thy face this day, and were reveal'd,
There would be then no talk of fighting more.
But being what I am, I tell thee this —

105

Do thou record it in thine inmost soul:
Either thou shalt renounce thy vaunt and yield, 375
Or else thy bones shall strew this sand, till winds
Bleach them, or Oxus with his summer-floods,
Oxus in summer wash them all away.'

　　He spoke; and Sohrab answer'd, on his feet: –
'Art thou so fierce? Thou wilt not fright me so! 380
I am no girl, to be made pale by words.
Yet this thou hast said well, did Rustum stand
Here on this field, there were no fighting then.
But Rustum is far hence, and we stand here.
Begin! thou art more vast, more dread than I, 385
And thou art proved, I know, and I am young –
But yet success sways with the breath of Heaven.
And though thou thinkest that thou knowest sure
Thy victory, yet thou canst not surely know.
For we are all, like swimmers in the sea, 390
Poised on the top of a huge wave of fate,
Which hangs uncertain to which side to fall.
And whether it will heave us up to land,
Or whether it will roll us out to sea,
Back out to sea, to the deep waves of death, 395
We know not, and no search will make us know;
Only the event will teach us in its hour.'

　　He spoke, and Rustum answer'd not, but hurl'd
His spear; down from the shoulder, down it came,
As on some partridge in the corn a hawk, 400
That long has tower'd in the airy clouds,
Drops like a plummet; Sohrab saw it come,
And sprang aside, quick as a flash; the spear
Hiss'd, and went quivering down into the sand,
Which it sent flying wide; – then Sohrab threw 405
In turn, and full struck Rustum's shield; sharp rang,
The iron plates rang sharp, but turn'd the spear.
And Rustum seized his club, which none but he
Could wield; an unlopp'd trunk it was, and huge,
Still rough – like those which men in treeless plains 410
To build them boats fish from the flooded rivers,

Hyphasis or Hydaspes, when, high up
By their dark springs, the wind in winter-time
Hath made in Himalayan forests wrack,
And strewn the channels with torn boughs – so huge   415
The club which Rustum lifted now, and struck
One stroke; but again Sohrab sprang aside,
Lithe as the glancing snake, and the club came
Thundering to earth, and leapt from Rustum's hand.
And Rustum follow'd his own blow, and fell   420
To his knees, and with his fingers clutch'd the sand;
And now might Sohrab have unsheathed his sword,
And pierced the mighty Rustum while he lay
Dizzy, and on his knees, and choked with sand;
But he look'd on, and smiled, nor bared his sword,   425
But courteously drew back, and spoke, and said: –
    'Thou strik'st too hard! that club of thine will float
Upon the summer-floods, and not my bones.
But rise, and be not wroth! not wroth am I;
No, when I see thee, wrath forsakes my soul.   430
Thou say'st, thou art not Rustum; be it so!
Who art thou then, that canst so touch my soul?
Boy as I am, I have seen battles too –
Have waded foremost in their bloody waves,
And heard their hollow roar of dying men;   435
But never was my heart thus touch'd before.
Are they from Heaven, these softenings of the heart?
O thou old warrior, let us yield to Heaven!
Come, plant we here in earth our angry spears,
And make a truce, and sit upon this sand,   440
And pledge each other in red wine, like friends,
And thou shalt talk to me of Rustum's deeds.
There are enough foes in the Persian host,
Whom I may meet, and strike, and feel no pang;
Champions enough Afrasiab has, whom thou   445
Mayst fight; fight *them*, when they confront thy spear!
But oh, let there be peace 'twixt thee and me!'
    He ceased, but while he spake, Rustum had risen,
And stood erect, trembling with rage; his club

He left to lie, but had regain'd his spear,   450
Whose fiery point now in his mail'd right-hand
Blazed bright and baleful, like that autumn-star,
The baleful sign of fevers: dust had soil'd
His stately crest, and dimm'd his glittering arms.
His breast heaved, his lips foam'd, and twice his voice   455
Was choked with rage; at last these words broke way: —
  'Girl! nimble with thy feet, not with thy hands!
Curl'd minion, dancer, coiner of sweet words!
Fight, let me hear thy hateful voice no more!
Thou art not in Afrasiab's gardens now   460
With Tartar girls, with whom thou art wont to dance;
But on the Oxus-sands, and in the dance
Of battle, and with me, who make no play
Of war; I fight it out, and hand to hand.
Speak not to me of truce, and pledge, and wine!   465
Remember all thy valour; try thy feints
And cunning! all the pity I had is gone;
Because thou hast shamed me before both the hosts
With thy light skipping tricks, and thy girl's wiles.'
  He spoke, and Sohrab kindled at his taunts,   470
And he too drew his sword; at once they rush'd
Together, as two eagles on one prey
Come rushing down together from the clouds,
One from the east, one from the west; their shields
Dash'd with a clang together, and a din   475
Rose, such as that the sinewy woodcutters
Make often in the forest's heart at morn,
Of hewing axes, crashing trees — such blows
Rustum and Sohrab on each other hail'd.
And you would say that sun and stars took part   480
In that unnatural conflict; for a cloud
Grew suddenly in Heaven, and dark'd the sun
Over the fighters' heads; and a wind rose
Under their feet, and moaning swept the plain,
And in a sandy whirlwind wrapp'd the pair.   485
In gloom they twain were wrapp'd, and they alone;
For both the on-looking hosts on either hand

Stood in broad daylight, and the sky was pure,
And the sun sparkled on the Oxus stream.
But in the gloom they fought, with bloodshot eyes   490
And labouring breath; first Rustum struck the shield
Which Sohrab held stiff out; the steel-spiked spear
Rent the tough plates, but fail'd to reach the skin,
And Rustum pluck'd it back with angry groan.
Then Sohrab with his sword smote Rustum's helm,   495
Nor clove its steel quite through; but all the crest
He shore away, and that proud horsehair plume,
Never till now defiled, sank to the dust;
And Rustum bow'd his head; but then the gloom
Grew blacker, thunder rumbled in the air,   500
And lightnings rent the cloud; and Ruksh, the horse,
Who stood at hand, utter'd a dreadful cry; –
No horse's cry was that, most like the roar
Of some pain'd desert-lion, who all day
Hath trail'd the hunter's javelin in his side,   505
And comes at night to die upon the sand.
The two hosts heard that cry, and quaked for fear,
And Oxus curdled as it cross'd his stream.
But Sohrab heard, and quail'd not, but rush'd on,
And struck again; and again Rustum bow'd   510
His head; but this time all the blade, like glass,
Sprang in a thousand shivers on the helm,
And in the hand the hilt remain'd alone.
Then Rustum raised his head; his dreadful eyes
Glared, and he shook on high his menacing spear,   515
And shouted: *Rustum!* – Sohrab heard that shout,
And shrank amazed; back he recoil'd one step,
And scann'd with blinking eyes the advancing form;
And then he stood bewilder'd; and he dropp'd
His covering shield, and the spear pierced his side.   520
He reel'd, and staggering back, sank to the ground;
And then the gloom dispersed, and the wind fell,
And the bright sun broke forth, and melted all
The cloud; and the two armies saw the pair –
Saw Rustum standing, safe upon his feet,   525

And Sohrab, wounded, on the bloody sand.
   Then, with a bitter smile, Rustum began: —
'Sohrab, thou thoughtest in thy mind to kill
A Persian lord this day, and strip his corpse,
And bear thy trophies to Afrasiab's tent.   530
Or else that the great Rustum would come down
Himself to fight, and that thy wiles would move
His heart to take a gift, and let thee go.
And then that all the Tartar host would praise
Thy courage or thy craft, and spread thy fame,   535
To glad thy father in his weak old age.
Fool, thou art slain, and by an unknown man!
Dearer to the red jackals shalt thou be
Than to thy friends, and to thy father old.'
   And, with a fearless mien, Sohrab replied: —   540
'Unknown thou art; yet thy fierce vaunt is vain.
Thou dost not slay me, proud and boastful man!
No! Rustum slays me, and this filial heart.
For were I match'd with ten such men as thee,
And I were that which till to-day I was,   545
They should be lying here, I standing there.
But that belovéd name unnerved my arm —
That name, and something, I confess, in thee,
Which troubles all my heart, and made my shield
Fall; and thy spear transfix'd an unarm'd foe.   550
And now thou boastest, and insult'st my fate.
But hear thou this, fierce man, tremble to hear:
The mighty Rustum shall avenge my death!
My father, whom I seek through all the world,
He shall avenge my death, and punish thee!'   555
   As when some hunter in the spring hath found
A breeding eagle sitting on her nest,
Upon the craggy isle of a hill-lake,
And pierced her with an arrow as she rose,
And follow'd her to find her where she fell   560
Far off; — anon her mate comes winging back
From hunting, and a great way off descries
His huddling young left sole; at that, he checks

His pinion, and with short uneasy sweeps
Circles above his eyry, with loud screams   565
Chiding his mate back to her nest; but she
Lies dying, with the arrow in her side,
In some far stony gorge out of his ken,
A heap of fluttering feathers – never more
Shall the lake glass her, flying over it;   570
Never the black and dripping precipices
Echo her stormy scream as she sails by –
As that poor bird flies home, nor knows his loss,
So Rustum knew not his own loss, but stood
Over his dying son, and knew him not.   575

    But, with a cold incredulous voice, he said: –
'What prate is this of fathers and revenge?
The mighty Rustum never had a son.'
    And, with a failing voice, Sohrab replied: –
'Ah yes, he had! and that lost son am I.   580
Surely the news will one day reach his ear,
Reach Rustum, where he sits, and tarries long,
Somewhere, I know not where, but far from here;
And pierce him like a stab, and make him leap
To arms, and cry for vengeance upon thee.   585
Fierce man, bethink thee, for an only son!
What will that grief, what will that vengeance be?
Oh, could I live, till I that grief had seen!
Yet him I pity not so much, but her,
My mother, who in Ader-baijan dwells   590
With that old king, her father, who grows grey
With age, and rules over the valiant Koords.
Her most I pity, who no more will see
Sohrab returning from the Tartar camp,
With spoils and honour, when the war is done.   595
But a dark rumour will be bruited up,
From tribe to tribe, until it reach her ear;
And then will that defenceless woman learn
That Sohrab will rejoice her sight no more,
But that in battle with a nameless foe,   600
By the far-distant Oxus, he is slain.'

He spoke; and as he ceased, he wept aloud,
Thinking of her he left, and his own death.
He spoke; but Rustum listen'd, plunged in thought.
Nor did he yet believe it was his son   605
Who spoke, although he call'd back names he knew;
For he had had sure tidings that the babe,
Which was in Ader-baijan born to him,
Had been a puny girl, no boy at all –
So that sad mother sent him word, for fear   610
Rustum should seek the boy, to train in arms.
And so he deem'd that either Sohrab took,
By a false boast, the style of Rustum's son;
Or that men gave it him, to swell his fame.
So deem'd he; yet he listen'd, plunged in thought 615
And his soul set to grief, as the vast tide
Of the bright rocking Ocean sets to shore
At the full moon; tears gather'd in his eyes;
For he remember'd his own early youth,
And all its bounding rapture; as, at dawn,   620
The shepherd from his mountain-lodge descries
A far, bright city, smitten by the sun,
Through many rolling clouds – so Rustum saw
His youth; saw Sohrab's mother, in her bloom;
And that old king, her father, who loved well   625
His wandering guest, and gave him his fair child
With joy; and all the pleasant life they led,
They three, in that long-distant summer-time –
The castle, and the dewy woods, and hunt
And hound, and morn on those delightful hills   630
In Ader-baijan. And he saw that youth,
Of age and looks to be his own dear son,
Piteous and lovely, lying on the sand,
Like some rich hyacinth which by the scythe
Of an unskilful gardener has been cut,   635
Mowing the garden grass-plots near its bed,
And lies, a fragrant tower of purple bloom,
On the mown, dying grass – so Sohrab lay,
Lovely in death, upon the common sand.

And Rustum gazed on him with grief, and said: –   640
  'O Sohrab, thou indeed art such a son
Whom Rustum, wert thou his, might well have loved.
Yet here thou errest, Sohrab, or else men
Have told thee false – thou art not Rustum's son.
For Rustum had no son; one child he had –   645
But one – a girl; who with her mother now
Plies some light female task, nor dreams of us –
Of us she dreams not, nor of wounds, nor war.'
    But Sohrab answer'd him in wrath; for now
The anguish of the deep-fix'd spear grew fierce,   650
And he desired to draw forth the steel,
And let the blood flow free, and so to die –
But first he would convince his stubborn foe;
And, rising sternly on one arm, he said: –
    'Man, who art thou who dost deny my words?   655
Truth sits upon the lips of dying men,
And falsehood, while I lived, was far from mine.
I tell thee, prick'd upon this arm I bear
That seal which Rustum to my mother gave,
That she might prick it on the babe she bore.'   660
    He spoke; and all the blood left Rustum's cheeks,
And his knees totter'd, and he smote his hand
Against his breast, his heavy mailed hand,
That the hard iron corslet clank'd aloud;
And to his heart he press'd the other hand,   665
And in a hollow voice he spake, and said: –
    'Sohrab, that were a proof which could not lie!
If thou show this, then art thou Rustum's son.'
    Then, with weak hasty fingers, Sohrab loosed
His belt, and near the shoulder bared his arm,   670
And show'd a sign in faint vermilion points
Prick'd; as a cunning workman, in Pekin,
Pricks with vermilion some clear porcelain vase,
An emperor's gift – at early morn he paints,
And all day long, and, when night comes, the lamp   675
Lights up his studious forehead and thin hands –
So delicately prick'd the sign appear'd

On Sohrab's arm, the sign of Rustum's seal.
It was that griffin, which of old rear'd Zal,
Rustum's great father, whom they left to die,   680
A helpless babe, among the mountain-rocks;
Him that kind creature found, and rear'd, and loved –
Then Rustum took it for his glorious sign.
And Sohrab bared that image on his arm,
And himself scann'd it long with mournful eyes,   685
And then he touch'd it with his hand and said: –
  'How say'st thou? Is that sign the proper sign
Of Rustum's son, or of some other man's?'
  He spoke; but Rustum gazed, and gazed, and stood
Speechless; and then he utter'd one sharp cry: 690
O boy – thy father! – and his voice choked there.
And then a dark cloud pass'd before his eyes,
And his head swam, and he sank down to earth.
But Sohrab crawl'd to where he lay, and cast
His arms about his neck, and kiss'd his lips,   695
And with fond faltering fingers stroked his cheeks,
Trying to call him back to life; and life
Came back to Rustum, and he oped his eyes,
And they stood wide with horror; and he seized
In both his hands the dust which lay around,   700
And threw it on his head, and smirch'd his hair, –
His hair, and face, and beard, and glittering arms;
And strong convulsive groanings shook his breast,
And his sobs choked him; and he clutch'd his sword,
To draw it, and for ever let life out.   705
But Sohrab saw his thought, and held his hands,
And with a soothing voice he spake, and said: –
  'Father, forbear! for I but meet to-day
The doom which at my birth was written down
In Heaven, and thou art Heaven's unconscious hand.   710
Surely my heart cried out that it was thou,
When first I saw thee; and thy heart spoke too,
I know it! but fate trod those promptings down
Under its iron heel; fate, fate engaged
The strife, and hurl'd me on my father's spear.   715

But let us speak no more of this! I find
My father; let me feel that I have found!
Come, sit beside me on this sand, and take
My head betwixt thy hands, and kiss my cheeks,
And wash them with thy tears, and say: *My son!*   720
Quick! quick! for number'd are my sands of life,
And swift; for like the lightning to this field
I came, and like the wind I go away —
Sudden, and swift, and like a passing wind.
But it was writ in Heaven that this should be.'   725
    So said he, and his voice released the heart
Of Rustum, and his tears broke forth; he cast
His arms round his son's neck, and wept aloud,
And kiss'd him. And awe fell on both the hosts,
When they saw Rustum's grief; and Ruksh, the horse,   730
With his head bowing to the ground and mane
Sweeping the dust, came near, and in mute woe
First to the one then to the other moved
His head, as if inquiring what their grief
Might mean; and from his dark, compassionate eyes,   735
The big warm tears roll'd down, and caked the sand.
But Rustum chid him with stern voice, and said: —
    'Ruksh, now thou grievest; but, O Ruksh, thy feet
Should first have rotted on their nimble joints,
Or ere they brought thy master to this field!'   740
    But Sohrab look'd upon the horse and said; —
'Is this, then, Ruksh? How often, in past days,
My mother told me of thee, thou brave steed,
My terrible father's terrible horse! and said,
That I should one day find thy lord and thee.   745
Come, let me lay my hand upon thy mane!
O Ruksh, thou art more fortunate than I;
For thou hast gone where I shall never go,
And snuff'd the breezes of my father's home.
And thou hast trod the sands of Seistan,   750
And seen the River of Helmund, and the Lake
Of Zirrah; and the aged Zal himself
Has often stroked thy neck, and given thee food,

Corn in a golden platter soak'd with wine,
And said: *O Ruksh! bear Rustum well!* – but I   755
Have never known my grandsire's furrow'd face,
Nor seen his lofty house in Seistan,
Nor slaked my thirst at the clear Helmund stream;
But lodged among my father's foes, and seen
Afrasiab's cities only, Samarcand,   760
Bokhara, and lone Khiva in the waste,
And the black Toorkmun tents; and only drunk
The desert rivers, Moorghab and Tejend,
Kohik, and where the Kalmuks feed their sheep,
The northern Sir; and this great Oxus stream,   765
The yellow Oxus, by whose brink I die.'
    Then, with a heavy groan, Rustum bewail'd: –
'Oh, that its waves were flowing over me!
Oh, that I saw its grains of yellow silt
Roll tumbling in the current o'er my head!'   770
    But, with a grave mild voice, Sohrab replied: –
'Desire not that, my father! thou must live.
For some are born to do great deeds, and live,
As some are born to be obscured, and die.
Do thou the deeds I die too young to do,   775
And reap a second glory in thine age;
Thou art my father, and thy gain is mine.
But come! thou seest this great host of men
Which follow me; I pray thee, slay not these!
Let me entreat for them; what have they done?   780
They follow'd me, my hope, my fame, my star.
Let them all cross the Oxus back in peace.
But me thou must bear hence, not send with them,
But carry me with thee to Seistan,
And place me on a bed, and mourn for me,   785
Thou, and the snow-hair'd Zal, and all thy friends.
And thou must lay me in that lovely earth,
And heap a stately mound above my bones,
And plant a far-seen pillar over all.
That so the passing horseman on the waste   790
May see my tomb a great way off, and cry:

Sohrab, the mighty Rustum's son, lies there,
Whom his great father did in ignorance kill!
And I be not forgotten in my grave.'
    And, with a mournful voice, Rustum replied: —   795
'Fear not! as thou hast said, Sohrab, my son,
So shall it be; for I will burn my tents,
And quit the host, and bear thee hence with me,
And carry thee away to Seistan,
And place thee on a bed, and mourn for thee,   800
With the snow-headed Zal, and all my friends.
And I will lay thee in that lovely earth,
And heap a stately mound above thy bones,
And plant a far-seen pillar over all,
And men shall not forget thee in thy grave.   805
And I will spare thy host; yea, let them go!
Let them all cross the Oxus back in peace!
What should I do with slaying any more?
For would that all whom I have ever slain
Might be once more alive; my bitterest foes,   810
And they who were call'd champions in their time,
And through whose death I won that fame I have —
And I were nothing but a common man,
A poor, mean soldier, and without renown,
So thou mightest live too, my son, my son!   815
Or rather would that I, even I myself,
Might now be lying on this bloody sand,
Near death, and by an ignorant stroke of thine,
Not thou of mine! and I might die, not thou;
And I, not thou, be borne to Seistan;   820
And Zal might weep above my grave, not thine;
And say: *O son, I weep thee not too sore,*
For willingly, I know, thou met'st thine end!
But now in blood and battles was my youth,
And full of blood and battles is my age,   825
And I shall never end this life of blood.'
    Then, at the point of death, Sohrab replied: —
'A life of blood indeed, thou dreadful man!
But thou shalt yet have peace; only not now,

Not yet! but thou shalt have it on that day,   830
When thou shalt sail in a high-masted ship,
Thou and the other peers of Kai Khosroo,
Returning home over the salt blue sea,
From laying thy dear master in his grave.'
   And Rustum gazed in Sohrab's face, and said: —   835
'Soon be that day, my son, and deep that sea!
Till then, if fate so wills, let me endure.'
   He spoke; and Sohrab smiled on him, and took
The spear, and drew it from his side, and eased
His wound's imperious anguish; but the blood   840
Came welling from the open gash, and life
Flow'd with the stream; — all down his cold white side
The crimson torrent ran, dim now and soil'd,
Like the soil'd tissue of white violets
Left, freshly gather'd, on their native bank,   845
By children whom their nurses call with haste
Indoors from the sun's eye; his head droop'd low,
His limbs grew slack; motionless, white, he lay —
White, with eyes closed; only when heavy gasps,
Deep heavy gasps quivering through all his frame,   850
Convulsed him back to life, he open'd them,
And fix'd them feebly on his father's face;
Till now all strength was ebb'd, and from his limbs
Unwillingly the spirit fled away,
Regretting the warm mansion which it left,   855
And youth, and bloom, and this delightful world.
  So, on the bloody sand, Sohrab lay dead;
And the great Rustum drew his horseman's cloak
Down o'er his face, and sate by his dead son.
As those black granite pillars, once high-rear'd   860
By Jemshid in Persepolis, to bear
His house, now 'mid their broken flights of steps
Lie prone, enormous, down the mountain side —
So in the sand lay Rustum by his son.
   And night came down over the solemn waste,   865
And the two gazing hosts, and that sole pair,
And darken'd all; and a cold fog, with night,

Crept from the Oxus. Soon a hum arose,
As of a great assembly loosed, and fires
Began to twinkle through the fog; for now   870
Both armies moved to camp, and took their meal;
The Persians took it on the open sands
Southward, the Tartars by the river marge;
And Rustum and his son were left alone.

But the majestic river floated on,   875
Out of the mist and hum of that low land,
Into the frosty starlight, and there moved,
Rejoicing, through the hush'd Chorasmian waste,
Under the solitary moon; – he flow'd
Right for the polar star, past Orgunjè,   880
Brimming, and bright, and large; then sands begin
To hem his watery march, and dam his streams,
And split his currents; that for many a league
The shorn and parcell'd Oxus strains along
Through beds of sand and matted rushy isles –   885
Oxus, forgetting the bright speed he had
In his high mountain cradle in Pamere,
A foil'd circuitous wanderer – till at last
The long'd-for dash of waves is heard, and wide
His luminous home of waters opens, bright   890
And tranquil, from whose floor the new-bathed stars
Emerge, and shine upon the Aral Sea.

A TOMB AMONG THE MOUNTAINS*

So rest, for ever rest, O princely Pair!
In your high church, 'mid the still mountain-air,
Where horn, and hound, and vassals, never come.
Only the blessed Saints are smiling dumb,
From the rich painted windows of the nave,   5
On aisle, and transept, and your marble grave;
Where thou, young Prince! shalt never more arise
From the fringed mattress where thy Duchess lies,
On autumn-mornings, when the bugle sounds,
And ride across the drawbridge with thy hounds   10
To hunt the boar in the crisp woods till eve;
And thou, O Princess! shalt no more receive,
Thou and thy ladies, in the hall of state,
The jaded hunters with their bloody freight,
Coming benighted to the castle-gate.   15
  So sleep, for ever sleep, O marble Pair!
Or, if ye wake, let it be then, when fair
On the carved western front a flood of light
Streams from the setting sun, and colours bright
Prophets, transfigured Saints, and Martyrs brave,   20
In the vast western window of the nave;
And on the pavement round the Tomb there glints
A chequer-work of glowing sapphire-tints
And amethyst, and ruby – then unclose
Your eyelids on the stone where ye repose,   25
And from your broider'd pillows lift your heads,
And rise upon your cold white marble beds;
And, looking down on the warm rosy tints,
Which chequer, at your feet, the illumined flints,
Say: *What is this? we are in bliss – forgiven –*   30
Behold the pavement of the courts of Heaven!

* Arnold's title in 1877. The poem is the third part of 'The Church of Brou'.

Or let it be on autumn nights, when rain
Doth rustlingly above your heads complain
On the smooth leaden roof, and on the walls
Shedding her pensive light at intervals   35
The moon through the clere-story windows shines,
And the wind washes through the mountain-pines.
Then, gazing up 'mid the dim pillars high,
The foliaged marble forest where ye lie,
Hush, ye will say, *it is eternity!*   40
This is the glimmering verge of Heaven, and these
The columns of the heavenly palaces!
And, in the sweeping of the wind, your ear
The passage of the Angels' wings will hear,
And on the lichen-crusted leads above   45
The rustle of the eternal rain of love.

SONNETS

SHAKESPEARE

OTHERS abide our question. Thou art free.
We ask and ask – Thou smilest and art still,
Out-topping knowledge. For the loftiest hill,
Who to the stars uncrowns his majesty,

Planting his stedfast footsteps in the sea,   5
Making the heaven of heavens his dwelling-place,
Spares but the cloudy border of his base
To the foil'd searching of mortality;

And thou, who didst the stars and sunbeams know,
Self-school'd, self-scann'd, self-honour'd, self-secure, 10
Didst tread on earth unguess'd at. – Better so!

All pains the immortal spirit must endure,
All weakness which impairs, all griefs which bow,
Find their sole speech in that victorious brow.

TO A REPUBLICAN FRIEND, 1848

GOD knows it, I am with you. If to prize
Those virtues, prized and practised by too few,
But prized, but loved, but eminent in you,
Man's fundamental life; if to despise

The barren optimistic sophistries   5
Of comfortable moles, whom what they do
Teaches the limit of the just and true
(And for such doing they require not eyes);

If sadness at the long heart-wasting show
Wherein earth's great ones are disquieted; 10
If thoughts, not idle, while before me flow

The armies of the homeless and unfed —
If these are yours, if this is what you are,
Them am I yours, and what you feel, I share.

CONTINUED

YET, when I muse on what life is, I seem
Rather to patience prompted, than that proud
Prospect of hope which France proclaims so loud —
France, famed in all great arts, in none supreme;

Seeing this vale, this earth, whereon we dream, 5
Is on all sides o'ershadow'd by the high
Uno'erleap'd Mountains of Necessity,
Sparing us narrower margin than we deem.

Nor will that day dawn at a human nod,
When, bursting through the network superposed 10
By selfish occupation — plot and plan,

Lust, avarice, envy — liberated man,
All difference with his fellow-mortal closed,
Shall be left standing face to face with God.

YOUTH'S AGITATIONS

WHEN I shall be divorced, some ten years hence,
From this poor present self which I am now;
When youth has done its tedious vain expense
Of passions that for ever ebb and flow;

Shall I not joy youth's heats are left behind, 5
And breathe more happy in an even clime? —
Ah no, for then I shall begin to find
A thousand virtues in this hated time!

Then I shall wish its agitations back,
And all its thwarting currents of desire;   10
Then I shall praise the heat which then I lack,
And call this hurrying fever, generous fire;

And sigh that one thing only has been lent
To youth and age in common — discontent.

RACHEL

I

IN Paris all look'd hot and like to fade.
Sere, in the garden of the Tuileries,
Sere with September, droop'd the chestnut-trees.
'Twas dawn; a brougham roll'd through the streets and
       made

Halt at the white and silent colonnade   5
Of the French Theatre. Worn with disease,
Rachel, with eyes no gazing can appease,
Sate in the brougham and those blank walls survey'd.

She follows the gay world, whose swarms have fled
To Switzerland, to Baden, to the Rhine;   10
Why stops she by this empty play-house drear?

Ah, where the spirit its highest life hath led,
All spots, match'd with that spot, are less divine;
And Rachel's Switzerland, her Rhine, is here!

LOVE POEMS

A MEMORY-PICTURE

Laugh, my friends, and without blame
Lightly quit what lightly came;
Rich to-morrow as to-day,
Spend as madly as you may!
I, with little land to stir,   5
Am the exacter labourer.
    Ere the parting hour go by,
    Quick, thy tablets, Memory!

Once I said: 'A face is gone
If too hotly mused upon;   10
And our best impressions are
Those that do themselves repair.'
Many a face I so let flee,
Ah! is faded utterly.
    Ere the parting hour go by,   15
    Quick, thy tablets, Memory!

Marguerite says: 'As last year went,
So the coming year'll be spent;
Some day next year, I shall be,
Entering heedless, kiss'd by thee.'   20
Ah, I hope – yet, once away,
What may chain us, who can say?
    Ere the parting hour go by,
    Quick, thy tablets, Memory!

Paint that lilac kerchief, bound   25
Her soft face, her hair around;
Tied under the archest chin
Mockery ever ambush'd in.

Let the fluttering fringes streak
All her pale, sweet-rounded cheek.   30
   Ere the parting hour go by,
   Quick, thy tablets, Memory!

Paint that figure's pliant grace
As she tow'rd me lean'd her face,
Half refused and half resign'd   35
Murmuring: 'Art thou still unkind?'
Many a broken promise then
Was new made – to break again.
   Ere the parting hour go by,
   Quick, thy tablets, Memory!   40

Paint those eyes, so blue, so kind,
Eager tell-tales of her mind;
Paint, with their impetuous stress
Of inquiring tenderness,
Those frank eyes, where deep I see   45
An angelic gravity.
   Ere the parting hour go by,
   Quick, thy tablets, Memory!

What, my friends, these feeble lines
Show, you say, my love declines?   50
To paint ill as I have done,
Proves forgetfulness begun?
Time's gay minions, pleased you see,
Time, your master, governs me;
   Pleased, you mock the fruitless cry: 55
   'Quick, thy tablets, Memory!'

Ah, too true! Time's current strong
Leaves us fixt to nothing long.
Yet, if little stays with man,
Ah, retain we all we can!   60
If the clear impression dies,
Ah, the dim remembrance prize!
   Ere the parting hour go by,
   Quick, thy tablets, Memory!

SWITZERLAND

1. MEETING

AGAIN I see my bliss at hand,
The town, the lake are here;
My Marguerite smiles upon the strand,
Unalter'd with the year.

I know that graceful figure fair,   5
That cheek of languid hue;
I know that soft, enkerchief'd hair,
And those sweet eyes of blue.

Again I spring to make my choice;
Again in tones of ire   10
I hear a God's tremendous voice:
'Be counsell'd, and retire.'

Ye guiding Powers who join and part,
What would ye have with me?
Ah, warn some more ambitious heart,   15
And let the peaceful be!

2. PARTING

YE storm-winds of Autumn!
Who rush by, who shake
The window, and ruffle
The gleam-lighted lake;
Who cross to the hill-side   5
Thin-sprinkled with farms,
Where the high woods strip sadly
Their yellowing arms —
Ye are bound for the mountains!
Ah! with you let me go   10
Where your cold, distant barrier,
The vast range of snow,

Through the loose clouds lifts dimly
Its white peaks in air –
How deep is their stillness!   15
Ah, would I were there!

But on the stairs what voice is this I hear,
Buoyant as morning, and as morning clear?
Say, has some wet bird-haunted English lawn
Lent it the music of its trees at dawn?   20
Or was it from some sun-fleck'd mountain-brook
That the sweet voice its upland clearness took?
          Ah! it comes nearer –
          Sweet notes, this way!

      Hark! fast by the window   25
      The rushing winds go,
      To the ice-cumber'd gorges,
      The vast seas of snow!
      There the torrents drive upward
      Their rock-strangled hum;   30
      There the avalanche thunders
      The hoarse torrent dumb.
      – I come, O ye mountains!
      Ye torrents, I come!

But who is this, by the half-open'd door,   35
Whose figure casts a shadow on the floor?
The sweet blue eyes – the soft, ash-colour'd hair –
The cheeks that still their gentle paleness wear –
The lovely lips, with their arch smile that tells
The unconquer'd joy in which her spirit dwells –   40
          Ah! they bend nearer –
          Sweet lips, this way!

      Hark! the wind rushes past us!
      Ah! with that let me go
      To the clear, waning hill-side,   45
      Unspotted by snow,
      There to watch, o'er the sunk vale,

The frore mountain-wall,
Where the niched snow-bed sprays down
Its powdery fall. 50
There its dusky blue clusters
The aconite spreads;
There the pines slope, the cloud-strips
Hung soft in their heads.
No life but, at moments, 55
The mountain-bee's hum.
– I come, O ye mountains!
Ye pine-woods, I come!

Forgive me! forgive me!
Ah, Marguerite, fain 60
Would these arms reach to clasp thee!
But see! 'tis in vain.

In the void air, towards thee,
My stretch'd arms are cast;
But a sea rolls between us – 65
Our different past!

To the lips, ah! of others
Those lips have been prest,
And others, ere I was,
Were strain'd to that breast; 70

Far, far from each other
Our spirits have grown;
And what heart knows another?
Ah! who knows his own?

Blow, ye winds! lift me with you! 75
I come to the wild.
Fold closely, O Nature!
Thine arms round thy child.

To thee only God granted
A heart ever new – 80
To all always open,
To all always true.

Ah! calm me, restore me;
  And dry up my tears
On thy high mountain-platforms,   85
  Where morn first appears;

Where the white mists, for ever,
  Are spread and upfurl'd –
In the stir of the forces
  Whence issued the world.   90

3. A FAREWELL

MY horse's feet beside the lake,
Where sweet the unbroken moonbeams lay,
Sent echoes through the night to wake
Each glistening strand, each heath-fringed bay.

The poplar avenue was pass'd,   5
And the roof'd bridge that spans the stream;
Up the steep street I hurried fast,
Led by thy taper's starlike beam.

I came! I saw thee rise! – the blood
Pour'd flushing to thy languid cheek.   10
Lock'd in each other's arms we stood,
In tears, with hearts too full to speak.

Days flew; – ah, soon I could discern
A trouble in thine alter'd air!
Thy hand lay languidly in mine,   15
Thy cheek was grave, thy speech grew rare.

I blame thee not! – this heart, I know,
To be long loved was never framed;
For something in its depths doth glow
Too strange, too restless, too untamed.   20

And women – things that live and move
Mined by the fever of the soul –
They seek to find in those they love
Stern strength, and promise of control.

They ask not kindness, gentle ways –   25
These they themselves have tried and known;
They ask a soul which never sways
With the blind gusts that shake their own.

I too have felt the load I bore
In a too strong emotion's sway;   30
I too have wish'd, no woman more,
This starting, feverish heart away.

I too have long'd for trenchant force,
And will like a dividing spear;
Have praised the keen, unscrupulous course,   35
Which knows no doubt, which feels no fear.

But in the world I learnt, what there
Thou too wilt surely one day prove,
That will, that energy, though rare,
Are yet far, far less rare than love.   40

Go, then! – till time and fate impress
This truth on thee, be mine no more!
They will! – for thou, I feel, not less
Than I, wast destined to this lore.

We school our manners, act our parts –   45
But He, who sees us through and through,
Knows that the bent of both our hearts
Was to be gentle, tranquil, true.

And though we wear out life, alas!
Distracted as a homeless wind,   50
In beating where we must not pass,
In seeking what we shall not find;

Yet we shall one day gain, life past,
Clear prospect o'er our being's whole;
Shall see ourselves, and learn at last   55
Our true affinities of soul.

We shall not then deny a course
To every thought the mass ignore;
We shall not then call hardness force,
Nor lightness wisdom any more.   60

Then, in the eternal Father's smile,
Our soothed, encouraged souls will dare
To seem as free from pride and guile,
As good, as generous, as they are.

Then we shall know our friends! – though
    much   65
Will have been lost – the help in strife,
The thousand sweet, still joys of such
As hand in hand face earthly life –

Though these be lost, there will be yet
A sympathy august and pure;   70
Ennobled by a vast regret,
And by contrition seal'd thrice sure.

And we, whose ways were unlike here,
May then more neighbouring courses ply;
May to each other be brought near,   75
And greet across infinity.

How sweet, unreach'd by earthly jars,
My sister! to maintain with thee
The hush among the shining stars,
The calm upon the moonlit sea!   80

How sweet to feel, on the boon air,
All our unquiet pulses cease!
To feel that nothing can impair
The gentleness, the thirst for peace –

The gentleness too rudely hurl'd   85
On this wild earth of hate and fear;
The thirst for peace a raving world
Would never let us satiate here.

4. ISOLATION. TO MARGUERITE

WE were apart; yet, day by day,
I bade my heart more constant be.
I bade it keep the world away,
And grow a home for only thee;
Nor fear'd but thy love likewise grew,   5
Like mine, each day, more tried, more true.

The fault was grave! I might have known,
What far too soon, alas! I learn'd –
The heart can bind itself alone,
And faith may oft be unreturn'd.   10
Self-sway'd our feelings ebb and swell –
Thou lov'st no more; – Farewell! Farewell!

Farewell! – and thou, thou lonely heart,
Which never yet without remorse
Even for a moment didst depart   15
From thy remote and spheréd course
To haunt the place where passions reign –
Back to thy solitude again!

Back! with the conscious thrill of shame
Which Luna felt, that summer-night,   20
Flash through her pure immortal frame,
When she forsook the starry height
To hang over Endymion's sleep
Upon the pine-grown Latmian steep.

Yet she, chaste queen, had never proved   25
How vain a thing is mortal love,
Wandering in Heaven, far removed.
But thou hast long had place to prove
This truth – to prove, and make thine
    own:
'Thou hast been, shalt be, art, alone.'   30

Or, if not quite alone, yet they
Which touch thee are unmating things –
Ocean and clouds and night and day;
Lorn autumns and triumphant springs;
And life, and others' joy and pain,   35
And love, if love, of happier men.

Of happier men – for they, at least,
Have *dream'd* two human hearts might
    blend
In one, and were through faith released
From isolation without end   40
Prolong'd; nor knew, although not less
Alone than thou, their loneliness.

5. TO MARGUERITE – CONTINUED

YES! in the sea of life enisled,
With echoing straits between us thrown,
Dotting the shoreless watery wild,
We mortal millions live *alone*.
The islands feel the enclasping flow,   5
And then their endless bounds they know.

But when the moon their hollows lights,
And they are swept by balms of spring,
And in their glens, on starry nights,
The nightingales divinely sing;   10
And lovely notes, from shore to shore,
Across the sounds and channels pour –

Oh! then a longing like despair
Is to their farthest caverns sent;
For surely once, they feel, we were   15
Parts of a single continent!
Now round us spreads the watery plain –
Oh might our marges meet again!

Who order'd, that their longing's fire
Should be, as soon as kindled, cool'd? 20
Who renders vain their deep desire? –
A God, a God their severance ruled!
And bade betwixt their shores to be
The unplumb'd, salt, estranging sea.

6. ABSENCE

In this fair stranger's eyes of grey
Thine eyes, my love! I see.
I shiver; for the passing day
Had borne me far from thee.

This is the curse of life! that not 5
A nobler, calmer train
Of wiser thoughts and feelings blot
Our passions from our brain;

But each day brings its petty dust
Our soon-choked souls to fill, 10
And we forget because we must
And not because we will.

I struggle towards the light; and ye,
Once-long'd-for storms of love!
If with the light ye cannot be, 15
I bear that ye remove.

I struggle towards the light – but oh,
While yet the night is chill,
Upon time's barren, stormy flow,
Stay with me, Marguerite, still! 20

7. THE TERRACE AT BERNE

(COMPOSED TEN YEARS AFTER THE PRECEDING.)

Ten years! – and to my waking eye
Once more the roofs of Berne appear;
The rocky banks, the terrace high,
The stream! – and do I linger here?

The clouds are on the Oberland,   5
The Jungfrau snows look faint and far;
But bright are those green fields at hand,
And through those fields comes down the Aar,

And from the blue twin-lakes it comes,
Flows by the town, the churchyard fair;   10
And 'neath the garden-walk it hums,
The house! – and is my Marguerite there?

Ah, shall I see thee, while a flush
Of startled pleasure floods thy brow,
Quick through the oleanders brush,   15
And clap thy hands, and cry: *'Tis thou!*

Or hast thou long since wander'd back,
Daughter of France! to France, thy home;
And flitted down the flowery track
Where feet like thine too lightly come?   20

Doth riotous laughter now replace
Thy smile; and rouge, with stony glare,
Thy cheek's soft hue; and fluttering lace
The kerchief that enwound thy hair?

Or is it over? – art thou dead? –   25
Dead! – and no warning shiver ran
Across my heart, to say thy thread
Of life was cut, and closed thy span!

Could from earth's ways that figure slight
Be lost, and I not feel 'twas so?   30
Of that fresh voice the gay delight
Fail from earth's air, and I not know?

Or shall I find thee still, but changed,
But not the Marguerite of thy prime?
With all thy being re-arranged,   35
Pass'd through the crucible of time;

With spirit vanish'd, beauty waned,
And hardly yet a glance, a tone,
A gesture – anything – retain'd
Of all that was my Marguerite's own?   40

I will not know! For wherefore try,
To things by mortal course that live,
A shadowy durability,
For which they were not meant, to give?

Like driftwood spars, which meet and pass   45
Upon the boundless ocean-plain,
So on the sea of life, alas!
Man meets man – meets, and quits again.

I knew it when my life was young;
I feel it still, now youth is o'er.   50
– The mists are on the mountain hung,
And Marguerite I shall see no more.

FADED LEAVES

1. THE RIVER

STILL glides the stream, slow drops the boat
Under the rustling poplars' shade;
Silent the swans beside us float —
None speaks, none heeds; ah, turn thy head!

Let those arch eyes now softly shine, 5
That mocking mouth grow sweetly bland;
Ah, let them rest, those eyes, on mine!
On mine let rest that lovely hand!

My pent-up tears oppress my brain,
My heart is swoln with love unsaid. 10
Ah, let me weep, and tell my pain,
And on thy shoulder rest my head!

Before I die — before the soul,
Which now is mine, must re-attain
Immunity from my control, 15
And wander round the world again;

Before this teased o'erlabour'd heart
For ever leaves its vain employ,
Dead to its deep habitual smart,
And dead to hopes of future joy. 20

2. TOO LATE

EACH on his own strict line we move,
And some find death ere they find love;
So far apart their lives are thrown
From the twin soul which halves their own.

And sometimes, by still harder fate, 5
The lovers meet, but meet too late.
— Thy heart is mine! — *True, true! ah, true!*
— Then, love, thy hand! — *Ah no! adieu!*

140

3. SEPARATION

STOP! – not to me, at this bitter departing,
  Speak of the sure consolations of time!
Fresh be the wound, still-renew'd be its smarting,
  So but thy image endure in its prime.

But, if the stedfast commandment of Nature   5
  Wills that remembrance should always decay –
If the loved form and the deep-cherish'd feature
  Must, when unseen, from the soul fade away –

Me let no half-effaced memories cumber!
  Fled, fled at once, be all vestige of thee!   10
Deep be the darkness and still be the slumber –
  Dead be the past and its phantoms to me!

Then, when we meet, and thy look strays toward me,
  Scanning my face and the changes wrought there:
Who, let me say, *is this stranger regards me,*   15
  With the grey eyes, and the lovely brown hair?

4. ON THE RHINE

VAIN is the effort to forget.
Some day I shall be cold, I know,
As is the eternal moonlit snow
Of the high Alps, to which I go –
But ah, not yet, not yet!   5

Vain is the agony of grief.
'Tis true, indeed, an iron knot
Ties straitly up from mine thy lot,
And were it snapt – thou lov'st me not!
But is despair relief?   10

Awhile let me with thought have done.
And as this brimm'd unwrinkled Rhine,
And that far purple mountain-line,
Lie sweetly in the look divine
Of the slow-sinking sun;   15

So let me lie, and, calm as they,
Let beam upon my inward view
Those eyes of deep, soft, lucent hue –
Eyes too expressive to be blue,
Too lovely to be grey.   20

Ah, Quiet, all things feel thy balm!
Those blue hills too, this river's flow,
Were restless once, but long ago.
Tamed is their turbulent youthful glow;
Their joy is in their calm.   25

5. LONGING

COME to me in my dreams, and then
By day I shall be well again!
For then the night will more than pay
The hopeless longing of the day.

Come, as thou cam'st a thousand times,   5
A messenger from radiant climes,
And smile on thy new world, and be
As kind to others as to me!

Or, as thou never cam'st in sooth,
Come now, and let me dream it truth;   10
And part my hair, and kiss my brow,
And say: *My love! why sufferest thou?*

Come to me in my dreams, and then
By day I shall be well again!
For then the night will more than pay   15
The hopeless longing of the day.

LYRIC POEMS

THE STRAYED REVELLER

THE PORTICO OF CIRCE'S PALACE. EVENING.

A Youth. Circe.

The Youth

FASTER, faster,
O Circe, Goddess,
Let the wild, thronging train,
The bright procession
Of eddying forms,   5
Sweep through my soul!

Thou standest, smiling
Down on me! thy right arm,
Lean'd up against the column there,
Props thy soft cheek;   10
Thy left holds, hanging loosely,
The deep cup, ivy-cinctured,
I held but now.

   Is it, then, evening
So soon? I see, the night-dews,   15
Cluster'd in thick beads, dim
The agate brooch-stones
On thy white shoulder;
The cool night-wind, too,
Blows through the portico,   20
Stirs thy hair, Goddess,
Waves thy white robe!

Circe

Whence art thou, sleeper?

The Youth

When the white dawn first
Through the rough fir-planks   25
Of my hut, by the chestnuts,
Up at the valley-head,
Came breaking, Goddess!
I sprang up, I threw round me
My dappled fawn-skin;   30
Passing out, from the wet turf,
Where they lay, by the hut door,
I snatch'd up my vine-crown, my fir-staff,
All drench'd in dew —
Came swift down to join   35
The rout early gather'd
In the town, round the temple,
Iacchus' white fane
On yonder hill.

Quick I pass'd, following   40
The wood-cutters' cart-track
Down the dark valley; — I saw
On my left, through the beeches,
Thy palace, Goddess,
Smokeless, empty!   45
Trembling, I enter'd; beheld
The court all silent,
The lions sleeping,
On the altar this bowl.
I drank, Goddess!   50
And sank down here, sleeping,
On the steps of thy portico.

Circe

Foolish boy! Why tremblest thou?
Thou lovest it, then, my wine?
Wouldst more of it? See, how glows, 55
Through the delicate, flush'd marble
The red, creaming liquor,

144

Strown with dark seeds!
Drink, then! I chide thee not,
Deny thee not my bowl.   60
Come, stretch forth thy hand, then – so!
Drink – drink again!

The Youth

Thanks, gracious one!
Ah, the sweet fumes again!
More soft, ah me,   65
More subtle-winding
Than Pan's flute-music!
Faint – faint! Ah me,
Again the sweet sleep!

Circe

Hist! Thou – within there!   70
Come forth, Ulysses!
Art tired with hunting?
While we range the woodland,
See what the day brings.

Ulysses

Ever new magic!   75
Hast thou then lured hither,
Wonderful Goddess, by thy art,
The young, languid-eyed Ampelus,
Iacchus' darling –
Or some youth beloved of Pan,   80
Of Pan and the Nymphs?
That he sits, bending downward
His white, delicate neck
To the ivy-wreathed marge
Of thy cup; the bright, glancing vine-leaves   85
That crown his hair,
Falling forward, mingling
With the dark ivy-plants –

His fawn-skin, half untied,
Smear'd with red wine-stains? Who is he,   90
That he sits, overweigh'd
By fumes of wine and sleep,
So late, in thy portico?
What youth, Goddess, – what guest
Of Gods or mortals?   95

Circe

Hist! he wakes!
I lured him not hither, Ulysses.
Nay, ask him!

The Youth

Who speaks? Ah, who comes forth
To thy side, Goddess, from within?   100
How shall I name him?
This spare, dark-featured,
Quick-eyed stranger?
Ah, and I see too
His sailor's bonnet,   105
His short coat, travel-tarnish'd,
With one arm bare! –
Art thou not he, whom fame
This long time rumours
The favour'd guest of Circe, brought by
   the waves?   110
Art thou he, stranger?
The wise Ulysses,
Laertes' son?

Ulysses

I am Ulysses.
And thou, too, sleeper?   115
Thy voice is sweet.
It may be thou hast follow'd
Through the islands some divine bard,
By age taught many things,

Age and the Muses; 120
And heard him delighting
The chiefs and people
In the banquet, and learn'd his songs,
Of Gods and Heroes,
Of war and arts, 125
And peopled cities,
Inland, or built
By the grey sea. – If so, then hail!
I honour and welcome thee.

The Youth

The Gods are happy. 130
They turn on all sides
Their shining eyes,
And see below them
The earth and men.

They see Tiresias 135
Sitting, staff in hand,
On the warm, grassy
Asopus bank,
His robe drawn over
His old, sightless head, 140
Revolving inly
The doom of Thebes.

They see the Centaurs
In the upper glens
Of Pelion, in the streams, 145
Where red-berried ashes fringe
The clear-brown shallow pools,
With streaming flanks, and heads
Rear'd proudly, snuffing
The mountain wind. 150

They see the Indian
Drifting, knife in hand,
His frail boat moor'd to

A floating isle thick-matted
With large-leaved, low-creeping melon-plants, 155
And the dark cucumber.
He reaps, and stows them,
Drifting – drifting; – round him,
Round his green harvest-plot,
Flow the cool lake-waves, 160
The mountains ring them.

They see the Scythian
On the wide stepp, unharnessing
His wheel'd house at noon.
He tethers his beast down, and makes his meal –
Mares' milk, and bread 166
Baked on the embers; – all around
The boundless, waving grass-plains stretch, thick-
  starr'd
With saffron and the yellow hollyhock
And flag-leaved iris-flowers. 170
Sitting in his cart
He makes his meal; before him, for long miles,
Alive with bright green lizards,
And the springing bustard-fowl,
The track, a straight black line, 175
Furrows the rich soil; here and there
Clusters of lonely mounds
Topp'd with rough-hewn,
Grey, rain-blear'd statues, overpeer
The sunny waste. 180

They see the ferry
On the broad, clay-laden
Lone Chorasmian stream; – thereon,
With snort and strain,
Two horses, strongly swimming, tow 185
The ferry-boat, with woven ropes
To either bow
Firm harness'd by the mane; a chief,
With shout and shaken spear,

Stands at the prow, and guides them; but astern
The cowering merchants, in long robes,   191
Sit pale beside their wealth
Of silk-bales and of balsam-drops,
Of gold and ivory,
Of turquoise-earth and amethyst,   195
Jasper and chalcedony,
And milk-barr'd onyx-stones.
The loaded boat swings groaning
In the yellow eddies;
The Gods behold them.   200

They see the Heroes
Sitting in the dark ship
On the foamless, long-heaving,
Violet sea,
At sunset nearing   205
The Happy Islands.

    These things, Ulysses,
The wise bards also
Behold and sing.
But oh, what labour!   210
O prince, what pain!

They too can see
Tiresias; – but the Gods,
Who give them vision,
Added this law: 215
That they should bear too
His groping blindness,
His dark foreboding,
His scorn'd white hairs;
Bear Hera's anger   220
Through a life lengthen'd
To seven ages.

They see the Centaurs
On Pelion; – then they feel,

They too, the maddening wine   225
Swell their large veins to bursting; in wild pain
They feel the biting spears
Of the grim Lapithae, and Theseus, drive,
Drive crashing through their bones; they feel
High on a jutting rock in the red stream   230
Alcmena's dreadful son
Ply his bow; – such a price
The Gods exact for song:
To become what we sing.

They see the Indian   235
On his mountain lake; but squalls
Make their skiff reel, and worms
In the unkind spring have gnawn
Their melon-harvest to the heart. – They see
The Scythian; but long frosts   240
Parch them in winter-time on the bare stepp,
Till they too fade like grass; they crawl
Like shadows forth in spring.

They see the merchants
On the Oxus stream; – but care   245
Must visit first them too, and make them pale.
Whether, through whirling sand,
A cloud of desert robber-horse have burst
Upon their caravan; or greedy kings,
In the wall'd cities the way passes through,   250
Crush'd them with tolls; or fever-airs,
On some great river's marge,
Mown them down, far from home.

They see the Heroes
Near harbour; – but they share   255
Their lives, and former violent toil in Thebes,
Seven-gated Thebes, or Troy;
Or where the echoing oars
Of Argo first
Startled the unknown sea.   260

The old Silenus
Came, lolling in the sunshine,
From the dewy forest-coverts,
This way, at noon.
Sitting by me, while his Fauns   265
Down at the water-side
Sprinkled and smoothed
His drooping garland,
He told me these things.

But I, Ulysses,   270
Sitting on the warm steps,
Looking over the valley,
All day long, have seen,
Without pain, without labour,
Sometimes a wild-hair'd Maenad –   275
Sometimes a Faun with torches –
And sometimes, for a moment,
Passing through the dark stems
Flowing-robed, the beloved,
The desired, the divine,   280
Beloved Iacchus.

Ah, cool night-wind, tremulous stars!
Ah, glimmering water,
Fitful earth-murmur,
Dreaming woods!   285
Ah, golden-hair'd, strangely smiling Goddess,
And thou, proved, much enduring,
Wave-toss'd Wanderer!
Who can stand still?
Ye fade, ye swim, ye waver before me –   290
The cup again!

Faster, faster,
O Circe, Goddess,
Let the wild, thronging train,
The bright procession   295
Of eddying forms,
Sweep through my soul!

IN UTRUMQUE PARATUS

IF, in the silent mind of One all-pure,
　　At first imagined lay
The sacred world; and by procession sure
From those still deeps, in form and colour drest,
　　Seasons alternating, and night and day,　　　　5
The long-mused thought to north, south, east and west,
　　Took then its all-seen way;

O waking on a world which thus-wise springs!
　　Whether it needs thee count
Betwixt thy waking and the birth of things　　　　10
Ages or hours – O waking on life's stream!
By lonely pureness to the all-pure fount
(Only by this thou canst) the colour'd dream
　　Of life remount!

Thin, thin the pleasant human noises grow,　　　　15
　　And faint the city gleams;
Rare the lone pastoral huts – marvel not thou!
The solemn peaks but to the stars are known,
But to the stars, and the cold lunar beams;
Alone the sun arises, and alone　　　　　　　　　20
　　Spring the great streams.

But, if the wild unfather'd mass no birth
　　In divine seats hath known;
In the blank, echoing solitude if Earth,
Rocking her obscure body to and fro,　　　　　　25
Ceases not from all time to heave and groan,
Unfruitful oft, and at her happiest throe
　　Forms, what she forms, alone;

O seeming sole to awake, thy sun-bathed head
　　Piercing the solemn cloud　　　　　　　　30
Round thy still dreaming brother-world outspread!
O man, whom Earth, thy long-vext mother, bare
Not without joy – so radiant, so endow'd
(Such happy issue crown'd her painful care) –
　　Be not too proud!　　　　　　　　　　35

Oh when most self-exalted most alone,
　　Chief dreamer, own thy dream!
Thy brother-world stirs at thy feet unknown,
Who hath a monarch's hath no brother's part;
Yet doth thine inmost soul with yearning teem.　　　40
– Oh, what a spasm shakes the dreamer's heart!
　　'*I, too, but seem.*'

RESIGNATION

TO FAUSTA

To die be given us, or attain!
Fierce work it were, to do again.
So pilgrims, bound for Mecca, pray'd
At burning noon; so warriors said,
Scarf'd with the cross, who watch'd the miles　　　5
Of dust which wreathed their struggling files
Down Lydian mountains; so, when snows
Round Alpine summits, eddying, rose,
The Goth, bound Rome-wards; so the Hun,
Crouch'd on his saddle, while the sun　　　10
Went lurid down o'er flooded plains
Through which the groaning Danube strains
To the drear Euxine; – so pray all,
Whom labours, self-ordain'd, enthrall;
Because they to themselves propose　　　15
On this side the all-common close
A goal which, gain'd, may give repose.
So pray they; and to stand again
Where they stood once, to them were pain;
Pain to thread back and to renew　　　20
Past straits, and currents long steer'd through.

But milder natures, and more free –
Whom an unblamed serenity
Hath freed from passions, and the state
Of struggle these necessitate;　　　25

Whom schooling of the stubborn mind
Hath made, or birth hath found, resign'd –
These mourn not, that their goings pay
Obedience to the passing day.
These claim not every laughing Hour   30
For handmaid to their striding power;
Each in her turn, with torch uprear'd,
To await their march; and when appear'd,
Through the cold gloom, with measured race,
To usher for a destined space   35
(Her own sweet errands all forgone)
The too imperious traveller on.
These, Fausta, ask not this; nor thou,
Time's chafing prisoner, ask it now!

  We left, just ten years since, you say,   40
That wayside inn we left to-day.
Our jovial host, as forth we fare,
Shouts greeting from his easy chair.
High on a bank our leader stands,
Reviews and ranks his motley bands,   45
Makes clear our goal to every eye –
The valley's western boundary.
A gate swings to! our tide hath flow'd
Already from the silent road.
The valley-pastures, one by one,   50
Are threaded, quiet in the sun;
And now beyond the rude stone bridge
Slopes gracious up the western ridge.
Its woody border, and the last
Of its dark upland farms is past –   55
Cool farms, with open-lying stores,
Under their burnish'd sycamores;
All past! and through the trees we glide,
Emerging on the green hill-side.
There climbing hangs, a far-seen sign,   60
Our wavering, many-colour'd line;

There winds, upstreaming slowly still
Over the summit of the hill.
And now, in front, behold outspread
Those upper regions we must tread!   65
Mild hollows, and clear heathy swells,
The cheerful silence of the fells.
Some two hours' march with serious air,
Through the deep noontide heats we fare;
The red-grouse, springing at our sound,   70
Skims, now and then, the shining ground;
No life, save his and ours, intrudes
Upon these breathless solitudes.
O joy! again the farms appear.
Cool shade is there, and rustic cheer;   75
There springs the brook will guide us down,
Bright comrade, to the noisy town.
Lingering, we follow down; we gain
The town, the highway, and the plain.
And many a mile of dusty way,   80
Parch'd and road-worn, we made that day;
But, Fausta, I remember well,
That as the balmy darkness fell
We bathed our hands with speechless glee,
That night, in the wide-glimmering sea.   85

Once more we tread this self-same road,
Fausta, which ten years since we trod;
Alone we tread it, you and I,
Ghosts of that boisterous company.
Here, where the brook shines, near its head,   90
In its clear, shallow, turf-fringed bed;
Here, whence the eye first sees, far down,
Capp'd with faint smoke, the noisy town;
Here sit we, and again unroll,
Though slowly, the familiar whole.   95
The solemn wastes of heathy hill
Sleep in the July sunshine still;

The self-same shadows now, as then,
Play through this grassy upland glen;
The loose dark stones on the green way   100
Lie strewn, it seems, where then they lay;
On this mild bank above the stream,
(You crush them!) the blue gentians gleam.
Still this wild brook, the rushes cool,
The sailing foam, the shining pool!   105
These are not changed; and we, you say,
Are scarce more changed, in truth, than
    they.

The gipsies, whom we met below,
They, too, have long roam'd to and fro;
They ramble, leaving, where they pass,   110
Their fragments on the cumber'd grass.
And often to some kindly place
Chance guides the migratory race,
Where, though long wanderings intervene,
They recognise a former scene.   115
The dingy tents are pitch'd; the fires
Give to the wind their wavering spires;
In dark knots crouch round the wild flame
Their children, as when first they came;
They see their shackled beasts again   120
Move, browsing, up the gray-wall'd lane.
Signs are not wanting, which might raise
The ghost in them of former days —
Signs are not wanting, if they would;
Suggestions to disquietude.   125
For them, for all, time's busy touch,
While it mends little, troubles much.
Their joints grow stiffer — but the year
Runs his old round of dubious cheer;
Chilly they grow — yet winds in March,   130
Still, sharp as ever, freeze and parch;
They must live still — and yet, God knows,
Crowded and keen the country grows;

It seems as if, in their decay,
The law grew stronger every day.   135
So might they reason, so compare,
Fausta, times past with times that are.
But no! – they rubb'd through yesterday
In their hereditary way,
And they will rub through, if they can,   140
To-morrow on the self-same plan,
Till death arrive to supersede,
For them, vicissitude and need.

The poet, to whose mighty heart
Heaven doth a quicker pulse impart,   145
Subdues that energy to scan
Not his own course, but that of man.
Though he move mountains, though his day
Be pass'd on the proud heights of sway,
Though he hath loosed a thousand chains,   150
Though he hath borne immortal pains,
Action and suffering though he know –
He hath not lived, if he lives so.
He sees, in some great-historied land,
A ruler of the people stand,   155
Sees his strong thought in fiery flood
Roll through the heaving multitude;
Exults – yet for no moment's space
Envies the all-regarded place.
Beautiful eyes meet his – and he   160
Bears to admire uncravingly;
They pass – he, mingled with the crowd,
Is in their far-off triumphs proud.
From some high station he looks down,
At sunset, on a populous town;   165
Surveys each happy group, which fleets,
Toil ended, through the shining streets,
Each with some errand of its own –
And does not say: *I am alone.*

He sees the gentle stir of birth   170
When morning purifies the earth;
He leans upon a gate and sees
The pastures, and the quiet trees.
Low, woody hill, with gracious bound,
Folds the still valley almost round;   175
The cuckoo, loud on some high lawn,
Is answer'd from the depth of dawn;
In the hedge straggling to the stream,
Pale, dew-drench'd, half-shut roses gleam;
But, where the farther side slopes down,   180
He sees the drowsy new-waked clown
In his white quaint-embroider'd frock
Make, whistling, tow'rd his mist-wreathed flock –
Slowly, behind his heavy tread,
The wet, flower'd grass heaves up its head.   185
Lean'd on his gate, he gazes – tears
Are in his eyes, and in his ears
The murmur of a thousand years.
Before him he sees life unroll,
A placid and continuous whole –   190
That general life, which does not cease,
Whose secret is not joy, but peace;
That life, whose dumb wish is not miss'd
If birth proceeds, if things subsist;
The life of plants, and stones, and rain,   195
The life he craves – if not in vain
Fate gave, what chance shall not control,
His sad lucidity of soul.

You listen – but that wandering smile,
Fausta, betrays you cold the while!   200
Your eyes pursue the bells of foam
Wash'd, eddying, from this bank, their home.
Those gipsies, so your thoughts I scan,
Are less, the poet more, than man.
They feel not, though they move and see;   205
Deeper the poet feels; but he

Breathes, when he will, immortal air,
Where Orpheus and where Homer are.
In the day's life, whose iron round
Hems us all in, he is not bound;   210
He leaves his kind, o'erleaps their pen,
And flees the common life of men.
He escapes thence, but we abide —
Not deep the poet sees, but wide.

The world in which we live and move   215
Outlasts aversion, outlasts love,
Outlasts each effort, interest, hope,
Remorse, grief, joy; — and were the scope
Of these affections wider made,
Man still would see, and see dismay'd,   220
Beyond his passion's widest range,
Far regions of eternal change.
Nay, and since death, which wipes out man,
Finds him with many an unsolved plan,
With much unknown, and much untried,   225
Wonder not dead, and thirst not dried,
Still gazing on the ever full
Eternal mundane spectacle —
This world in which we draw our breath,
In some sense, Fausta, outlasts death.   230

   Blame thou not, therefore, him who dares
Judge vain beforehand human cares;
Whose natural insight can discern
What through experience others learn;
Who needs not love and power, to know   235
Love transient, power an unreal show;
Who treads at ease life's uncheer'd ways —
Him blame not, Fausta, rather praise!
Rather thyself for some aim pray
Nobler than this, to fill the day;   240
Rather that heart, which burns in thee,
Ask, not to amuse, but to set free;
Be passionate hopes not ill resign'd

For quiet, and a fearless mind.
And though fate grudge to thee and me   245
The poet's rapt security,
Yet they, believe me, who await
No gifts from chance, have conquer'd fate.
They, winning room to see and hear,
And to men's business not too near,   250
Through clouds of individual strife
Draw homeward to the general life.
Like leaves by suns not yet uncurl'd;
To the wise, foolish; to the world,
Weak; — yet not weak, I might reply,   255
Not foolish, Fausta, in His eye,
To whom each moment in its race,
Crowd as we will its neutral space,
Is but a quiet watershed
Whence, equally, the seas of life and death are fed.   260

Enough, we live! — and if a life,
With large results so little rife,
Though bearable, seem hardly worth
This pomp of worlds, this pain of birth;
Yet, Fausta, the mute turf we tread,   265
The solemn hills around us spread,
This stream which falls incessantly,
The strange-scrawl'd rocks, the lonely sky,
If I might lend their life a voice,
Seem to bear rather than rejoice.   270
And even could the intemperate prayer
Man iterates, while these forbear,
For movement, for an ampler sphere,
Pierce Fate's impenetrable ear;
Not milder is the general lot   275
Because our spirits have forgot,
In action's dizzying eddy whirl'd,
The something that infects the world.

A SUMMER NIGHT

In the deserted, moon-blanch'd street,
How lonely rings the echo of my feet!
Those windows, which I gaze at, frown,
Silent and white, unopening down,
Repellent as the world; – but see,   5
A break between the housetops shows
The moon! and, lost behind her, fading dim
Into the dewy dark obscurity
Down at the far horizon's rim,
Doth a whole tract of heaven disclose!   10

And to my mind the thought
Is on a sudden brought
Of a past night, and a far different scene.
Headlands stood out into the moonlit deep
As clearly as at noon;   15
The spring-tide's brimming flow
Heaved dazzlingly between;
Houses, with long white sweep,
Girdled the glistening bay;
Behind, through the soft air,   20
The blue haze-cradled mountains spread away,
That night was far more fair –
But the same restless pacings to and fro,
And the same vainly throbbing heart was there,
And the same bright, calm moon.   25

And the calm moonlight seems to say:
Hast thou then still the old unquiet breast,
Which neither deadens into rest,
Nor ever feels the fiery glow
That whirls the spirit from itself away,   30
But fluctuates to and fro,
Never by passion quite possess'd
And never quite benumb'd by the world's sway? –
And I, I know not if to pray
Still to be what I am, or yield and be   35
Like all the other men I see.

For most men in a brazen prison live,
Where, in the sun's hot eye,
With heads bent o'er their toil, they languidly
Their lives to some unmeaning taskwork give,   40
Dreaming of nought beyond their prison-wall.
And as, year after year,
Fresh products of their barren labour fall
From their tired hands, and rest
Never yet comes more near,   45
Gloom settles slowly down over their breast;
And while they try to stem
The waves of mournful thought by which they are prest,
Death in their prison reaches them,
Unfreed, having seen nothing, still unblest.   50

And the rest, a few,
Escape their prison and depart
On the wide ocean of life anew.
There the freed prisoner, where'er his heart
Listeth, will sail;   55
Nor doth he know how there prevail,
Despotic on that sea,
Trade-winds which cross it from eternity.
Awhile he holds some false way, undebarr'd
By thwarting signs, and braves   60
The freshening wind and blackening waves.
And then the tempest strikes him; and between
The lightning-bursts is seen
Only a driving wreck,
And the pale master on his spar-strewn deck   65
With anguish'd face and flying hair
Grasping the rudder hard,
Still bent to make some port he knows not where,
Still standing for some false, impossible shore.
And sterner comes the roar   70
Of sea and wind, and through the deepening gloom
Fainter and fainter wreck and helmsman loom,
And he too disappears, and comes no more.

Is there no life, but these alone?
Madman or slave, must man be one?   75

Plainness and clearness without shadow of stain!
Clearness divine!
Ye heavens, whose pure dark regions have no sign
Of languor, though so calm, and, though so great,
Are yet untroubled and unpassionate;   80
Who, though so noble, share in the world's toil,
And, though so task'd, keep free from dust and soil!
I will not say that your mild deeps retain
A tinge, it may be, of their silent pain
Who have long'd deeply once, and long'd in vain –   85
But I will rather say that you remain
A world above man's head, to let him see
How boundless might his soul's horizons be,
How vast, yet of what clear transparency!
How it were good to abide there, and breathe free;   90
How fair a lot to fill
Is left to each man still!

THE BURIED LIFE

LIGHT flows our war of mocking words, and yet,
Behold, with tears mine eyes are wet!
I feel a nameless sadness o'er me roll.
Yes, yes, we know that we can jest,
We know, we know that we can smile!   5
But there's a something in this breast,
To which thy light words bring no rest,
And thy gay smiles no anodyne.
Give me thy hand, and hush awhile,
And turn those limpid eyes on mine,   10
And let me read there, love! thy inmost soul.

Alas! is even love too weak
To unlock the heart, and let it speak?
Are even lovers powerless to reveal
To one another what indeed they feel?   15

I knew the mass of men conceal'd
Their thoughts, for fear that if reveal'd
They would by other men be met
With blank indifference, or with blame reproved;
I knew they lived and moved   20
Trick'd in disguises, alien to the rest
Of men, and alien to themselves — and yet
The same heart beats in every human breast!

But we, my love! — doth a like spell benumb
Our hearts, our voices? — must we too be dumb?   25

Ah! well for us, if even we,
Even for a moment, can get free
Our heart, and have our lips unchain'd;
For that which seals them hath been deep-ordain'd!

Fate, which foresaw   30
How frivolous a baby man would be —
By what distractions he would be possess'd,
How he would pour himself in every strife,
And well-nigh change his own identity —
That it might keep from his capricious play   35
His genuine self, and force him to obey
Even in his own despite his being's law,
Bade through the deep recesses of our breast
The unregarded river of our life
Pursue with indiscernible flow its way;   40
And that we should not see
The buried stream, and seem to be
Eddying at large in blind uncertainty,
Though driving on with it eternally.

But often, in the world's most crowded streets,   45
But often, in the din of strife,
There rises an unspeakable desire
After the knowledge of our buried life;
A thirst to spend our fire and restless force
In tracking out our true, original course;   50

A longing to inquire
Into the mystery of this heart which beats
So wild, so deep in us — to know
Whence our lives come and where they go.
And many a man in his own breast then delves,   55
But deep enough, alas! none ever mines.
And we have been on many thousand lines,
And we have shown, on each, spirit and power;
But hardly have we, for one little hour,
Been on our own line, have we been ourselves —   60
Hardly had skill to utter one of all
The nameless feelings that course through our
    breast,
But they course on for ever unexpress'd.
And long we try in vain to speak and act
Our hidden self, and what we say and do   65
Is eloquent, is well — but 'tis not true!
And then we will no more be rack'd
With inward striving, and demand
Of all the thousand nothings of the hour
Their stupefying power;   70
Ah yes, and they benumb us at our call!
Yet still, from time to time, vague and forlorn,
From the soul's subterranean depth upborne
As from an infinitely distant land,
Come airs, and floating echoes, and convey   75
A melancholy into all our day.

Only — but this is rare —
When a belovéd hand is laid in ours,
When, jaded with the rush and glare
Of the interminable hours,   80
Our eyes can in another's eyes read clear,
When our world-deafen'd ear
Is by the tones of a loved voice caress'd —
A bolt is shot back somewhere in our breast,
And a lost pulse of feeling stirs again.   85
The eye sinks inward, and the heart lies plain,

And what we mean, we say, and what we would,
  we know.
A man becomes aware of his life's flow,
And hears its winding murmur; and he sees
The meadows where it glides, the sun, the breeze.   90

And there arrives a lull in the hot race
Wherein he doth for ever chase
That flying and elusive shadow, rest.
An air of coolness plays upon his face,
And an unwonted calm pervades his breast.   95
And then he thinks he knows
The hills where his life rose,
And the sea where it goes.

LINES

WRITTEN IN KENSINGTON GARDENS

In this lone, open glade I lie,
Screen'd by deep boughs on either hand;
And at its end, to stay the eye,
Those black-crown'd, red-boled pine-trees stand!

Birds here make song, each bird has his,   5
Across the girdling city's hum.
How green under the boughs it is!
How thick the tremulous sheep-cries come!

Sometimes a child will cross the glade
To take his nurse his broken toy;   10
Sometimes a thrush flit overhead
Deep in her unknown day's employ.

Here at my feet what wonders pass,
What endless, active life is here!
What blowing daisies, fragrant grass!   15
An air-stirr'd forest, fresh and clear.

Scarce fresher is the mountain-sod
Where the tired angler lies, stretch'd out,
And, eased of basket and of rod,
Counts his day's spoil, the spotted trout.   20

In the huge world, which roars hard by,
Be others happy if they can!
But in my helpless cradle I
Was breathed on by the rural Pan.

I, on men's impious uproar hurl'd,   25
Think often, as I hear them rave,
That peace has left the upper world
And now keeps only in the grave.

Yet here is peace for ever new!
When I who watch them am away,   30
Still all things in this glade go through
The changes of their quiet day.

Then to their happy rest they pass!
The flowers upclose, the birds are fed,
The night comes down upon the grass,   35
The child sleeps warmly in his bed.

Calm soul of all things! make it mine
To feel, amid the city's jar,
That there abides a peace of thine,
Man did not make, and cannot mar.   40

The will to neither strive nor cry,
The power to feel with others give!
Calm, calm me more! nor let me die
Before I have begun to live.

THE YOUTH OF NATURE

RAISED are the dripping oars,
Silent the boat! the lake,
Lovely and soft as a dream,
Swims in the sheen of the moon.

The mountains stand at its head 5
Clear in the pure June-night,
But the valleys are flooded with haze.
Rydal and Fairfield are there;
In the shadow Wordsworth lies dead.
So it is, so it will be for aye. 10
Nature is fresh as of old,
Is lovely; a mortal is dead.

The spots which recall him survive,
For he lent a new life to these hills.
The Pillar still broods o'er the fields 15
Which border Ennerdale Lake,
And Egremont sleeps by the sea.
The gleam of The Evening Star
Twinkles on Grasmere no more,
But ruin'd and solemn and grey 20
The sheepfold of Michael survives;
And, far to the south, the heath
Still blows in the Quantock coombs,
By the favourite waters of Ruth.
These survive! – yet not without pain, 25
Pain and dejection to-night,
Can I feel that their poet is gone.

He grew old in an age he condemn'd.
He look'd on the rushing decay
Of the times which had shelter'd his youth; 30
Felt the dissolving throes
Of a social order he loved;
Outlived his brethren, his peers,
And, like the Theban seer,
Died in his enemies' day. 35

Cold bubbled the spring of Tilphusa,
Copais lay bright in the moon,
Helicon glass'd in the lake
Its firs, and afar rose the peaks
Of Parnassus, snowily clear; 40

Thebes was behind him in flames,
And the clang of arms in his ear,
When his awe-struck captors led
The Theban seer to the spring.
Tiresias drank and died.   45
Nor did reviving Thebes
See such a prophet again.

Well may we mourn, when the head
Of a sacred poet lies low
In an age which can rear them no more!   50
The complaining millions of men
Darken in labour and pain;
But he was a priest to us all
Of the wonder and bloom of the world,
Which we saw with his eyes, and were glad.   55
He is dead, and the fruit-bearing day
Of his race is past on the earth;
And darkness returns to our eyes.

For, oh! is it you, is it you,
Moonlight, and shadow, and lake,   60
And mountains, that fill us with joy,
Or the poet who sings you so well?
Is it you, O beauty, O grace,
O charm, O romance, that we feel,
Or the voice which reveals what you are?   65
Are ye, like daylight and sun,
Shared and rejoiced in by all?
Or are ye immersed in the mass
Of matter, and hard to extract,
Or sunk at the core of the world   70
Too deep for the most to discern?
Like stars in the deep of the sky,
Which arise on the glass of the sage,
But are lost when their watcher is gone.

'They are here' – I heard, as men heard   75
In Mysian Ida the voice
Of the Mighty Mother, or Crete,
The murmur of Nature reply –
'Loveliness, magic, and grace,
They are here! they are set in the world,   80
They abide; and the finest of souls
Hath not been thrill'd by them all,
Nor the dullest been dead to them quite.
The poet who sings them may die,
But they are immortal and live,   85
For they are the life of the world.
Will ye not learn it, and know,
When ye mourn that a poet is dead,
That the singer was less than his themes,
Life, and emotion, and I?   90

'More than the singer are these.
Weak is the tremor of pain
That thrills in his mournfullest chord
To that which once ran through his soul.
Cold the elation of joy   95
In his gladdest, airiest song,
To that which of old in his youth
Fill'd him and made him divine.
Hardly his voice at its best
Gives us a sense of the awe,   100
The vastness, the grandeur, the gloom
Of the unlit gulph of himself.

'Ye know not yourselves; and your bards –
The clearest, the best, who have read
Most in themselves – have beheld   105
Less than they left unreveal'd.
Ye express not yourselves; – can you make
With marble, with colour, with word,
What charm'd you in others re-live?
Can thy pencil, O artist! restore   110
The figure, the bloom of thy love,

As she was in her morning of spring?
Canst thou paint the ineffable smile
Of her eyes as they rested on thine?
Can the image of life have the glow,   115
The motion of life itself?

'Yourselves and your fellows ye know not; and me,
The mateless, the one, will ye know?
Will ye scan me, and read me, and tell
Of the thoughts that ferment in my breast,   120
My longing, my sadness, my joy?
Will ye claim for your great ones the gift
To have render'd the gleam of my skies,
To have echoed the moan of my seas,
Utter'd the voice of my hills?   125
When your great ones depart, will ye say:
All things have suffer'd a loss,
Nature is hid in their grave?

'Race after race, man after man,
Have thought that my secret was theirs,   130
Have dream'd that I lived but for them,
That they were my glory and joy.
– They are dust, they are changed, they are gone!
I remain.'

THE YOUTH OF MAN

WE, O Nature, depart,
Thou survivest us! this,
This, I know, is the law.
Yes! but more than this,
Thou who seest us die   5
Seest us change while we live;
Seest our dreams, one by one,
Seest our errors depart;
Watchest us, Nature! throughout,
Mild and inscrutably calm.   10

171

Well for us that we change!
Well for us that the power
Which in our morning-prime
Saw the mistakes of our youth,
Sweet, and forgiving, and good,   15
Sees the contrition of age!

Behold, O Nature, this pair!
See them to-night where they stand,
Not with the halo of youth
Crowning their brows with its light,   20
Not with the sunshine of hope,
Not with the rapture of spring,
Which they had of old, when they stood
Years ago at my side
In this self-same garden, and said: 25
'We are young, and the world is ours;
Man, man is the king of the world!
Fools that these mystics are
Who prate of Nature! for she
Hath neither beauty, nor warmth,   30
Nor life, nor emotion, nor power.
But man has a thousand gifts,
And the generous dreamer invests
The senseless world with them all.
Nature is nothing; her charm   35
Lives in our eyes which can paint,
Lives in our hearts which can feel.'

Thou, O Nature, wast mute,
Mute as of old! days flew,
Days and years; and Time   40
With the ceaseless stroke of his wings
Brush'd off the bloom from their soul.
Clouded and dim grew their eye,
Languid their heart – for youth
Quicken'd its pulses no more.   45
Slowly, within the walls
Of an ever-narrowing world,

They droop'd, they grew blind, they grew old.
Thee and their youth in thee,
Nature! they saw no more.   50

Murmur of living,
Stir of existence,
Soul of the world!
Make, oh, make yourselves felt
To the dying spirit of youth!   55
Come, like the breath of the spring!
Leave not a human soul
To grow old in darkness and pain!
Only the living can feel you,
But leave us not while we live!   60

Here they stand to-night —
Here, where this grey balustrade
Crowns the still valley; behind
Is the castled house, with its woods,
Which shelter'd their childhood — the sun   65
On its ivied windows; a scent
From the grey-wall'd gardens, a breath
Of the fragrant stock and the pink,
Perfumes the evening air.
Their children play on the lawns.   70
They stand and listen; they hear
The children's shouts, and at times,
Faintly, the bark of a dog
From a distant farm in the hills.
Nothing besides! in front   75
The wide, wide valley outspreads
To the dim horizon, reposed
In the twilight, and bathed in dew,
Corn-field and hamlet and copse
Darkening fast; but a light,   80
Far off, a glory of day,
Still plays on the city spires;
And there in the dusk by the walls,
With the grey mist marking its course

Through the silent, flowery land,   85
On, to the plains, to the sea,
Floats the imperial stream.

  Well I know what they feel!
They gaze, and the evening wind
Plays on their faces; they gaze –   90
Airs from the Eden of youth
Awake and stir in their soul;
The past returns – they feel
What they are, alas! what they were.
They, not Nature, are changed.   95
Well I know what they feel!

Hush, for tears
Begin to steal to their eyes!
Hush, for fruit
Grows from such sorrow as theirs!   100

And they remember,
With piercing, untold anguish,
The proud boasting of their youth.
And they feel how Nature was fair.
And the mists of delusion,   105
And the scales of habit,
Fall away from their eyes;
And they see, for a moment,
Stretching out, like the desert
In its weary, unprofitable length,   110
Their faded, ignoble lives.

While the locks are yet brown on thy head,
While the soul still looks through thine eyes,
While the heart still pours
The mantling blood to thy cheek,   115
Sink, O youth, in thy soul!
Yearn to the greatness of Nature;
Rally the good in the depths of thyself!

YOUTH AND CALM

'Tis death! and peace, indeed, is here,
And ease from shame, and rest from fear.
There's nothing can dismarble now
The smoothness of that limpid brow.
But is a calm like this, in truth,   5
The crowning end of life and youth,
And when this boon rewards the dead,
Are all debts paid, has all been said?
And is the heart of youth so light,
Its step so firm, its eye so bright,   10
Because on its hot brow there blows
A wind of promise and repose
From the far grave, to which it goes;
Because it hath the hope to come,
One day, to harbour in the tomb?   15
Ah no, the bliss youth dreams is one
For daylight, for the cheerful sun,
For feeling nerves and living breath –
Youth dreams a bliss on this side death.
It dreams a rest, if not more deep,   20
More grateful than this marble sleep;
It hears a voice within it tell:
Calm's not life's crown, though calm is well.
'Tis all perhaps which man acquires,
But 'tis not what our youth desires.   25

THE FUTURE

A wanderer is man from his birth.
He was born in a ship
On the breast of the river of Time;
Brimming with wonder and joy
He spreads out his arms to the light,   5
Rivets his gaze on the banks of the stream.

As what he sees is, so have his thoughts
   been.
Whether he wakes,
Where the snowy mountainous pass,
Echoing the screams of the eagles,   10
Hems in its gorges the bed
Of the new-born clear-flowing stream;
Whether he first sees light
Where the river in gleaming rings
Sluggishly winds through the plain;   15
Whether in sound of the swallowing sea –
As is the world on the banks,
So is the mind of the man.

   Vainly does each, as he glides,
Fable and dream   20
Of the lands which the river of Time
Had left ere he woke on its breast,
Or shall reach when his eyes have been
   closed.
Only the tract where he sails
He wots of; only the thoughts,   25
Raised by the objects he passes, are his.

Who can see the green earth any more
As she was by the sources of Time?
Who imagines her fields as they lay
In the sunshine, unworn by the plough?   30
Who thinks as they thought,
The tribes who then roam'd on her breast,
Her vigorous, primitive sons?

What girl
Now reads in her bosom as clear   35
As Rebekah read, when she sate
At eve by the palm-shaded well?
Who guards in her breast
As deep, as pellucid a spring
Of feeling, as tranquil, as sure?   40

 What bard,
At the height of his vision, can deem
Of God, of the world, of the soul,
With a plainness as near,
As flashing as Moses felt   45
When he lay in the night by his flock
On the starlit Arabian waste?
Can rise and obey
The beck of the Spirit like him?

This tract which the river of Time   50
Now flows through with us, is the plain.
Gone is the calm of its earlier shore.
Border'd by cities and hoarse
With a thousand cries is its stream.
And we on its breast, our minds   55
Are confused as the cries which we hear,
Changing and shot as the sights which we
   see.

And we say that repose has fled
For ever the course of the river of Time.
That cities will crowd to its edge   60
In a blacker, incessanter line;
That the din will be more on its banks,
Denser the trade on its stream,
Flatter the plain where it flows,
Fiercer the sun overhead.   65
That never will those on its breast
See an ennobling sight,
Drink of the feeling of quiet again.

But what was before us we know not,
And we know not what shall succeed.   70

Haply, the river of Time –
As it grows, as the towns on its marge
Fling their wavering lights
On a wider, statelier stream –

May acquire, if not the calm   75
Of its early mountainous shore,
Yet a solemn peace of its own.

And the width of the waters, the hush
Of the grey expanse where he floats,
Freshening its current and spotted with foam   80
As it draws to the Ocean, may strike
Peace to the soul of the man on its breast –
As the pale waste widens around him,
As the banks fade dimmer away,
As the stars come out, and the night-wind   85
Brings up the stream
Murmurs and scents of the infinite sea.

REQUIESCAT

STREW on her roses, roses,
    And never a spray of yew!
In quiet she reposes;
    Ah, would that I did too!

Her mirth the world required;   5
    She bathed it in smiles of glee.
But her heart was tired, tired,
    And now they let her be.

Her life was turning, turning,
    In mazes of heat and sound.   10
But for peace her soul was yearning,
    And now peace laps her round.

Her cabin'd, ample spirit,
    It flutter'd and fail'd for breath.
To-night it doth inherit   15
    The vasty hall of death.

A DREAM

Was it a dream? We sail'd, I thought we sail'd,
Martin and I, down a green Alpine stream,
Border'd, each bank, with pines; the morning sun
On the wet umbrage of their glossy tops,
On the red pinings of their forest-floor,   5
Drew a warm scent abroad; behind the pines
The mountain-skirts, with all their sylvan change
Of bright-leaf'd chestnuts and moss'd walnut-trees
And the frail scarlet-berried ash, began.
Swiss chalets glitter'd on the dewy slopes,   10
And from some swarded shelf, high up, there came
Notes of wild pastoral music – over all
Ranged, diamond-bright, the eternal wall of snow.
Upon the mossy rocks at the stream's edge,
Back'd by the pines, a plank-built cottage stood,   15
Bright in the sun; the climbing gourd-plant's leaves
Muffled its walls, and on the stone-strewn roof
Lay the warm golden gourds; golden, within,
Under the eaves, peer'd rows of Indian corn.
We shot beneath the cottage with the stream.   20
On the brown, rude-carved balcony, two forms
Came forth – Olivia's, Marguerite! and thine.
Clad were they both in white, flowers in their breast;
Straw hats bedeck'd their heads, with ribbons blue,
Which danced, and on their shoulders, fluttering, play'd. 25
They saw us, they conferr'd; their bosoms heaved,
And more than mortal impulse fill'd their eyes.
Their lips moved; their white arms, waved eagerly,
Flash'd once, like falling streams; we rose, we gazed.
One moment, on the rapid's top, our boat   30
Hung poised – and then the darting river of Life
(Such now, methought, it was), the river of Life,
Loud thundering, bore us by; swift, swift it foam'd,
Black under cliffs it raced, round headlands shone.
Soon the plank'd cottage by the sun-warm'd pines   35
Faded – the moss – the rocks; us burning plains,
Bristled with cities, us the sea received.

PHILOMELA

Hark! ah, the nightingale –
The tawny-throated!
Hark, from that moonlit cedar what a burst!
What triumph! hark! – what pain!

O wanderer from a Grecian shore,   5
Still, after many years, in distant lands,
Still nourishing in thy bewilder'd brain
That wild, unquench'd, deep-sunken, old-world pain –
Say, will it never heal?
And can this fragrant lawn   10
With its cool trees, and night,
And the sweet, tranquil Thames,
And moonshine, and the dew,
To thy rack'd heart and brain
Afford no balm?   15

Dost thou to-night behold,
Here, through the moonlight on this English grass,
The unfriendly palace in the Thracian wild?
Dost thou again peruse
With hot cheeks and sear'd eyes   20
The too clear web, and thy dumb sister's shame?
Dost thou once more assay
Thy flight, and feel come over thee,
Poor fugitive, the feathery change
Once more, and once more seem to make resound   25
With love and hate, triumph and agony,
Lone Daulis, and the high Cephissian vale?
Listen, Eugenia –
How thick the bursts come crowding through the leaves!
Again – thou hearest?   30
Eternal passion!
Eternal pain!

DOVER BEACH

THE sea is calm to-night.
The tide is full, the moon lies fair
Upon the straits; – on the French coast the light
Gleams and is gone; the cliffs of England stand,
Glimmering and vast, out in the tranquil bay.   5
Come to the window, sweet is the night-air!
Only, from the long line of spray
Where the sea meets the moon-blanch'd land,
Listen! you hear the grating roar
Of pebbles which the waves draw back, and fling,   10
At their return, up the high strand,
Begin, and cease, and then again begin,
With tremulous cadence slow, and bring
The eternal note of sadness in.

Sophocles long ago   15
Heard it on the Aegaean, and it brought
Into his mind the turbid ebb and flow
Of human misery; we
Find also in the sound a thought,
Hearing it by this distant northern sea.   20

The Sea of Faith ·
Was once, too, at the full, and round earth's shore
Lay like the folds of a bright girdle furl'd.
But now I only hear
Its melancholy, long, withdrawing roar,   25
Retreating, to the breath
Of the night-wind, down the vast edges drear
And naked shingles of the world.

Ah, love, let us be true
To one another! for the world, which seems   30
To lie before us like a land of dreams,
So various, so beautiful, so new,
Hath really neither joy, nor love, nor light,
Nor certitude, nor peace, nor help for pain;

And we are here as on a darkling plain   35
Swept with confused alarms of struggle and flight,
Where ignorant armies clash by night.

GROWING OLD

WHAT is it to grow old?
Is it to lose the glory of the form,
The lustre of the eye?
Is it for beauty to forego her wreath?
– Yes, but not this alone.   5

Is it to feel our strength –
Not our bloom only, but our strength – decay?
Is it to feel each limb
Grow stiffer, every function less exact,
Each nerve more loosely strung?   10

Yes, this, and more; but not
Ah, 'tis not what in youth we dream'd 'twould be!
'Tis not to have our life
Mellow'd and soften'd as with sunset-glow,
A golden day's decline.   15

'Tis not to see the world
As from a height, with rapt prophetic eyes,
And heart profoundly stirr'd;
And weep, and feel the fulness of the past,
The years that are no more.   20

It is to spend long days
And not once feel that we were ever young;
It is to add, immured
In the hot prison of the present, month
To month with weary pain.   25

It is to suffer this,
And feel but half, and feebly, what we feel.
Deep in our hidden heart
Festers the dull remembrance of a change,
But no emotion – none.   30

It is – last stage of all –
When we are frozen up within, and quite
The phantom of ourselves,
To hear the world applaud the hollow ghost
Which blamed the living man.   35

THE PROGRESS OF POESY

A VARIATION

YOUTH rambles on life's arid mount,
And strikes the rock, and finds the vein,
And brings the water from the fount,
The fount which shall not flow again.

The man mature with labour chops   5
For the bright stream a channel grand,
And sees not that the sacred drops
Ran off and vanish'd out of hand.

And then the old man totters nigh,
And feebly rakes among the stones.   10
The mount is mute, the channel dry;
And down he lays his weary bones.

THE LAST WORD

CREEP into thy narrow bed,
Creep, and let no more be said!
Vain thy onset! all stands fast.
Thou thyself must break at last.

Let the long contention cease!   5
Geese are swans, and swans are geese.
Let them have it how they will!
Thou art tired; best be still.

They out-talk'd thee, hiss'd thee, tore thee?
Better men fared thus before thee;   10
Fired their ringing shot and pass'd,
Hotly charged – and sank at last.

Charge once more, then, and be dumb!
Let the victors, when they come,
When the forts of folly fall,   15
Find thy body by the wall!

A WISH

I ASK not that my bed of death
From bands of greedy heirs be free;
For these besiege the latest breath
Of fortune's favour'd sons, not me.

I ask not each kind soul to keep   5
Tearless, when of my death he hears.
Let those who will, if any, weep!
There are worse plagues on earth than tears.

I ask but that my death may find
The freedom to my life denied;   10
Ask but the folly of mankind
Then, then at last, to quit my side.

Spare me the whispering, crowded room,
The friends who come, and gape, and go;
The ceremonious air of gloom —   15
All, which makes death a hideous show!

Nor bring, to see me cease to live,
Some doctor full of phrase and fame,
To shake his sapient head, and give
The ill he cannot cure a name.   20

Nor fetch, to take the accustom'd toll
Of the poor sinner bound for death,
His brother-doctor of the soul,
To canvass with official breath

The future and its viewless things —   25
That undiscover'd mystery
Which one who feels death's winnowing wings
Must needs read clearer, sure, than he!

A WISH

Bring none of these; but let me be,
While all around in silence lies,   30
Moved to the window near, and see
Once more, before my dying eyes,

Bathed in the sacred dews of morn
The wide aerial landscape spread –
The world which was ere I was born,   35
The world which lasts when I am dead;

Which never was the friend of *one*,
Nor promised love it could not give,
But lit for all its generous sun,
And lived itself, and made us live.   40

There let me gaze, till I become
In soul, with what I gaze on, wed!
To feel the universe my home;
To have before my mind – instead

Of the sick room, the mortal strife,   45
The turmoil for a little breath –
The pure eternal course of life,
Not human combatings with death!

Thus feeling, gazing, might I grow
Composed, refresh'd, ennobled, clear;   50
Then willing let my spirit go
To work or wait elsewhere or here!

PALLADIUM

SET where the upper streams of Simois flow
Was the Palladium, high 'mid rock and wood;
And Hector was in Ilium, far below,
And fought, and saw it not – but there it stood!

It stood, and sun and moonshine rain'd their light   5
On the pure columns of its glen-built hall.
Backward and forward roll'd the waves of fight
Round Troy – but while this stood, Troy could not fall.

So, in its lovely moonlight, lives the soul.
Mountains surround it, and sweet virgin air;   10
Cold plashing, past it, crystal waters roll;
We visit it by moments, ah, too rare!

We shall renew the battle in the plain
To-morrow; – red with blood will Xanthus be;
Hector and Ajax will be there again,   15
Helen will come upon the wall to see.

Then we shall rust in shade, or shine in strife,
And fluctuate 'twixt blind hopes and blind despairs,
And fancy that we put forth all our life,
And never know how with the soul it fares.   20

Still doth the soul, from its lone fastness high,
Upon our life a ruling effluence send.
And when it fails, fight as we will, we die;
And while it lasts, we cannot wholly end.

From

BACCHANALIA;

OR,

THE NEW AGE

The evening comes, the fields are still.
The tinkle of the thirsty rill,
Unheard all day, ascends again;
Deserted is the half-mown plain,
Silent the swaths! the ringing wain,   5
The mower's cry, the dog's alarms,
All housed within the sleeping farms!
The business of the day is done,
The last-left haymaker is gone.
And from the thyme upon the height,   10
And from the elder-blossom white
And pale dog-roses in the hedge,
And from the mint-plant in the sedge,

BACCHANALIA

In puffs of balm the night-air blows
The perfume which the day forgoes.   15
And on the pure horizon far,
See, pulsing with the first-born star,
The liquid sky above the hill!
The evening comes, the fields are still.

ELEGIAC POEMS

STANZAS IN MEMORY OF THE AUTHOR OF 'OBERMANN'

NOVEMBER, 1849

IN front the awful Alpine track
Crawls up its rocky stair;
The autumn storm-winds drive the rack,
Close o'er it, in the air.

Behind are the abandon'd baths   5
Mute in their meadows lone;
The leaves are on the valley-paths,
The mists are on the Rhone —

The white mists rolling like a sea!
I hear the torrents roar.   10
— Yes, Obermann, all speaks of thee;
I feel thee near once more!

I turn thy leaves! I feel their breath
Once more upon me roll;
That air of languor, cold, and death,   15
Which brooded o'er thy soul.

Fly hence, poor wretch, whoe'er thou art,
Condemn'd to cast about,
All shipwreck in thy own weak heart,
For comfort from without!   20

A fever in these pages burns
Beneath the calm they feign;
A wounded human spirit turns,
Here, on its bed of pain.

Yes, though the virgin mountain-air   25
Fresh through these pages blows;
Though to these leaves the glaciers spare
The soul of their white snows;

Though here a mountain-murmur swells
Of many a dark-bough'd pine;   30
Though, as you read, you hear the bells
Of the high-pasturing kine –

Yet, through the hum of torrent lone,
And brooding mountain-bee,
There sobs I know not what ground-tone   35
Of human agony.

Is it for this, because the sound
Is fraught too deep with pain,
That, Obermann! the world around
So little loves thy strain?   40

Some secrets may the poet tell,
For the world loves new ways;
To tell too deep ones is not well –
It knows not what he says.

Yet of the spirits who have reign'd   45
In this our troubled day,
I know but two, who have attain'd,
Save thee, to see their way.

By England's lakes, in grey old age,
His quiet home one keeps;   50
And one, the strong much-toiling sage,
In German Weimar sleeps.

But Wordsworth's eyes avert their ken
From half of human fate;
And Goethe's course few sons of men   55
May think to emulate.

For he pursued a lonely road,
His eyes on Nature's plan;
Neither made man too much a God,
Nor God too much a man.   60

Strong was he, with a spirit free
From mists, and sane, and clear;
Clearer, how much! than ours – yet we
Have a worse course to steer.

For though his manhood bore the blast   65
Of a tremendous time,
Yet in a tranquil world was pass'd
His tenderer youthful prime.

But we, brought forth and rear'd in hours
Of change, alarm, surprise –   70
What shelter to grow ripe is ours?
What leisure to grow wise?

Like children bathing on the shore,
Buried a wave beneath,
The second wave succeeds, before   75
We have had time to breathe.

Too fast we live, too much are tried,
Too harass'd, to attain
Wordsworth's sweet calm, or Goethe's wide
And luminous view to gain.   80

And then we turn, thou sadder sage,
To thee! we feel thy spell!
– The hopeless tangle of our age,
Thou too hast scann'd it well!

Immoveable thou sittest, still   85
As death, composed to bear!
Thy head is clear, thy feeling chill,
And icy thy despair.

Yes, as the son of Thetis said,
I hear thee saying now: 90
Greater by far than thou are dead;
Strive not! die also thou!

Ah! two desires toss about
The poet's feverish blood.
One drives him to the world without,   95
And one to solitude.

The glow, he cries, *the thrill of life,*
Where, where do these abound? –
Not in the world, not in the strife
Of men, shall they be found.   100

He who hath watch'd, not shared, the strife,
Knows how the day hath gone.
He only lives with the world's life,
Who hath renounced his own.

To thee we come, then! Clouds are roll'd   105
Where thou, O seer! art set;
Thy realm of thought is drear and cold –
The world is colder yet!

And thou hast pleasures, too, to share
With those who come to thee –   110
Balms floating on thy mountain-air,
And healing sights to see.

How often, where the slopes are green
On Jaman, hast thou sate
By some high chalet-door, and seen   115
The summer-day grow late;

And darkness steal o'er the wet grass
With the pale crocus starr'd,
And reach that glimmering sheet of glass
Beneath the piny sward,   120

Lake Leman's waters, far below!
And watch'd the rosy light
Fade from the distant peaks of snow;
And on the air of night

Heard accents of the eternal tongue   125
Through the pine branches play –
Listen'd, and felt thyself grow young!
Listen'd and wept – Away!

Away the dreams that but deceive
And thou, sad guide, adieu!   130
I go, fate drives me; but I leave
Half of my life with you.

We, in some unknown Power's employ,
Move on a rigorous line;
Can neither, when we will, enjoy,   135
Nor, when we will, resign.

I in the world must live; but thou,
Thou melancholy shade!
Wilt not, if thou canst see me now,
Condemn me, nor upbraid.   140

For thou art gone away from earth,
And place with those dost claim,
The Children of the Second Birth,
Whom the world could not tame;

And with that small, transfigured band,   145
Whom many a different way
Conducted to their common land,
Thou learn'st to think as they.

Christian and pagan, king and slave,
Soldier and anchorite,   150
Distinctions we esteem so grave,
Are nothing in their sight.

They do not ask, who pined unseen,
Who was on action hurl'd,
Whose one bond is, that all have been   155
Unspotted by the world.

There without anger thou wilt see
Him who obeys thy spell
No more, so he but rest, like thee,
Unsoil'd! – and so, farewell.   160

Farewell! – Whether thou now liest near
That much-loved inland sea,
The ripples of whose blue waves cheer
Vevey and Meillerie:

And in that gracious region bland,   165
Where with clear-rustling wave
The scented pines of Switzerland
Stand dark round thy green grave,

Between the dusty vineyard-walls
Issuing on that green place   170
The early peasant still recalls
The pensive stranger's face,

And stoops to clear thy moss-grown date
Ere he plods on again; –
Or whether, by maligner fate,   175
Among the swarms of men,

Where between granite terraces
The blue Seine rolls her wave,
The Capital of Pleasure sees
The hardly-heard-of grave; –   180

Farewell! Under the sky we part,
In this stern Alpine dell.
O unstrung will! O broken heart!
A last, a last farewell!

MEMORIAL VERSES

APRIL, 1850

Goethe in Weimar sleeps, and Greece,
Long since, saw Byron's struggle cease.
But one such death remain'd to come;
The last poetic voice is dumb –
We stand to-day by Wordsworth's tomb.   5

When Byron's eyes were shut in death,
We bow'd our head and held our breath.
He taught us little; but our soul
Had *felt* him like the thunder's roll.
With shivering heart the strife we saw   10
Of passion with eternal law;
And yet with reverential awe
We watch'd the fount of fiery life
Which served for that Titanic strife.

    When Goethe's death was told, we said: 15
Sunk, then, is Europe's sagest head.
Physician of the iron age,
Goethe has done his pilgrimage.
He took the suffering human race,
He read each wound, each weakness clear;   20
And struck his finger on the place,
And said: *Thou ailest here, and here!*
He look'd on Europe's dying hour
Of fitful dream and feverish power;
His eye plunged down the weltering strife,   25
The turmoil of expiring life –
He said: *The end is everywhere,*
Art still has truth, take refuge there!
And he was happy, if to know
Causes of things, and far below   30
His feet to see the lurid flow
Of terror, and insane distress,
And headlong fate, be happiness.

And Wordsworth! – Ah, pale ghosts, rejoice!
For never has such soothing voice   35
Been to your shadowy world convey'd,
Since erst, at morn, some wandering shade
Heard the clear song of Orpheus come
Through Hades, and the mournful gloom.
Wordsworth has gone from us – and ye,   40
Ah, may ye feel his voice as we!
He too upon a wintry clime
Had fallen – on this iron time
Of doubts, disputes, distractions, fears.
He found us when the age had bound   45
Our souls in its benumbing round;
He spoke, and loosed our heart in tears.
He laid us as we lay at birth
On the cool flowery lap of earth,
Smiles broke from us and we had ease;   50
The hills were round us, and the breeze
Went o'er the sun-lit fields again;
Our foreheads felt the wind and rain.
Our youth return'd; for there was shed
On spirits that had long been dead,   55
Spirits dried up and closely furl'd,
The freshness of the early world.

Ah! since dark days still bring to light
Man's prudence and man's fiery might,
Time may restore us in his course   60
Goethe's sage mind and Byron's force;
But where will Europe's latter hour
Again find Wordsworth's healing power?
Others will teach us how to dare,
And against fear our breast to steel;   65
Others will strengthen us to bear –
But who, ah! who, will make us feel?
The cloud of mortal destiny,
Others will front it fearlessly –
But who, like him, will put it by?   70

Keep fresh the grass upon his grave,
O Rotha, with thy living wave!
Sing him thy best! for few or none
Hears thy voice right, now he is gone.

THE SCHOLAR-GIPSY

Go, for they call you, shepherd, from the hill;
  Go, shepherd, and untie the wattled cotes!
    No longer leave thy wistful flock unfed,
  Nor let thy bawling fellows rack their throats,
    Nor the cropp'd herbage shoot another head.   5
      But when the fields are still,
  And the tired men and dogs all gone to rest,
    And only the white sheep are sometimes seen
    Cross and recross the strips of moon-blanch'd green,
Come, shepherd, and again begin the quest!   10

Here, where the reaper was at work of late –
  In this high field's dark corner, where he leaves
    His coat, his basket, and his earthen cruse,
  And in the sun all morning binds the sheaves,
    Then here, at noon, comes back his stores to use –   15
      Here will I sit and wait,
  While to my ear from uplands far away
    The bleating of the folded flocks is borne,
    With distant cries of reapers in the corn –
All the live murmur of a summer's day.   20

Screen'd is this nook o'er the high, half-reap'd field,
  And here till sun-down, shepherd! will I be.
    Through the thick corn the scarlet poppies peep,
  And round green roots and yellowing stalks I see
    Pale pink convolvulus in tendrils creep;   25
      And air-swept lindens yield
  Their scent, and rustle down their perfumed showers
    Of bloom on the bent grass where I am laid,
    And bower me from the August sun with shade;
And the eye travels down to Oxford's towers.   30

And near me on the grass lies Glanvil's book –
   Come, let me read the oft-read tale again!
    The story of the Oxford scholar poor,
  Of pregnant parts and quick inventive brain,
     Who, tired of knocking at preferment's door,   35
      One summer-morn forsook
  His friends, and went to learn the gipsy-lore,
    And roam'd the world with that wild brotherhood,
    And came, as most men deem'd, to little good,
But came to Oxford and his friends no more.   40

But once, years after, in the country-lanes,
   Two scholars, whom at college erst he knew,
    Met him, and of his way of life enquired;
  Whereat he answer'd, that the gipsy-crew,
     His mates, had arts to rule as they desired   45
      The workings of men's brains,
  And they can bind them to what thoughts they will.
    'And I,' he said, 'the secret of their art,
    When fully learn'd, will to the world impart;
But it needs heaven-sent moments for this skill.'   50

This said, he left them, and return'd no more. –
   But rumours hung about the country-side,
    That the lost Scholar long was seen to stray,
  Seen by rare glimpses, pensive and tongue-tied,
     In hat of antique shape, and cloak of grey,   55
      The same the gipsies wore.
  Shepherds had met him on the Hurst in spring;
    At some lone alehouse in the Berkshire moors,
    On the warm ingle-bench, the smock-frock'd boors
Had found him seated at their entering,   60

But, 'mid their drink and clatter, he would fly.
   And I myself seem half to know thy looks,
    And put the shepherds, wanderer! on thy trace;
  And boys who in lone wheatfields scare the rooks
     I ask if thou hast pass'd their quiet place;   65

    Or in my boat I lie
Moor'd to the cool bank in the summer-heats,
  'Mid wide grass meadows which the sunshine fills,
  And watch the warm, green-muffled Cumner hills,
And wonder if thou haunt'st their shy retreats.   70

For most, I know, thou lov'st retired ground!
  Thee at the ferry Oxford riders blithe,
    Returning home on summer-nights, have met
  Crossing the stripling Thames at Bab-lock-hithe,
    Trailing in the cool stream thy fingers wet,   75
      As the punt's rope chops round;
  And leaning backward in a pensive dream,
    And fostering in thy lap a heap of flowers
    Pluck'd in shy fields and distant Wychwood bowers,
  And thine eyes resting on the moonlit stream.   80

And then they land, and thou art seen no more! –
  Maidens, who from the distant hamlets come
    To dance around the Fyfield elm in May,
  Oft through the darkening fields have seen thee roam,
    Or cross a stile into the public way.   85
      Oft thou hast given them store
  Of flowers – the frail-leaf'd, white anemony,
    Dark bluebells drench'd with dews of summer eves,
    And purple orchises with spotted leaves –
  But none hath words she can report of thee.   90

And, above Godstow Bridge, when hay-time's here
  In June, and many a scythe in sunshine flames,
    Men who through those wide fields of breezy grass
  Where black-wing'd swallows haunt the glittering
      Thames,
    To bathe in the abandon'd lasher pass,   95
      Have often pass'd thee near
  Sitting upon the river bank o'ergrown;
    Mark'd thine outlandish garb, thy figure spare,
    Thy dark vague eyes, and soft abstracted air –
  But, when they came from bathing, thou wast gone!   100

At some lone homestead in the Cumner hills,
  Where at her open door the housewife darns,
    Thou hast been seen, or hanging on a gate
  To watch the threshers in the mossy barns.
      Children, who early range these slopes and late   105
        For cresses from the rills,
  Have known thee eying, all an April-day,
    The springing pastures and the feeding kine;
    And mark'd thee, when the stars come out and shine,
  Through the long dewy grass move slow away.   110

In autumn, on the skirts of Bagley Wood –
  Where most the gipsies by the turf-edged way
    Pitch their smoked tents, and every bush you see
  With scarlet patches tagg'd and shreds of grey,
      Above the forest-ground called Thessaly –   115
        The blackbird, picking food,
  Sees thee, nor stops his meal, nor fears at all;
    So often has he known thee past him stray,
    Rapt, twirling in thy hand a wither'd spray,
  And waiting for the spark from heaven to fall.   120

And once, in winter, on the causeway chill
  Where home through flooded fields foot-travellers go,
    Have I not pass'd thee on the wooden bridge,
  Wrapt in thy cloak and battling with the snow,
      Thy face tow'rd Hinksey and its wintry ridge?   125
        And thou hast climb'd the hill,
  And gain'd the white brow of the Cumner range;
    Turn'd once to watch, while thick the snowflakes fall,
    The line of festal light in Christ-Church hall –
  Then sought thy straw in some sequester'd grange.   130

But what – I dream! Two hundred years are flown
  Since first thy story ran through Oxford halls,
    And the grave Glanvil did the tale inscribe
  That thou wert wander'd from the studious walls
      To learn strange arts, and join a gipsy-tribe;   135
        And thou from earth art gone

Long since, and in some quiet churchyard laid —
  Some country-nook, where o'er thy unknown grave
  Tall grasses and white flowering nettles wave,
Under a dark, red-fruited yew-tree's shade.   140

— No, no, thou hast not felt the lapse of hours!
  For what wears out the life of mortal men?
    'Tis that from change to change their being rolls;
  'Tis that repeated shocks, again, again,
    Exhaust the energy of strongest souls   145
      And numb the elastic powers.
Till having used our nerves with bliss and teen,
  And tired upon a thousand schemes our wit,
  To the just-pausing Genius we remit
Our worn-out life, and are — what we have been.   150

Thou hast not lived, why should'st thou perish, so?
  Thou hadst *one* aim, *one* business, *one* desire;
    Else wert thou long since number'd with the dead!
  Else hadst thou spent, like other men, thy fire!
    The generations of thy peers are fled,   155
      And we ourselves shall go;
But thou possessest an immortal lot,
  And we imagine thee exempt from age
  And living as thou liv'st on Glanvil's page,
Because thou hadst — what we, alas! have not.   160

For early didst thou leave the world, with powers
  Fresh, undiverted to the world without,
    Firm to their mark, not spent on other things;
  Free from the sick fatigue, the languid doubt,
    Which much to have tried, in much been baffled,
       brings.   165
      O life unlike to ours!
Who fluctuate idly without term or scope,
  Of whom each strives, nor knows for what he strives,
  And each half lives a hundred different lives;
Who wait like thee, but not, like thee, in hope.   170

Thou waitest for the spark from heaven! and we,
　Light half-believers of our casual creeds,
　　Who never deeply felt, nor clearly will'd,
　Whose insight never has borne fruit in deeds,
　　Whose vague resolves never have been fulfill'd;　　175
　　　For whom each year we see
　Breeds new beginnings, disappointments new;
　　Who hesitate and falter life away,
　　And lose to-morrow the ground won to-day –
Ah! do not we, wanderer! await it too?　　180

Yes, we await it! – but it still delays,
　And then we suffer! and amongst us one,
　　Who most has suffer'd, takes dejectedly
　His seat upon the intellectual throne;
　　And all his store of sad experience he　　185
　　　Lays bare of wretched days;
　Tells us his misery's birth and growth and signs,
　　And how the dying spark of hope was fed,
　　And how the breast was soothed, and how the head,
And all his hourly varied anodynes.　　190

This for our wisest! and we others pine,
　And wish the long unhappy dream would end,
　　And waive all claim to bliss, and try to bear;
　With close-lipp'd patience for our only friend,
　　Sad patience, too near neighbour to despair –　　195
　　　But none has hope like thine!
　Thou through the fields and through the woods dost stray,
　　Roaming the country-side, a truant boy,
　　Nursing thy project in unclouded joy,
And every doubt long blown by time away.　　200

O born in days when wits were fresh and clear,
　And life ran gaily as the sparkling Thames;
　　Before this strange disease of modern life,
　With its sick hurry, its divided aims,
　　Its heads o'ertax'd, its palsied hearts, was rife –　　205
　　　Fly hence, our contact fear!

Still fly, plunge deeper in the bowering wood!
  Averse, as Dido did with gesture stern
  From her false friend's approach in Hades turn,
Wave us away, and keep thy solitude!   210

Still nursing the unconquerable hope,
  Still clutching the inviolable shade,
    With a free, onward impulse brushing through,
  By night, the silver'd branches of the glade –
    Far on the forest-skirts, where none pursue,   215
      On some mild pastoral slope
  Emerge, and resting on the moonlit pales
    Freshen thy flowers as in former years
    With dew, or listen with enchanted ears,
From the dark dingles, to the nightingales!   220

But fly our paths, our feverish contact fly!
  For strong the infection of our mental strife,
    Which, though it gives no bliss, yet spoils for
      rest;
  And we should win thee from thy own fair life,
    Like us distracted, and like us unblest.   225
      Soon, soon thy cheer would die,
  Thy hopes grow timorous, and unfix'd thy powers,
    And thy clear aims be cross and shifting made;
    And then thy glad perennial youth would fade,
Fade, and grow old at last, and die like ours.   230

Then fly our greetings, fly our speech and smiles!
  – As some grave Tyrian trader, from the sea,
    Descried at sunrise an emerging prow
  Lifting the cool-hair'd creepers stealthily,
    The fringes of a southward-facing brow   235
      Among the Aegaean isles;
  And saw the merry Grecian coaster come,
    Freighted with amber grapes, and Chian wine,
    Green, bursting figs, and tunnies steep'd in brine –
And knew the intruders on his ancient home,   240

The young light-hearted masters of the waves –
  And snatch'd his rudder, and shook out more sail;
  And day and night held on indignantly
O'er the blue Midland waters with the gale,
  Betwixt the Syrtes and soft Sicily,   245
      To where the Atlantic raves
Outside the western straits; and unbent sails
  There, where down cloudy cliffs, through sheets
      of foam,
  Shy traffickers, the dark Iberians come;
And on the beach undid his corded bales.   250

STANZAS FROM THE GRANDE CHARTREUSE

THROUGH Alpine meadows soft-suffused
With rain, where thick the crocus blows,
Past the dark forges long disused,
The mule-track from Saint Laurent goes.
The bridge is cross'd, and slow we ride,   5
Through forest, up the mountain-side.

The autumnal evening darkens round,
The wind is up, and drives the rain;
While, hark! far down, with strangled sound
Doth the Dead Guier's stream complain,   10
Where that wet smoke, among the woods,
Over his boiling cauldron broods.

Swift rush the spectral vapours white
Past limestone scars with ragged pines,
Showing – then blotting from our sight! –   15
Halt – through the cloud-drift something shines!
High in the valley, wet and drear,
The huts of Courrerie appear.

Strike leftward! cries our guide; and higher
Mounts up the stony forest-way.   20
At last the encircling trees retire;
Look! through the showery twilight grey
What pointed roofs are these advance? –
A palace of the Kings of France?

Approach, for what we seek is here!   25
Alight, and sparely sup, and wait
For rest in this outbuilding near;
Then cross the sward and reach that gate.
Knock; pass the wicket! Thou art come
To the Carthusians' world-famed home.   30

The silent courts, where night and day
Into their stone-carved basins cold
The splashing icy fountains play –
The humid corridors behold!
Where, ghostlike in the deepening night,   35
Cowl'd forms brush by in gleaming white.

The chapel, where no organ's peal
Invests the stern and naked prayer –
With penitential cries they kneel
And wrestle; rising then, with bare   40
And white uplifted faces stand,
Passing the Host from hand to hand;

Each takes, and then his visage wan
Is buried in his cowl once more.
The cells! – the suffering Son of Man   45
Upon the wall – the knee-worn floor –
And where they sleep, that wooden bed,
Which shall their coffin be, when dead!

The library, where tract and tome
Not to feed priestly pride are there,   50
To hymn the conquering march of Rome,
Nor yet to amuse, as ours are!
They paint of souls the inner strife,
Their drops of blood, their death in life.

The garden, overgrown – yet mild,   55
See, fragrant herbs are flowering there!
Strong children of the Alpine wild
Whose culture is the brethren's care;
Of human tasks their only one,
And cheerful works beneath the sun.   60

Those halls, too, destined to contain
Each its own pilgrim-host of old,
From England, Germany, or Spain –
All are before me! I behold
The House, the Brotherhood austere!   65
– And what am I, that I am here?

For rigorous teachers seized my youth,
And purged its faith, and trimm'd its fire,
Show'd me the high, white star of Truth,
There bade me gaze, and there aspire.   70
Even now their whispers pierce the gloom:
What dost thou in this living tomb?

Forgive me, masters of the mind!
At whose behest I long ago
So much unlearnt, so much resign'd –   75
I come not here to be your foe!
I seek these anchorites, not in ruth,
To curse and to deny your truth;

Not as their friend, or child, I speak!
But as, on some far northern strand,   80
Thinking of his own Gods, a Greek
In pity and mournful awe might stand
Before some fallen Runic stone –
For both were faiths, and both are gone.

Wandering between two worlds, one dead,   85
The other powerless to be born,
With nowhere yet to rest my head,
Like these, on earth I wait forlorn.
Their faith, my tears, the world deride –
I come to shed them at their side.   90

Oh, hide me in your gloom profound,
Ye solemn seats of holy pain!
Take me, cowl'd forms, and fence me round,
Till I possess my soul again;
Till free my thoughts before me roll,   95
Not chafed by hourly false control!

For the world cries your faith is now
But a dead time's exploded dream;
My melancholy, sciolists say,
Is a pass'd mode, an outworn theme —   100
As if the world had ever had
A faith, or sciolists been sad!

Ah, if it *be* pass'd, take away,
At least, the restlessness, the pain;
Be man henceforth no more a prey   105
To these out-dated stings again!
The nobleness of grief is gone —
Ah, leave us not the fret alone!

But — if you cannot give us ease —
Last of the race of them who grieve   110
Here leave us to die out with these
Last of the people who believe!
Silent, while years engrave the brow;
Silent — the best are silent now.

Achilles ponders in his tent,   115
The kings of modern thought are dumb;
Silent they are, though not content,
And wait to see the future come.
They have the grief men had of yore,
But they contend and cry no more.   120

Our fathers water'd with their tears
This sea of time whereon we sail,
Their voices were in all men's ears
Who pass'd within their puissant hail.
Still the same ocean round us raves,   125
But we stand mute, and watch the waves.

For what avail'd it, all the noise
And outcry of the former men? –
Say, have their sons achieved more joys,
Say, is life lighter now than then? 130
The sufferers died, they left their pain –
The pangs which tortured them remain.

What helps it now, that Byron bore,
With haughty scorn which mock'd the smart,
Through Europe to the Aetolian shore 135
The pageant of his bleeding heart?
That thousands counted every groan,
And Europe made his woe her own?

What boots it, Shelley! that the breeze
Carried thy lovely wail away, 140
Musical through Italian trees
Which fringe thy soft blue Spezzian bay?
Inheritors of thy distress
Have restless hearts one throb the less?

Or are we easier, to have read, 145
O Obermann! the sad, stern page,
Which tells us how thou hidd'st thy head
From the fierce tempest of thine age
In the lone brakes of Fontainebleau,
Or chalets near the Alpine snow? 150

Ye slumber in your silent grave! –
The world, which for an idle day
Grace to your mood of sadness gave,
Long since hath flung her weeds away.
The eternal trifler breaks your spell; 155
But we – we learnt your lore too well!

Years hence, perhaps, may dawn an age,
More fortunate, alas! than we,
Which without hardness will be sage,
And gay without frivolity. 160
Sons of the world, oh, speed those years;
But, while we wait, allow our tears!

Allow them! We admire with awe
The exulting thunder of your race;
You give the universe your law,   165
You triumph over time and space!
Your pride of life, your tireless powers,
We laud them, but they are not ours.

We are like children rear'd in shade
Beneath some old-world abbey wall,   170
Forgotten in a forest-glade,
And secret from the eyes of all.
Deep, deep the greenwood round them waves,
Their abbey, and its close of graves!

But, where the road runs near the stream,   175
Oft through the trees they catch a glance
Of passing troops in the sun's beam –
Pennon, and plume, and flashing lance!
Forth to the world those soldiers fare,
To life, to cities, and to war!   180

And through the wood, another way,
Faint bugle-notes from far are borne,
Where hunters gather, staghounds bay,
Round some fair forest-lodge at morn.
Gay dames are there, in sylvan green;   185
Laughter and cries – those notes between!

The banners flashing through the trees
Make their blood dance and chain their eyes;
That bugle-music on the breeze
Arrests them with a charm'd surprise.   190
Banner by turns and bugle woo:
Ye shy recluses, follow too!

O children, what do ye reply? –
'Action and pleasure, will ye roam
Through these secluded dells to cry   195
And call us? – but too late ye come!
Too late for us your call ye blow,
Whose bent was taken long ago.

'Long since we pace this shadow'd nave;
We watch those yellow tapers shine, 200
Emblems of hope over the grave,
In the high altar's depth divine;
The organ carries to our ear
Its accents of another sphere.

'Fenced early in this cloistral round 205
Of reverie, of shade, of prayer,
How should we grow in other ground?
How can we flower in foreign air?
— Pass, banners, pass, and bugles, cease;
And leave our desert to its peace!' 210

RUGBY CHAPEL

NOVEMBER 1857

COLDLY, sadly descends
The autumn-evening. The field
Strewn with its dank yellow drifts
Of wither'd leaves, and the elms,
Fade into dimness apace, 5
Silent; — hardly a shout
From a few boys late at their play!
The lights come out in the street,
In the school-room windows; — but cold,
Solemn, unlighted, austere, 10
Through the gathering darkness, arise
The chapel-walls, in whose bound
Thou, my father! art laid.

There thou dost lie, in the gloom
Of the autumn evening. But ah! 15
That word, *gloom*, to my mind
Brings thee back, in the light
Of thy radiant vigour, again;

In the gloom of November we pass'd
Days not dark at thy side;   20
Seasons impair'd not the ray
Of thy buoyant cheerfulness clear.
Such thou wast! and I stand
In the autumn evening, and think
Of bygone autumns with thee.   25

Fifteen years have gone round
Since thou arosest to tread,
In the summer-morning, the road
Of death, at a call unforeseen,
Sudden. For fifteen years,   30
We who till then in thy shade
Rested as under the boughs
Of a mighty oak, have endured
Sunshine and rain as we might,
Bare, unshaded, alone,   35
Lacking the shelter of thee.

O strong soul, by what shore
Tarriest thou now? For that force,
Surely, has not been left vain!
Somewhere, surely, afar,   40
In the sounding labour-house vast
Of being, is practised that strength,
Zealous, beneficent, firm!

Yes, in some far-shining sphere,
Conscious or not of the past,   45
Still thou performest the word
Of the Spirit in whom thou dost live –
Prompt, unwearied, as here!
Still thou upraisest with zeal
The humble good from the ground,   50
Sternly repressest the bad!
Still, like a trumpet, dost rouse
Those who with half-open eyes
Tread the border-land dim

'Twixt vice and virtue; reviv'st,   55
Succourest! – this was thy work,
This was thy life upon earth.

What is the course of the life
Of mortal men on the earth? –
Most men eddy about   60
Here and there – eat and drink,
Chatter and love and hate,
Gather and squander, are raised
Aloft, are hurl'd in the dust,
Striving blindly, achieving   65
Nothing; and then they die –
Perish; – and no one asks
Who or what they have been,
More than he asks what waves,
In the moonlit solitudes mild   70
Of the midmost Ocean, have swell'd,
Foam'd for a moment, and gone.

And there are some, whom a thirst
Ardent, unquenchable, fires,
Not with the crowd to be spent,   75
Not without aim to go round
In an eddy of purposeless dust,
Effort unmeaning and vain.
Ah yes! some of us strive
Not without action to die   80
Fruitless, but something to snatch
From dull oblivion, nor all
Glut the devouring grave!
We, we have chosen our path –
Path to a clear-purposed goal,   85
Path of advance! – but it leads
A long, steep journey, through sunk
Gorges, o'er mountains in snow.
Cheerful, with friends, we set forth –
Then, on the height, comes the storm.   90

Thunder crashes from rock
To rock, the cataracts reply,
Lightnings dazzle our eyes.
Roaring torrents have breach'd
The track, the stream-bed descends   95
In the place where the wayfarer once
Planted his footstep – the spray
Boils o'er its borders! aloft
The unseen snow-beds dislodge
Their hanging ruin; alas,   100
Havoc is made in our train!
Friends, who set forth at our side,
Falter, are lost in the storm.
We, we only are left!
With frowning foreheads, with lips   105
Sternly compress'd, we strain on,
On – and at nightfall at last
Come to the end of our way,
To the lonely inn 'mid the rocks;
Where the gaunt and taciturn host   110
Stands on the threshold, the wind
Shaking his thin white hairs –
Holds his lantern to scan
Our storm-beat figures, and asks:
Whom in our party we bring?   115
Whom we have left in the snow?

Sadly we answer: We bring
Only ourselves! we lost
Sight of the rest in the storm.
Hardly ourselves we fought through,   120
Stripp'd, without friends, as we are.
Friends, companions, and train,
The avalanche swept from our side.

But thou would'st not *alone*
Be saved, my father! *alone*   125
Conquer and come to thy goal,
Leaving the rest in the wild.

We were weary, and we
Fearful, and we in our march
Fain to drop down and to die.   130
Still thou turnedst, and still
Beckonedst the trembler, and still
Gavest the weary thy hand.

If, in the paths of the world,
Stones might have wounded thy feet,   135
Toil or dejection have tried
Thy spirit, of that we saw
Nothing – to us thou wast still
Cheerful, and helpful, and firm!
Therefore to thee it was given   140
Many to save with thyself;
And, at the end of thy day,
O faithful shepherd! to come,
Bringing thy sheep in thy hand.

And through thee I believe   145
In the noble and great who are gone;
Pure souls honour'd and blest
By former ages, who else –
Such, so soulless, so poor,
Is the race of men whom I see –   150
Seem'd but a dream of the heart,
Seem'd but a cry of desire.
Yes! I believe that there lived
Others like thee in the past,
Not like the men of the crowd   155
Who all round me to-day
Bluster or cringe, and make life
Hideous, and arid, and vile;
But souls temper'd with fire,
Fervent, heroic, and good,   160
Helpers and friends of mankind.

Servants of God! – or sons
Shall I not call you? because

Not as servants ye knew
Your Father's innermost mind,   165
His, who unwillingly sees
One of his little ones lost –
Yours is the praise, if mankind
Hath not as yet in its march
Fainted, and fallen, and died!   170

See! In the rocks of the world
Marches the host of mankind,
A feeble, wavering line.
Where are they tending? – A God
Marshall'd them, gave them their goal.   175
Ah, but the way is so long!
Years they have been in the wild!
Sore thirst plagues them, the rocks,
Rising all round, overawe;
Factions divide them, their host   180
Threatens to break, to dissolve.
– Ah, keep, keep them combined!
Else, of the myriads who fill
That army, not one shall arrive;
Sole they shall stray; in the rocks   185
Stagger for ever in vain,
Die one by one in the waste.

Then, in such hour of need
Of your fainting, dispirited race,
Ye, like angels, appear,   190
Radiant with ardour divine!
Beacons of hope, ye appear!
Languor is not in your heart,
Weakness is not in your word,
Weariness not on your brow.   195
Ye alight in our van! at your voice,
Panic, despair, flee away.
Ye move through the ranks, recall
The stragglers, refresh the outworn,

Praise, re-inspire the brave! 200
Order, courage, return.
Eyes rekindling, and prayers,
Follow your steps as ye go.
Ye fill up the gaps in our files,
Strengthen the wavering line, 205
Stablish, continue our march,
On, to the bound of the waste,
On, to the City of God.

STANZAS FROM CARNAC

FAR on its rocky knoll descried
Saint Michael's chapel cuts the sky.
I climb'd; – beneath me, bright and wide,
Lay the lone coast of Brittany.

Bright in the sunset, weird and still, 5
It lay beside the Atlantic wave,
As though the wizard Merlin's will
Yet charm'd it from his forest-grave.

Behind me on their grassy sweep,
Bearded with lichen, scrawl'd and grey, 10
The giant stones of Carnac sleep,
In the mild evening of the May.

No priestly stern procession now
Moves through their rows of pillars old;
No victims bleed, no Druids bow – 15
Sheep make the daisied aisles their fold.

From bush to bush the cuckoo flies,
The orchis red gleams everywhere;
Gold furze with broom in blossom vies,
The blue-bells perfume all the air. 20

And o'er the glistening, lonely land,
Rise up, all round, the Christian spires;
The church of Carnac, by the strand,
Catches the westering sun's last fires.

And there, across the watery way,   25
See, low above the tide at flood,
The sickle-sweep of Quiberon Bay,
Whose beach once ran with loyal blood!

And beyond that, the Atlantic wide! —
All round, no soul, no boat, no hail;   30
But, on the horizon's verge descried,
Hangs, touch'd with light, one snowy sail!

Ah! where is he, who should have come
Where that far sail is passing now,
Past the Loire's mouth, and by the foam   35
Of Finistère's unquiet brow,

Home, round into the English wave?
— He tarries where the Rock of Spain
Mediterranean waters lave;
He enters not the Atlantic main.   40

Oh, could he once have reach'd this air
Freshen'd by plunging tides, by showers!
Have felt this breath he loved, of fair
Cool northern fields, and grass, and flowers!

He long'd for it — press'd on. — In vain!   45
At the Straits fail'd that spirit brave.
The south was parent of his pain,
The south is mistress of his grave.

A SOUTHERN NIGHT

THE sandy spits, the shore-lock'd lakes,
    Melt into open, moonlit sea;
The soft Mediterranean breaks
    At my feet, free.

217

Dotting the fields of corn and vine,   5
   Like ghosts the huge, gnarl'd olives stand.
Behind, that lovely mountain-line!
      While, by the strand,

Cette, with its glistening houses white,
   Curves with the curving beach away   10
To where the lighthouse beacons bright
      Far in the bay.

Ah! such a night, so soft, so lone,
   So moonlit, saw me once of yore
Wander unquiet, and my own   15
      Vext heart deplore.

But now that trouble is forgot;
   Thy memory, thy pain, to-night,
My brother! and thine early lot,
      Possess me quite.   20

The murmur of this Midland deep
   Is heard to-night around thy grave,
There, where Gibraltar's cannon'd steep
      O'erfrowns the wave.

For there, with bodily anguish keen,   25
   With Indian heats at last fordone,
With public toil and private teen –
      Thou sank'st, alone.

Slow to a stop, at morning grey,
   I see the smoke-crown'd vessel come;   30
Slow round her paddles dies away
      The seething foam.

A boat is lower'd from her side;
   Ah, gently place him on the bench!
That spirit – if all have not yet died –   35
      A breath might quench.

Is this the eye, the footstep fast,
   The mien of youth we used to see,
Poor, gallant boy! – for such thou wast,
     Still art, to me.   **40**

The limbs their wonted tasks refuse;
   The eyes are glazed, thou canst not speak;
And whiter than thy white burnous
     That wasted cheek!

Enough! The boat, with quiet shock,   **45**
   Unto its haven coming nigh,
Touches, and on Gibraltar's rock
     Lands thee to die.

Ah me! Gibraltar's strand is far,
   But farther yet across the brine   **50**
Thy dear wife's ashes buried are,
     Remote from thine.

For there, where morning's sacred fount
   Its golden rain on earth confers,
The snowy Himalayan Mount   **55**
     O'ershadows hers.

Strange irony of fate, alas,
   Which, for two jaded English, saves,
When from their dusty life they pass,
     Such peaceful graves!   **60**

In cities should we English lie,
   Where cries are rising ever new,
And men's incessant stream goes by –
     We who pursue

Our business with unslackening stride,   **65**
   Traverse in troops, with care-fill'd breast,
The soft Mediterranean side,
     The Nile, the East,

And see all sights from pole to pole,
　　And glance, and nod, and bustle by,　　　70
And never once possess our soul
　　　　Before we die.

Not by those hoary Indian hills,
　　Not by this gracious Midland sea
Whose floor to-night sweet moonshine fills,　　75
　　　　Should our graves be.

Some sage, to whom the world was dead,
　　And men were specks, and life a play;
Who made the roots of trees his bed,
　　　　And once a day　　　　　　　80

With staff and gourd his way did bend
　　To villages and homes of man,
For food to keep him till he end
　　　　His mortal span

And the pure goal of being reach;　　　　85
　　Hoar-headed, wrinkled, clad in white,
Without companion, without speech,
　　　　By day and night

Pondering God's mysteries untold,
　　And tranquil as the glacier-snows　　　90
He by those Indian mountains old
　　　　Might well repose.

Some grey crusading knight austere,
　　Who bore Saint Louis company,
And came home hurt to death, and here　　　95
　　　　Landed to die;

Some youthful troubadour, whose tongue
　　Fill'd Europe once with his love-pain,
Who here outworn had sunk, and sung
　　　　His dying strain;　　　　　　100

Some girl, who here from castle-bower,
    With furtive step and cheek of flame,
'Twixt myrtle-hedges all in flower
        By moonlight came

To meet her pirate-lover's ship;   105
    And from the wave-kiss'd marble stair
Beckon'd him on, with quivering lip
        And floating hair;

And lived some moons in happy trance,
    Then learnt his death and pined away –   110
Such by these waters of romance
        'Twas meet to lay.

But you – a grave for knight or sage,
    Romantic, solitary, still,
O spent ones of a work-day age!   115
        Befits you ill.

So sang I; but the midnight breeze,
    Down to the brimm'd, moon-charmed main,
Comes softly through the olive-trees,
        And checks my strain.   120

I think of her, whose gentle tongue
    All plaint in her own cause controll'd;
Of thee I think, my brother! young
        In heart, high-soul'd –

That comely face, that cluster'd brow,   125
    That cordial hand, that bearing free,
I see them still, I see them now,
        Shall always see!

And what but gentleness untired,
    And what but noble feeling warm,   130
Wherever shown, howe'er inspired,
        Is grace, is charm?

What else is all these waters are,
    What else is steep'd in lucid sheen,
What else is bright, what else is fair,   135
    What else serene?

Mild o'er her grave, ye mountains, shine!
    Gently by his, ye waters, glide!
To that in you which is divine
    They were allied.   140

THYRSIS

A MONODY, *to commemorate the author's friend,*
ARTHUR HUGH CLOUGH, *who died at Florence,* 1861

How changed is here each spot man makes or fills!
    In the two Hinkseys nothing keeps the same;
      The village street its haunted mansion lacks,
    And from the sign is gone Sibylla's name,
      And from the roofs the twisted chimney-stacks –   5
      Are ye too changed, ye hills?
    See, 'tis no foot of unfamiliar men
    To-night from Oxford up your pathway strays!
    Here came I often, often, in old days –
Thyrsis and I; we still had Thyrsis then.   10

Runs it not here, the track by Childsworth Farm,
    Past the high wood, to where the elm-tree crowns
      The hill behind whose ridge the sunset flames?
    The signal-elm, that looks on Ilsley Downs,
      The Vale, the three lone weirs, the youthful Thames? –
      This winter-eve is warm,   16
    Humid the air! leafless, yet soft as spring,
    The tender purple spray on copse and briers!
    And that sweet city with her dreaming spires,
She needs not June for beauty's heightening,

Lovely all times she lies, lovely to-night! –
  Only, methinks, some loss of habit's power
    Befalls me wandering through this upland dim.
  Once pass'd I blindfold here, at any hour;
    Now seldom come I, since I came with him.   25
      That single elm-tree bright
  Against the west – I miss it! is it gone?
    We prized it dearly; while it stood, we said,
    Our friend, the Gipsy-Scholar, was not dead;
  While the tree lived, he in these fields lived on.   30

Too rare, too rare, grow now my visits here,
  But once I knew each field, each flower, each stick;
    And with the country-folk acquaintance made
  By barn in threshing-time, by new-built rick.
    Here, too, our shepherd-pipes we first assay'd.   35
      Ah me! this many a year
  My pipe is lost, my shepherd's holiday!
    Needs must I lose them, needs with heavy heart
    Into the world and wave of men depart;
  But Thyrsis of his own will went away.   40

It irk'd him to be here, he could not rest.
  He loved each simple joy the country yields,
    He loved his mates; but yet he could not keep,
  For that a shadow lour'd on the fields,
    Here with the shepherds and the silly sheep.   45
      Some life of men unblest
  He knew, which made him droop, and fill'd his head.
    He went; his piping took a troubled sound
    Of storms that rage outside our happy ground;
  He could not wait their passing, he is dead.   50

So, some tempestuous morn in early June,
  When the year's primal burst of bloom is o'er,
    Before the roses and the longest day –
  When garden-walks and all the grassy floor
    With blossoms red and white of fallen May   55
      And chestnut-flowers are strewn –

So have I heard the cuckoo's parting cry,
   From the wet field, through the vext garden-trees,
    Come with the volleying rain and tossing breeze:
The bloom is gone, and with the bloom go I!   60

Too quick despairer, wherefore wilt thou go?
   Soon will the high Midsummer pomps come on,
    Soon will the musk carnations break and swell,
Soon shall we have gold-dusted snapdragon,
   Sweet-William with his homely cottage-smell,   65
    And stocks in fragrant blow;
Roses that down the alleys shine afar,
   And open, jasmine-muffled lattices,
   And groups under the dreaming garden-trees,
And the full moon, and the white evening-star.   70

He hearkens not! light comer, he is flown!
   What matters it? next year he will return,
    And we shall have him in the sweet spring-days,
With whitening hedges, and uncrumpling fern,
   And blue-bells trembling by the forest-ways,   75
    And scent of hay new-mown.
But Thyrsis never more we swains shall see;
   See him come back, and cut a smoother reed,
   And blow a strain the world at last shall heed –
For Time, not Corydon, hath conquer'd thee!   80

Alack, for Corydon no rival now! –
   But when Sicilian shepherds lost a mate,
    Some good survivor with his flute would go,
Piping a ditty sad for Bion's fate;
   And cross the unpermitted ferry's flow,   85
    And relax Pluto's brow,
And make leap up with joy the beauteous head
   Of Proserpine, among whose crowned hair
   Are flowers first open'd on Sicilian air,
And flute his friend, like Orpheus, from the dead.   90

224

O easy access to the hearer's grace
  When Dorian shepherds sang to Proserpine!
    For she herself had trod Sicilian fields,
She knew the Dorian water's gush divine,
    She knew each lily white which Enna yields,   95
      Each rose with blushing face;
She loved the Dorian pipe, the Dorian strain.
    But ah, of our poor Thames she never heard!
    Her foot the Cumner cowslips never stirr'd;
And we should tease her with our plaint in vain!   100

Well! wind-dispersed and vain the words will be,
  Yet, Thyrsis, let me give my grief its hour
    In the old haunt, and find our tree-topp'd hill!
Who, if not I, for questing here hath power?
    I know the wood which hides the daffodil,   105
      I know the Fyfield tree,
I know what white, what purple fritillaries
    The grassy harvest of the river-fields,
    Above by Ensham, down by Sandford, yields,
And what sedged brooks are Thames's tributaries;   110

I know these slopes; who knows them if not I? –
  But many a dingle on the loved hill-side,
    With thorns once studded, old, white-blossom'd trees,
Where thick the cowslips grew, and far descried
    High tower'd the spikes of purple orchises,   115
      Hath since our day put by
The coronals of that forgotten time;
    Down each green bank hath gone the ploughboy's team,
    And only in the hidden brookside gleam
Primroses, orphans of the flowery prime.   120

Where is the girl, who by the boatman's door,
  Above the locks, above the boating throng,
    Unmoor'd our skiff when through the Wytham flats,
Red loosestrife and blond meadow-sweet among

And darting swallows and light water-gnats,   125
  We track'd the shy Thames shore?
Where are the mowers, who, as the tiny swell
  Of our boat passing heaved the river-grass,
    Stood with suspended scythe to see us pass? –
They all are gone, and thou art gone as well!   130

Yes, thou art gone! and round me too the night
  In ever-nearing circle weaves her shade.
    I see her veil draw soft across the day,
  I feel her slowly chilling breath invade
    The cheek grown thin, the brown hair sprent with grey;
      I feel her finger light   136
Laid pausefully upon life's headlong train; –
    The foot less prompt to meet the morning dew,
    The heart less bounding at emotion new,
And hope, once crush'd, less quick to spring again.   140

And long the way appears, which seem'd so short
  To the less practised eye of sanguine youth;
    And high the mountain-tops, in cloudy air,
  The mountain-tops where is the throne of Truth,
    Tops in life's morning-sun so bright and bare!   145
      Unbreachable the fort
Of the long-batter'd world uplifts its wall;
    And strange and vain the earthly turmoil grows,
    And near and real the charm of thy repose,
And night as welcome as a friend would fall.   150

But hush! the upland hath a sudden loss
  Of quiet! – Look, adown the dusk hill-side,
    A troop of Oxford hunters going home,
  As in old days, jovial and talking, ride!
    From hunting with the Berkshire hounds they come.   155
      Quick! let me fly, and cross
Into yon farther field! – 'Tis done; and see,
    Back'd by the sunset, which doth glorify
    The orange and pale violet evening-sky,
Bare on its lonely ridge, the Tree! the Tree!   160

I take the omen! Eve lets down her veil,
  The white fog creeps from bush to bush about,
    The west unflushes, the high stars grow bright,
And in the scatter'd farms the lights come out.
    I cannot reach the signal-tree to-night,   165
      Yet, happy omen, hail!
Hear it from thy broad lucent Arno-vale
  (For there thine earth-forgetting eyelids keep
  The morningless and unawakening sleep
Under the flowery oleanders pale),   170

Hear it, O Thyrsis, still our tree is there! –
  Ah, vain! These English fields, this upland dim,
    These brambles pale with mist engarlanded,
That lone, sky-pointing tree, are not for him;
    To a boon southern country he is fled,   175
      And now in happier air,
Wandering with the great Mother's train divine
  (And purer or more subtle soul than thee,
  I trow, the mighty Mother doth not see)
Within a folding of the Apennine,   180

Thou hearest the immortal chants of old! –
  Putting his sickle to the perilous grain
    In the hot cornfield of the Phrygian king,
For thee the Lityerses-song again
    Young Daphnis with his silver voice doth sing; 185
      Sings his Sicilian fold,
His sheep, his hapless love, his blinded eyes –
  And how a call celestial round him rang,
  And heavenward from the fountain-brink he sprang,
And all the marvel of the golden skies.   190

There thou art gone, and me thou leavest here
  Sole in these fields! yet will I not despair.
    Despair I will not, while I yet descry
'Neath the mild canopy of English air
    That lonely tree against the western sky.   195
      Still, still these slopes, 'tis clear,

Our Gipsy-Scholar haunts, outliving thee!
  Fields where soft sheep from cages pull the hay,
  Woods with anemonies in flower till May,
Know him a wanderer still; then why not me?   200

A fugitive and gracious light he seeks,
  Shy to illumine; and I seek it too.
    This does not come with houses or with gold,
  With place, with honour, and a flattering crew;
    'Tis not in the world's market bought and sold —   205
      But the smooth-slipping weeks
  Drop by, and leave its seeker still untired;
    Out of the heed of mortals he is gone,
    He wends unfollow'd, he must house alone;
Yet on he fares, by his own heart inspired.   210

Thou too, O Thyrsis, on like quest wast bound;
  Thou wanderedst with me for a little hour!
    Men gave thee nothing; but this happy quest,
  If men esteem'd thee feeble, gave thee power,
    If men procured thee trouble, gave thee rest.   215
      And this rude Cumner ground,
  Its fir-topped Hurst, its farms, its quiet fields,
    Here camst thou in thy jocund youthful time,
    Here was thine height of strength, thy golden
        prime!
And still the haunt beloved a virtue yields.   220

What though the music of thy rustic flute
  Kept not for long its happy, country tone;
    Lost it too soon, and learnt a stormy note
  Of men contention-tost, of men who groan,
    Which task'd thy pipe too sore, and tired thy throat — 225
      It fail'd, and thou wast mute!
  Yet hadst thou alway visions of our light,
    And long with men of care thou couldst not stay,
    And soon thy foot resumed its wandering way,
Left human haunt, and on alone till night.   230

Too rare, too rare, grow now my visits here!
　'Mid city-noise, not, as with thee of yore,
　　Thyrsis! in reach of sheep-bells is my home.
－ Then through the great town's harsh, heart-wearying
　　　roar,
　　Let in thy voice a whisper often come,　　　　　235
　　　To chase fatigue and fear:
Why faintest thou? I wander'd till I died.
Roam on! The light we sought is shining still.
Dost thou ask proof? Our tree yet crowns the hill,
Our Scholar travels yet the loved hill-side.　　　240

OBERMANN ONCE MORE *

Savez-vous quelque bien qui console du regret d'un monde? OBERMANN

　　Glion? － Ah, twenty years, it cuts
　　All meaning from a name!
　　White houses prank where once were huts.
　　Glion, but not the same!

　　And yet I know not! All unchanged　　　5
　　The turf, the pines, the sky!
　　The hills in their old order ranged;
　　The lake, with Chillon by!

　　And, 'neath those chestnut-trees, where stiff
　　And stony mounts the way,　　　　　10
　　The crackling husk-heaps burn, as if
　　I left them yesterday!

　　Across the valley, on that slope,
　　The huts of Avant shine!
　　Its pines, under their branches, ope　　　15
　　Ways for the pasturing kine.

* In the Library Edition this poem follows 'Stanzas in Memory of
the Author of "Obermann" ' and has this subtitle: (Composed many
years after the preceding).

Full-foaming milk-pails, Alpine fare,
Sweet heaps of fresh-cut grass,
Invite to rest the traveller there
Before he climb the pass -   20

The gentian-flower'd pass, its crown
With yellow spires aflame;
Whence drops the path to Allière down,
And walls where Byron came,

By their green river, who doth change   25
His birth-name just below;
Orchard, and croft, and full-stored grange
Nursed by his pastoral flow.

But stop! - to fetch back thoughts that stray
Beyond this gracious bound,   30
The cone of Jaman, pale and grey,
See, in the blue profound!

Ah, Jaman! delicately tall
Above his sun-warm'd firs -
What thoughts to me his rocks recall,   35
What memories he stirs!

And who but thou must be, in truth,
Obermann! with me here?
Thou master of my wandering youth,
But left this many a year!   40

Yes, I forget the world's work wrought,
Its warfare waged with pain;
An eremite with thee, in thought
Once more I slip my chain,

And to thy mountain-chalet come,   45
And lie beside its door,
And hear the wild bee's Alpine hum,
And thy sad, tranquil lore!

Again I feel the words inspire
Their mournful calm; serene,   50
Yet tinged with infinite desire
For all that *might* have been —

The harmony from which man swerved
Made his life's rule once more!
The universal order served,   55
Earth happier than before!

— While thus I mused, night gently ran
Down over hill and wood.
Then, still and sudden, Obermann
On the grass near me stood.   60

Those pensive features well I knew,
On my mind, years before,
Imaged so oft! imaged so true!
— A shepherd's garb he wore,

A mountain-flower was in his hand,   65
A book was in his breast.
Bent on my face, with gaze which scann'd
My soul, his eyes did rest.

'And is it thou,' he cried, 'so long
Held by the world which we   70
Loved not, who turnest from the throng
Back to thy youth and me?

'And from thy world, with heart opprest,
Choosest thou *now* to turn? —
Ah me! we anchorites read things best,   75
Clearest their course discern!

'Thou fledst me when the ungenial earth,
Man's work-place, lay in gloom.
Return'st thou in her hour of birth,
Of hopes and hearts in bloom?   80

'Perceiv'st thou not the change of day?
  Ah! Carry back thy ken,
What, some two thousand years! Survey
The world as it was then!

'Like ours it look'd in outward air.   85
Its head was clear and true,
Sumptuous its clothing, rich its fare,
No pause its action knew;

'Stout was its arm, each thew and bone
Seem'd puissant and alive —   90
But, ah! its heart, its heart was stone,
And so it could not thrive!

'On that hard Pagan world disgust
And secret loathing fell.
Deep weariness and sated lust   95
Made human life a hell.

'In his cool hall, with haggard eyes,
The Roman noble lay;
He drove abroad, in furious guise,
Along the Appian way.   100

'He made a feast, drank fierce and fast,
And crown'd his hair with flowers —
No easier nor no quicker pass'd
The impracticable hours.

'The brooding East with awe beheld   105
Her impious younger world.
The Roman tempest swell'd and swell'd,
And on her head was hurl'd.

'The East bow'd low before the blast
In patient, deep disdain;   110
She let the legions thunder past,
And plunged in thought again.

'So well she mused, a morning broke
Across her spirit grey;
A conquering, new-born joy awoke,   115
And fill'd her life with day.

' "Poor world," she cried, "so deep accurst,
That runn'st from pole to pole
To seek a draught to slake thy thirst –
Go, seek it in thy soul!"   120

'She heard it, the victorious West,
In crown and sword array'd!
She felt the void which mined her breast,
She shiver'd and obey'd.

'She veil'd her eagles, snapp'd her sword,   125
And laid her sceptre down;
Her stately purple she abhorr'd,
And her imperial crown.

'She broke her flutes, she stopp'd her sports,
Her artists could not please;   130
She tore her books, she shut her courts,
She fled her palaces;

'Lust of the eye and pride of life
She left it all behind,
And hurried, torn with inward strife,   135
The wilderness to find.

'Tears wash'd the trouble from her face!
She changed into a child!
'Mid weeds and wrecks she stood – a place
Of ruin – but she smiled!   140

'Oh, had I lived in that great day,
How had its glory new
Fill'd earth and heaven, and caught away
My ravish'd spirit too!

'No thoughts that to the world belong   145
Had stood against the wave
Of love which set so deep and strong
From Christ's then open grave.

'No cloister-floor of humid stone
Had been too cold for me.   150
For me no Eastern desert lone
Had been too far to flee.

'No lonely life had pass'd too slow,
When I could hourly scan
Upon his Cross, with head sunk low,   155
That nail'd, thorn-crowned Man!

'Could see the Mother with her Child
Whose tender winning arts
Have to his little arms beguiled
So many wounded hearts!   160

'And centuries came and ran their course,
And unspent all that time
Still, still went forth that Child's dear force,
And still was at its prime.

'Ay, ages long endured his span   165
Of life – 'tis true received –
That gracious Child, that thorn-crown'd Man!
– He lived while we believed.

'While we believed, on earth he went,
And open stood his grave.   170
Men call'd from chamber, church, and tent;
And Christ was by to save.

'Now he is dead! Far hence he lies
In the lorn Syrian town;
And on his grave, with shining eyes,   175
The Syrian stars look down.

'In vain men still, with hoping new,
Regard his death-place dumb,
And say the stone is not yet to,
And wait for words to come.   180

'Ah, o'er that silent sacred land,
Of sun, and arid stone,
And crumbling wall, and sultry sand,
Sounds now one word alone!

'Unduped of fancy, henceforth man   185
Must labour! — must resign
His all too human creeds, and scan
Simply the way divine!

'But slow that tide of common thought,
Which bathed our life, retired;   190
Slow, slow the old world wore to nought,
And pulse by pulse expired.

'Its frame yet stood without a breach
When blood and warmth were fled;
And still it spake its wonted speech —   195
But every word was dead.

'And oh, we cried, that on this corse
Might fall a freshening storm!
Rive its dry bones, and with new force
A new-sprung world inform!   200

' — Down came the storm! O'er France it pass'd
In sheets of scathing fire;
All Europe felt that fiery blast,
And shook as it rush'd by her.

'Down came the storm! In ruins fell   205
The worn-out world we knew.
    It pass'd, that elemental swell!
Again appear'd the blue;

'The sun shone in the new-wash'd sky,
And what from heaven saw he?   210
Blocks of the past, like icebergs high,
Float on a rolling sea!

'Upon them plies the race of man
All it before endeavour'd;
"Ye live," I cried, "ye work and plan,   215
And know not ye are sever'd!

' "Poor fragments of a broken world
Whereon men pitch their tent!
Why were ye too to death not hurl'd
When your world's day was spent?   220

' "That glow of central fire is done
Which with its fusing flame
Knit all your parts, and kept you one –
But ye, ye are the same!

' "The past, its mask of union on,   225
Had ceased to live and thrive.
The past, its mask of union gone,
Say, is it more alive?

' "Your creeds are dead, your rites are dead,
Your social order too!   230
Where tarries he, the Power who said:
See, I make all things new?

' "The millions suffer still, and grieve,
And what can helpers heal
With old-world cures men half believe   235
For woes they wholly feel?

' "And yet men have such need of joy!
But joy whose grounds are true;
And joy that should all hearts employ
As when the past was new.   240

‘ "Ah, not the emotion of that past,
Its common hope, were vain!
Some new such hope must dawn at last,
Or man must toss in pain.

‘ "But now the old is out of date,   245
The new is not yet born,
And who can be *alone* elate,
While the world lies forlorn?"

'Then to the wilderness I fled. —
There among Alpine snows   250
And pastoral huts I hid my head,
And sought and found repose.

'It was not yet the appointed hour.
Sad, patient, and resign'd,
I watch'd the crocus fade and flower,   255
I felt the sun and wind.

'The day I lived in was not mine,
Man gets no second day.
In dreams I saw the future shine —
But ah! I could not stay!   260

'Action I had not, followers, fame;
I pass'd obscure, alone.
The after-world forgets my name,
Nor do I wish it known.

'Composed to bear, I lived and died,   265
And knew my life was vain,
With fate I murmur not, nor chide,
At Sèvres by the Seine

'(If Paris that brief flight allow)
My humble tomb explore!   270
It bears: *Eternity, be thou
My refuge!* and no more.

'But thou, whom fellowship of mood
Did make from haunts of strife
Come to my mountain-solitude,   275
And learn my frustrate life;

'O thou, who, ere thy flying span
Was past of cheerful youth,
Didst find the solitary man
And love his cheerless truth –   280

'Despair not thou as I despair'd,
Nor be cold gloom thy prison!
Forward the gracious hours have fared,
And see! the sun is risen!

'He breaks the winter of the past;   285
A green, new earth appears.
Millions, whose life in ice lay fast,
Have thoughts, and smiles, and tears.

'What though there still need effort, strife?
Though much be still unwon?   290
Yet warm it mounts, the hour of life!
Death's frozen hour is done!

'The world's great order dawns in sheen,
After long darkness rude,
Divinelier imaged, clearer seen,   295
With happier zeal pursued.

'With hope extinct and brow composed
I mark'd the present die;
Its term of life was nearly closed,
Yet it had more than I.   300

'But thou, though to the world's new hour
Thou come with aspect marr'd,
Shorn of the joy, the bloom, the power
Which best befits its bard –

'Though more than half thy years be past,   305
And spent thy youthful prime;
Though, round thy firmer manhood cast,
Hang weeds of our sad time

'Whereof thy youth felt all the spell,
And traversed all the shade —   310
Though late, though dimm'd, though weak, yet tell
Hope to a world new-made!

'Help it to fill that deep desire,
The want which rack'd our brain,
Consumed our heart with thirst like fire,   315
Immedicable pain;

'Which to the wilderness drove out
Our life, to Alpine snow,
And palsied all our word with doubt,
And all our work with woe —   320

'What still of strength is left, employ
That end to help attain:
One common wave of thought and joy
Lifting mankind again!'

— The vision ended. I awoke   325
As out of sleep, and no
Voice moved; — only the torrent broke
The silence, far below.

Soft darkness on the turf did lie.
Solemn, o'er hut and wood,   330
In the yet star-sown nightly sky,
The peak of Jaman stood.

Still in my soul the voice I heard
Of Obermann! — — away
I turned; by some vague impulse stirr'd,   335
Along the rocks of Naye

Past Sonchaud's piny flanks I gaze
And the blanch'd summit bare
Of Malatrait, to where in haze
The Valais opens fair,   340

And the domed Velan, with his snows,
Behind the upcrowding hills,
Doth all the heavenly opening close
Which the Rhone's murmur fills; —

And glorious there, without a sound,   345
Across the glimmering lake,
High in the Valais-depth profound,
I saw the morning break.

PREFACE TO *POEMS*
(1853)

In two small volumes of Poems, published anonymously, one in 1849, the other in 1852, many of the poems which compose the present volume have already appeared. The rest are now published for the first time.

I have, in the present collection, omitted the poem from which the volume published in 1852 took its title. I have done so, not because the subject of it was a Sicilian Greek born between two and three thousand years ago, although many persons would think this a sufficient reason. Neither have I done so because I had, in my own opinion, failed in the delineation which I intended to effect. I intended to delineate the feelings of one of the last of the Greek religious philosophers, one of the family of Orpheus and Musaeus, having survived his fellows, living on into a time when the habits of Greek thought and feeling had begun fast to change, character to dwindle, the influence of the Sophists to prevail. Into the feelings of a man so situated there entered much that we are accustomed to consider as exclusively modern; how much, the fragments of Empedocles himself which remain to us are sufficient at least to indicate. What those who are familiar only with the great monuments of early Greek genius suppose to be its exclusive characteristics, have disappeared; the calm, the cheerfulness, the disinterested objectivity have disappeared; the dialogue of the mind with itself has commenced; modern problems have presented themselves; we hear already the doubts, we witness the discouragement, of Hamlet and of Faust.

The representation of such a man's feelings must be interesting, if consistently drawn. We all naturally take pleasure, says Aristotle, in any imitation or representation whatever; this is the basis of our love of poetry; and we take pleasure in them, he adds, because all knowledge is naturally agreeable to us; not to the philosopher only, but to mankind at large. Every representation therefore which is consistently drawn may be supposed to be interesting, inasmuch as it gratifies this natural interest in knowledge of all kinds. What is *not* interesting, is that which does not add to our knowledge of any kind; that which is vaguely conceived and loosely drawn; a representation which is general, indeterminate, and faint, instead of being particular, precise, and firm.

Any accurate representation may therefore be expected to be interesting; but, if the representation be a poetical one, more than this is demanded. It is demanded, not only that it shall interest, but also that it shall inspirit and rejoice the reader; that it shall convey a charm, and infuse delight. For the Muses, as Hesiod says, were born that they might be 'a forgetfulness of evils, and a truce from cares': and it is not enough that the poet should add to the knowledge of men, it is required of him also that he should add to their happiness. 'All art,' says Schiller, 'is dedicated to Joy, and there is no higher and no more serious problem, than how to make men happy. The right art is that alone, which creates the highest enjoyment.'

A poetical work, therefore, is not yet justified when it has been shown to be an accurate, and therefore interesting representation; it has to be shown also that it is a representation from which men can derive enjoyment. In presence of the most tragic circumstances, represented in a work of Art, the feeling of enjoyment, as is well known, may still subsist; the representation of the most utter calamity, of the liveliest anguish, is not sufficient to destroy it; the more tragic the situation, the deeper becomes the enjoyment; and the situation is more tragic in proportion as it becomes more terrible.

What then are the situations, from the representation of which, though accurate, no poetical enjoyment can be derived? They are those in which the suffering finds no vent in action; in which a continuous state of mental distress is prolonged, unrelieved by incident, hope, or resistance; in which there is everything to be endured, nothing to be done. In such situations there is inevitably something morbid, in the description of them something monotonous. When they occur in actual life, they are painful, not tragic; the representation of them in poetry is painful also.

To this class of situations, poetically faulty as it appears to me, that of Empedocles, as I have endeavoured to represent him, belongs; and I have therefore excluded the poem from the present collection.

And why, it may be asked, have I entered into this explanation respecting a matter so unimportant as the admission or exclusion of the poem in question? I have done so, because I was anxious to avow that the sole reason for its exclusion was that which has been stated above; and that it has not been excluded in deference to the opinion which many critics of the present day appear to entertain against subjects chosen from distant times and countries: against the choice, in short, of any subjects but modern ones.

'The poet,' it is said,[1] and by an intelligent critic, 'the poet who would really fix the public attention must leave the exhausted past, and draw his subjects from matters of present import, and *therefore* both of interest and novelty.'

Now this view I believe to be completely false. It is worth examining, inasmuch as it is a fair sample of a class of critical dicta everywhere current at the present day, having a philosophical form and air, but no real basis in fact; and which are calculated to vitiate the judgement of readers of poetry, while they exert, so far as they are adopted, a misleading influence on the practice of those who write it.

What are the eternal objects of poetry, among all nations and at all times? They are actions; human actions; possessing an inherent interest in themselves, and which are to be communicated in an interesting manner by the art of the poet. Vainly will the latter imagine that he has everything in his own power; that he can make an intrinsically inferior action equally delightful with a more excellent one by his treatment of it; he may indeed compel us to admire his

---

[1] In *The Spectator* of April 2nd, 1853. The words quoted were not used with reference to poems of mine.

skill, but his work will possess, within itself, an incurable defect.

The poet, then, has in the first place to select an excellent action; and what actions are the most excellent? Those, certainly, which most powerfully appeal to the great primary human affections: to those elementary feelings which subsist permanently in the race, and which are independent of time. These feelings are permanent and the same; that which interests them is permanent and the same also. The modernness or antiquity of an action, therefore, has nothing to do with its fitness for poetical representation; this depends upon its inherent qualities. To the elementary part of our nature, to our passions, that which is great and passionate is eternally interesting; and interesting solely in proportion to its greatness and to its passion. A great human action of a thousand years ago is more interesting to it than a smaller human action of to-day, even though upon the representation of this last the most consummate skill may have been expended, and though it has the advantage of appealing by its modern language, familiar manners, and contemporary allusions, to all our transient feelings and interests. These, however, have no right to demand of a poetical work that it shall satisfy them; their claims are to be directed elsewhere. Poetical works belong to the domain of our permanent passions; let them interest these, and the voice of all subordinate claims upon them is at once silenced.

Achilles, Prometheus, Clytemnestra, Dido – what modern poem presents personages as interesting, even to us moderns, as these personages of an 'exhausted past'? We have the domestic epic dealing with the details of modern life which pass daily under our eyes; we have poems representing modern personages in contact with the problems of modern life, moral, intellectual, and social; these works have been produced by poets the most distinguished of their nation and time; yet I fearlessly assert that Hermann and Dorothea, Childe Harold, Jocelyn, The Excursion, leave the reader cold in comparison with the effect produced upon him by the latter books of the Iliad, by the Oresteia, or by the episode of Dido.

And why is this? Simply because in the three last-named cases the action is greater, the personages nobler, the situations more intense: and this is the true basis of the interest in a poetical work, and this alone.

It may be urged, however, that past actions may be interesting in themselves, but that they are not to be adopted by the modern poet, because it is impossible for him to have them clearly present to his own mind, and he cannot therefore feel them deeply, nor represent them forcibly. But this is not necessarily the case. The externals of a past action, indeed, he cannot know with the precision of a contemporary; but his business is with its essentials. The outward man of Oedipus or of Macbeth, the houses in which they lived, the ceremonies of their courts, he cannot accurately figure to himself; but neither do they essentially concern him. His business is with their inward man; with their feelings and behaviour in certain tragic situations, which engage their passions as men; these have in them nothing local and casual; they are as accessible to the modern poet as to a contemporary.

The date of an action, then, signifies nothing: the action itself, its selection and construction, this is what is all-important. This the Greeks understood far more clearly than we do. The radical difference between their poetical theory and ours consists, as it appears to me, in this: that, with them, the poetical character of the action in itself, and the conduct of it, was the first consideration; with us, attention is fixed mainly on the value of the separate thoughts and images which occur in the treatment of an action. They regarded the whole; we regard the parts. With them, the action pre-dominated over the expression of it; with us, the expression predominates over the action. Not that they failed in expression, or were inattentive to it; on the contrary, they are the highest models of expression, the unapproached masters of the *grand style*: but their expression is so excellent because it is so admirably kept in its right degree of prominence; because it is so simple and so well subordinated; because it draws its force directly from the pregnancy of the matter which it conveys. For what reason was the Greek tragic poet confined to so limited a range of subjects? Because there are so few actions which unite in themselves, in the highest degree, the conditions of excellence: and it was not thought that on any but an excellent subject could an excellent poem be constructed. A few actions, therefore, eminently adapted for tragedy, maintained almost exclusive possession of the Greek tragic stage; their significance appeared inexhaustible; they were as permanent problems, perpetually offered to the genius of every fresh poet. This too is the reason of what appears to us moderns a certain baldness of expression in Greek tragedy; of the triviality with which we often reproach the remarks of the chorus, where it takes part in the dialogue: that the action itself, the situation of Orestes, or Merope, or Alcmaeon, was to stand the central point of interest, unforgotten, absorbing, principal; that no accessories were for a moment to distract the spectator's attention from this; that the tone of the parts was to be perpetually kept down, in order not to impair the grandiose effect of the whole. The terrible old mythic story on which the drama was founded stood, before he entered the theatre, traced in its bare outlines upon the spectator's mind; it stood in his memory, as a group of statuary, faintly seen, at the end of a long and dark vista: then came the poet, embodying outlines, developing situations, not a word wasted, not a sentiment capriciously thrown in: stroke upon stroke, the drama proceeded: the light deepened upon the group; more and more it revealed itself to the rivetted gaze of the spectator: until at last, when the final words were spoken, it stood before him in broad sunlight, a model of immortal beauty.

This was what a Greek critic demanded; this was what a Greek poet endeavoured to effect. It signified nothing to what time an action belonged; we do not find that the Persae occupied a particularly high rank among the dramas of Aeschylus, because it represented a matter of contemporary interest: this was not what a cultivated Athenian required; he required that the permanent elements of his nature should be moved; and dramas of which the action, though taken from a long-distant mythic time, yet was calculated to accomplish this in a higher degree than that of the Persae, stood higher in his estimation accordingly. The Greeks felt, no doubt, with their exquisite sagacity of taste, that an action of present times was too near them, too much mixed up with what was accidental and passing, to form a sufficiently grand, detached, and self-subsistent object for a tragic poem: such objects belonged to the domain of the comic poet, and of the lighter kinds of poetry. For the more serious kinds, for *pragmatic* poetry, to use an excellent expression of Polybius, they were more difficult and severe in the range of subjects which they permitted. Their theory and practice alike, the admirable treatise of Aristotle, and the unrivalled works of their poets, exclaim with a thousand tongues – 'All depends upon the subject; choose a fitting action, penetrate yourself with the feeling of its situations; this done, everything else will follow.'

But for all kinds of poetry alike there was one point on which they were rigidly exacting; the adaptability of the subject to the kind of poetry selected, and the careful construction of the poem.

How different a way of thinking from this is ours! We can hardly at the present day understand what Menander meant when he told a man who inquired as to the progress of his comedy that he had finished it, not having yet written a single line, because he had constructed the action of it in his mind. A modern critic would have assured him that the merit of his piece depended on the brilliant things which arose under his pen as he went along. We have poems which seem to exist merely for the sake of single lines and passages; not for the sake of producing any total-impression. We have critics who seem to direct their attention merely to detached expressions, to the language about the action, not to the action itself. I verily think that the majority of them do not in their hearts believe that there is such a thing as a total-impression to be derived from a poem at all, or to be demanded from a poet; they think the term a common-place of metaphysical criticism. They will permit the poet to select any action he pleases, and to suffer that action to go as it will, provided he gratifies them with occasional bursts of fine writing, and with a shower of isolated thoughts and images. That is, they permit him to leave their poetical sense ungratified, provided that he gratifies their rhetorical sense and their curiosity. Of his neglecting to gratify these, there is little danger. He needs rather to be warned against the danger of attempting to gratify these alone; he needs rather to be perpetually reminded to prefer his action to everything else; so to treat this, as to permit its inherent excellences to develop themselves, without interruption from the intrusion of his personal peculiarities; most fortunate, when he most entirely succeeds in effacing himself, and in enabling a noble action to subsist as it did in nature.

But the modern critic not only permits a false practice; he absolutely prescribes false aims. – 'A true allegory of the state of one's own mind in a representative history,' the poet is told, 'is perhaps the highest thing that one can attempt in the way of poetry.' – And accordingly he attempts it. An allegory of the state of one's own mind, the highest problem of an art which imitates actions! No assuredly, it is not, it never can be so: no great poetical work has ever been produced with such an aim. Faust itself, in which something of the kind is attempted, wonderful passages as it contains, and in spite of the unsurpassed beauty of the scenes which relate to Margaret, Faust itself, judged as a whole, and judged strictly as a poetical work, is defective: its illustrious author, the greatest poet of modern times, the greatest critic of all times, would have been the first to acknowledge it; he only defended his work, indeed, by asserting it to be 'something incommensurable.'

The confusion of the present times is great, the multitude of voices counselling different things bewildering, the number of existing works capable of attracting a young writer's attention and of becoming his models, immense. What he wants is a hand to guide him through the confusion, a voice to prescribe to him the aim which he should keep in view, and to explain to him that the value of the literary works which offer themselves to his attention is relative to their power of helping him forward on his road towards this aim. Such a guide the English writer at the present day will nowhere find. Failing this, all that can be looked for, all indeed that can be desired is, that his attention should be fixed on excellent models; that he may reproduce, at any rate, something of their excellence, by penetrating himself with their works and by catching their spirit, if he cannot be taught to produce what is excellent independently.

Foremost among these models for the English writer stands Shakespeare: a name the greatest perhaps of all poetical names; a name never to be mentioned without reverence. I will venture, however, to express a doubt, whether the influence of his works, excellent and fruitful for the readers of poetry, for the great majority, has been of unmixed advantage to the writers of it. Shakespeare indeed chose excellent subjects; the world could afford no better than Macbeth, or Romeo and Juliet, or Othello: he had no theory respecting the necessity of choosing subjects of present import, or the paramount interest attaching to allegories of the state of one's own mind; like all great poets, he knew well what constituted a poetical action; like them, wherever he found such an action, he took it; like them, too, he found his best in past times. But to these general characteristics of all great poets he added a special one of his own; a gift, namely, of happy, abundant, and ingenious expression, eminent and unrivalled: so eminent as irresistibly to strike the attention first in him, and even to throw into comparative shade his other excellences as a poet. Here has been the mischief. These other excellences were his fundamental excellences *as a poet*; what distinguishes the artist from the mere amateur, says Goethe, is *Architectonicè* in the highest sense; that power of execution, which creates, forms, and constitutes: not the profoundness of single thoughts, not the richness of imagery, not the abundance of illustration. But these attractive accessories of a poetical work being more easily seized than the spirit of the whole, and these accessories being possessed by Shakespeare in an unequalled degree, a young writer having recourse to Shakespeare as his model runs great risk of being vanquished and absorbed by them, and, in consequence, of reproducing, according to the measure of his power, these, and these alone. Of this preponderating quality of Shakespeare's genius, accordingly, almost the whole of modern English poetry has, it appears to me, felt the influence. To the exclusive attention on the part of his imitators to this it is in a great degree owing, that of the majority of modern poetical works the details alone are valuable, the composition worthless. In reading them one is perpetually reminded of that terrible sentence on a modern French poet: – *Il dit tout ce qu'il veut, mais malheureusement il n'a rien à dire.*

Let me give an instance of what I mean. I will take it from the works of the very chief among those who seem to have been formed in the school of Shakespeare: of one whose exquisite genius and pathetic death render him for ever interesting. I will take the poem of Isabella, or the Pot of Basil, by Keats. I choose this rather than the Endymion, because the latter work (which a modern critic has classed with the Fairy Queen!), although undoubtedly there blows through it the breath of genius, is yet as a whole so utterly incoherent, as not strictly to merit the name of a poem at all. The poem of Isabella, then, is a perfect treasure-house of graceful and felicitous words and images: almost in every stanza there occurs one of those vivid and picturesque turns of expression, by which the object is made to flash upon the eye of the mind, and which thrill the reader with a sudden delight. This one short poem contains, perhaps, a greater number of happy single expressions which one could quote than all the extant tragedies of Sophocles. But the action, the story? The action in itself is an excellent one; but so feebly is it conceived by the poet, so loosely constructed, that the effect produced by it, in and for itself, is absolutely null. Let the reader, after he has finished the poem of Keats, turn to the same story in the Decameron: he will then feel how pregnant and interesting the same action has become in the hands of a great artist, who above all things delineates his object; who subordinates expression to that which it is designed to express.

I have said that the imitators of Shakespeare, fixing their attention on his wonderful gift of expression, have directed their imitation to this, neglecting his other excellences. These excellences, the fundamental excellences of poetical art, Shakespeare no doubt possessed them — possessed many of them in a splendid degree; but it may perhaps be doubted whether even he himself did not sometimes give scope to his faculty of expression to the prejudice of a higher poetical duty. For we must never forget that Shakespeare is the great poet he is from his skill in discerning and firmly conceiving an excellent action, from his power of intensely feeling a situation, of intimately associating himself with a character; not from his gift of expression, which rather even leads him astray, degenerating sometimes into a fondness for curiosity of expression, into an irritability of fancy, which seems to make it impossible for him to say a thing plainly, even when the press of the action demands the very directest language, or its level character the very simplest. Mr. Hallam, than whom it is impossible to find a saner and more judicious critic, has had the courage (for at the present day it needs courage) to remark, how extremely and faultily difficult Shakespeare's language often is. It is so: you may find main scenes in some of his greatest tragedies, King *Lear* for instance, where the language is so artificial, so curiously tortured, and so difficult, that every speech has to be read two or three times before its meaning can be comprehended. This over-curiousness of expression is indeed but the excessive employment of a wonderful gift, — of the power of saying a thing in a happier way than any other man; nevertheless, it is carried so far that one understands what M. Guizot meant, when he said that Shakespeare appears in his language to have tried all styles except that of simplicity. He has not the severe and scrupulous self-restraint of the ancients, partly no doubt, because he had a far less cultivated and exacting audience. He has indeed a far wider range than they had, a far richer fertility of thought; in this respect he rises above them. In his strong conception of his subject, in the genuine way in which he is penetrated with it, he resembles them, and is unlike the moderns. But in the accurate limitation of it, the conscientious rejection of superfluities, the simple and rigorous development of it from the first line of his work to the last, he falls below them, and comes nearer to the moderns. In his chief works, besides what he has of his own, he has the elementary soundness of the ancients; he has their important action and their large and broad manner; but he has not their purity of method. He is therefore a less safe model; for what he has of his own is personal, and inseparable from his own rich nature; it may be imitated and exaggerated, it cannot be learned or applied as an art. He is above all suggestive; more valuable, therefore, to young writers as men than as artists. But clearness of arrangement, rigour of development, simplicity of style – these may to a certain extent be learned; and these may, I am convinced, be learned best from the ancients, who although infinitely less suggestive than Shakespeare, are thus, to the artist, more instructive.

What, then, it will be asked, are the ancients to be our sole models? the ancients with their comparatively narrow range of experience, and their widely different circumstances? Not, certainly, that which is narrow in the ancients, nor that in which we can no longer sympathise. An action like the action of the Antigone of Sophocles, which turns upon the conflict between the heroine's duty to her brother's corpse and that to the laws of her country, is no longer one in which it is possible that we should feel a deep interest. I am speaking too, it will be remembered, not of the best sources of intellectual stimulus for the general reader, but of the best models of instruction for the individual writer. This last may certainly learn of the ancients, better than anywhere else, three things which it is vitally important for him to know: – the all-importance of the choice of a subject; the necessity of accurate construction; and the subordinate character of expression. He will learn from them how unspeakably superior is the effect of the one moral impression left by a great action treated as a whole, to the effect produced by the most striking single thought or by the happiest image. As he penetrates into the spirit of the great classical works, as he becomes gradually aware of their intense significance, their noble simplicity, and their calm pathos, he will be convinced that it is this effect, unity and profoundness of moral impression, at which the ancient poets aimed; that it is this which constitutes the grandeur of their works, and which makes them immortal. He will desire to direct his own efforts towards producing the same effect. Above all, he will deliver himself from the jargon of modern criticism, and escape the danger of producing poetical works conceived in the spirit of the passing time, and which partake of its transitoriness.

The present age makes great claims upon us; we owe it service, it will not be satisfied without our admiration. I know not how it is, but their commerce with the ancients appears to me to produce, in those who constantly practise it, a steadying and composing effect upon their judgement, not of literary works only, but of men and events in general. They are like persons who have had a very weighty and impressive experience; they are more truly than others under the empire of facts, and more independent of the language current among those with whom they live. They wish neither to applaud nor to revile their age; they wish to know what it is, what it can give them, and whether this is what they want. What they want, they know very well; they want to educe and cultivate what is best and noblest in themselves; they know, too, that this is no easy task – χαλεπὸν, as Pittacus said, χαλεπὸν ἐσθλὸν ἔμμεναι – and they ask themselves sincerely whether their age and its literature can assist them in the attempt. If they are endeavouring to practise any art, they remember the plain and simple proceedings of the old artists, who attained their grand results by penetrating themselves with some noble and significant action, not by inflating themselves with a belief in the pre-eminent importance and greatness of their own times. They do not talk of their mission, nor of interpreting their age, nor of the coming poet; all this, they know, is the mere delirium of vanity; their business is not to praise their age, but to afford to the men who live in it the highest pleasure which they are capable of feeling. If asked to afford this by means of subjects drawn from the age itself, they ask what special fitness the present age has for supplying them. They are told that it is an era of progress, an age commissioned to carry out the great ideas of industrial development and social amelioration. They reply that with all this they can do nothing; that the elements they need for the exercise of their art are great actions, calculated powerfully and delightfully to affect what is permanent in the human soul; that so far as the present age can supply such actions, they will gladly make use of them; but that an age wanting in moral grandeur can with difficulty supply such, and an age of spiritual discomfort with difficulty be powerfully and delightfully affected by them.

A host of voices will indignantly rejoin that the present age is inferior to the past neither in moral grandeur nor in spiritual health. He who possesses the discipline I speak of will content himself with remembering the judgements passed upon the present age, in this respect, by the two men, the one of strongest head, the other of widest culture, whom it has produced; by Goethe and by Niebuhr. It will be sufficient for him that he knows the opinions held by these two great men respecting the present age and its literature; and that he feels assured in his own mind that their aims and demands upon life were such as he would wish, at any rate, his own to be; and their judgement as to what is impeding and disabling such as he may safely follow. He will not, however, maintain a hostile attitude towards the false pretensions of his age: he will content himself with not being overwhelmed by them. He will esteem himself fortunate if he can succeed in banishing from his mind all feelings of contradiction, and irritation, and impatience; in order to delight himself with the contemplation of some noble action of a heroic time, and to enable others, through his representation of it, to delight in it also.

I am far indeed from making any claim, for myself, that I

possess this discipline; or for the following poems, that they breathe its spirit. But I say, that in the sincere endeavour to learn and practise, amid the bewildering confusion of our times, what is sound and true in poetical art, I seemed to myself to find the only sure guidance, the only solid footing, among the ancients. They, at any rate, knew what they wanted in art, and we do not. It is this uncertainty which is disheartening, and not hostile criticism. How often have I felt this when reading words of disparagement or of cavil: that it is the uncertainty as to what is really to be aimed at which makes our difficulty, not the dissatisfaction of the critic, who himself suffers from the same uncertainty. *Non me tua fervida terrent Dicta; . . . Dii me terrent, et Jupiter hostis.*

Two kinds of *dilettanti*, says Goethe, there are in poetry: he who neglects the indispensable mechanical part, and thinks he has done enough if he shows spirituality and feeling; and he who seeks to arrive at poetry merely by mechanism, in which he can acquire an artisan's readiness, and is without soul and matter. And he adds, that the first does most harm to art, and the last to himself. If we must be *dilettanti*: if it is impossible for us, under the circumstances amidst which we live, to think clearly, to feel nobly, and to delineate firmly: if we cannot attain to the mastery of the great artists; — let us, at least, have so much respect for our art as to prefer it to ourselves. Let us not bewilder our successors; let us transmit to them the practice of poetry, with its boundaries and wholesome regulative laws, under which excellent works may again, perhaps, at some future time, be produced, not yet fallen into oblivion through our neglect, not yet condemned and cancelled by the influence of their eternal enemy, caprice.

PREFACE
TO THE SECOND EDITION
(1854)

I HAVE allowed the Preface to the former edition of these
Poems to stand almost without change, because I still believe
it to be, in the main, true. I must not, however, be supposed
insensible to the force of much that has been alleged against
portions of it, or unaware that it contains many things
incompletely stated, many things which need limitation. It
leaves, too, untouched the question, how far, and in what
manner, the opinions there expressed respecting the choice
of subjects apply to lyric poetry; that region of the poetical
field which is chiefly cultivated at present. But neither have
I time now to supply these deficiencies, nor is this the proper
place for attempting it. On one or two points alone I wish to
offer, in the briefest possible way, some explanation.

An objection has been ably urged to the classing together,
as subjects equally belonging to a past time, Oedipus and
Macbeth. And it is no doubt true that to Shakespeare,
standing on the verge of the middle ages, the epoch of
Macbeth was more familiar than that of Oedipus. But I was
speaking of actions as they presented themselves to us
moderns: and it will hardly be said that the European mind,
since Voltaire, has much more affinity with the times of
Macbeth than with those of Oedipus. As moderns, it seems
to me, we have no longer any direct affinity with the circum-
stances and feelings of either. As individuals, we are attracted
towards this or that personage, we have a capacity for
imagining him, irrespective of his times, solely according to
a law of personal sympathy; and those subjects for which
we feel this personal attraction most strongly, we may hope
to treat successfully. Prometheus or Joan of Arc, Charlemagne
or Agamemnon – one of these is not really nearer to us now
than another; each can be made present only by an act of

poetic imagination; but this man's imagination has an affinity for one of them, and that man's for another.

It has been said that I wish to limit the poet in his choice of subjects to the period of Greek and Roman antiquity; but it is not so. I only counsel him to choose for his subjects great actions, without regarding to what time they belong. Nor do I deny that the poetic faculty can and does manifest itself in treating the most trifling action, the most hopeless subject. But it is a pity that power should be wasted; and that the poet should be compelled to impart interest and force to his subject, instead of receiving them from it, and thereby doubling his impressiveness. There is, it has been excellently said, an immortal strength in the stories of great actions; the most gifted poet, then, may well be glad to supplement with it that mortal weakness, which, in presence of the vast spectacle of life and the world, he must for ever feel to be his individual portion.

Again, with respect to the study of the classical writers of antiquity; it has been said that we should emulate rather than imitate them. I make no objection; all I say is, let us study them. They can help to cure us of what is, it seems to me, the great vice of our intellect, manifesting itself in our incredible vagaries in literature, in art, in religion, in morals: namely, that it is *fantastic*, and wants *sanity*. Sanity – that is the great virtue of the ancient literature: the want of that is the great defect of the modern, in spite of all its variety and power. It is impossible to read carefully the great ancients, without losing something of our caprice and eccentricity; and to emulate them we must at least read them.

NOTES BY THE AUTHOR

[THE notes are in the order needed for this selection. The slight changes made necessary in two notes have been indicated.]

NOTE 1, PAGE 41

And that curst treachery on the Mount of Gore

Mount Hæmus, so called, said the legend, from Typho's blood spilt on it in his last battle with Zeus, when the giant's strength failed, owing to the Destinies having a short time before given treacherously to him, for his refreshment, perishable fruits. See APOLLODORUS, *Bibliotheca*, book i, chap. vi.

NOTE 2, PAGE 47

Ye Sun-born Virgins! on the road of truth

See the Fragments of Parmenides:

$$
\text{. . . } κοῦραι \ δ' \ ὁδὸν \ ἡγεμόνευον,
$$
$$
ἡλίαδες \ κοῦραι, \ προλιποῦσαι \ δώματα \ νυκτός,
$$
$$
εἰς \ φάος \text{ . . . . .}
$$

NOTE 3, PAGE 68

Mycerinus

'After Chephren, Mycerinus, son of Cheops, reigned over Egypt. He abhorred his father's courses, and judged his subjects more justly than any of their kings had done. – To him there came an oracle from the city of Buto, to the effect that he was to live but six years longer, and to die in the seventh year from that time.' – HERODOTUS.

NOTE 4, PAGE 72

Tristram and Iseult

'In the court of his uncle King Marc, the king of Cornwall, who at this time resided at the castle of Tyntagel, Tristram became expert in all knightly exercises. – The king of Ireland, at Tristram's solicitations, promised to bestow his daughter Iseult in marriage on King Marc. The mother of Iseult gave to her daughter's confidante a philtre, or love-potion, to be administered on the night of her nuptials. Of this beverage Tristram and Iseult, on their voyage to Cornwall, unfortunately partook. Its influence, during the remainder of their lives, regulated the affections and destiny of the lovers. –

'After the arrival of Tristram and Iseult in Cornwall, and the nuptials of the latter with King Marc, a great part of the romance is occupied with their contrivances to procure secret interviews. – Tristram, being forced to leave Cornwall, on account of the displeasure of his uncle, repaired to Brittany, where lived Iseult with the White Hands. – He married her – more out of gratitude than love. – Afterwards he proceeded to the dominions of Arthur, which became the theatre of unnumbered exploits.

'Tristram, subsequent to these events, returned to Brittany, and to his long-neglected wife. There, being wounded and sick, he was soon reduced to the lowest ebb. In this situation, he despatched a confidant to the queen of Cornwall, to try if he could induce her to follow him to Brittany, etc.' – DUNLOP's *History of Fiction*.

NOTE 5, PAGE 96

Sohrab and Rustum

The story of Sohrab and Rustum is told in Sir John Malcolm's *History of Persia*, as follows: –

'The young Sohrab was the fruit of one of Rustum's early amours. He had left his mother, and sought fame under the banners of Afrasiab, whose armies he commanded, and soon obtained a renown beyond that of all contemporary heroes but his father. He had carried death and dismay into the ranks of the Persians, and had terrified the boldest warriors of that country, before Rustum encountered him, which at last that hero resolved to do, under a feigned name. They met three times. The first time they parted by mutual consent, though Sohrab had the advantage; the second, the youth obtained a victory, but granted life to his unknown father; the third was fatal to Sohrab, who, when writhing in the pangs of death, warned his conqueror to shun the vengeance that is inspired by parental woes, and bade him dread the rage of the mighty Rustum, who must soon learn that he had slain his son Sohrab. These words, we are told, were as death to the aged hero; and when he recovered from a trance, he called in despair for proofs of what Sohrab had said. The afflicted and dying youth tore open his mail, and showed his father a seal which his mother had placed on his arm when she discovered to him the secret of his birth, and bade him seek his father. The sight of his own signet rendered Rustum quite frantic; he cursed himself, attempting to put an end to his existence, and was only prevented by the efforts of his expiring son. After Sohrab's death, he burnt his tents and all his goods, and carried the corpse to Seistan, where it was interred; the army of Turan was, agreeably to the last request of Sohrab, permitted to cross the Oxus unmolested. To reconcile us to the improbability of this tale, we are informed that Rustum could have no idea his son was in existence. The mother of Sohrab had written to him her child was a daughter, fearing to lose her darling infant if she revealed the truth; and Rustum, as before stated, fought under a feigned name, an usage not uncommon in the chivalrous combats of those days.'

NOTE 6, PAGE 129

My Marguerite smiles upon the strand

See . . . the poem called *A Memory-Picture*.

NOTE 7, PAGE 154

That wayside inn we left to-day

Those who have been long familiar with the English Lake-Country will find no difficulty in recalling, from the description in the text, the roadside inn at Wythburn on the descent from Dunmail Raise towards Keswick; its sedentary landlord of thirty years ago, and the passage over the Wythburn Fells to Watendlath.

[The note first appeared in this form in 1877.]

NOTE 8, PAGE 189

The author of *Obermann*, Étienne Pivert de Senancour, has little celebrity in France, his own country; and out of France he is almost unknown. But the profound inwardness, the austere sincerity, of his principal work, *Obermann*, the delicate feeling for nature which it exhibits, and the melancholy eloquence of many passages of it, have attracted and charmed some of the most remarkable spirits of this century, such as George Sand and Sainte-Beuve, and will probably always find a certain number of spirits whom they touch and interest.

Senancour was born in 1770. He was educated for the priesthood, and passed some time in the seminary of St. Sulpice; broke away from the Seminary and from France itself, and passed some years in Switzerland, where he married; returned to France in middle life, and followed thenceforward the career of a man of letters, but with hardly any fame or success. He died an old man in 1846, desiring that on his grave might be placed these words only: *Eternité, deviens mon asile!*

The influence of Rousseau, and certain affinities with more famous and fortunate authors of his own day, – Chateaubriand and Madame de Staël, – are everywhere visible in Senancour. But though, like these eminent personages, he may be called a sentimental writer, and though *Obermann,* a collection of letters from Switzerland treating almost entirely of nature and of the human soul, may be called a work of sentiment, Senancour has a gravity and severity which distinguish him from all other writers of the sentimental school. The world is with him in his solitude far less than it is with them; of all writers he is the most perfectly isolated and the least attitudinising. His chief work, too, has a value and power of its own, apart from these merits of its author. The stir of all the main forces, by which modern life is and has been impelled, lives in the letters of *Obermann;* the dissolving agencies of the eighteenth century; the fiery storm of the French Revolution, the first faint promise and dawn of that new world which our own time is but now more fully bringing to light, – all these are to be felt, almost to be touched, there. To me, indeed, it will always seem that the impressiveness of this production can hardly be rated too high.

Besides *Obermann* there is one other of Senancour's works which, for those spirits who feel his attraction, is very interesting; its title is, *Libres Méditations d'un Solitaire Inconnu.*

NOTE 9, PAGE 189

Behind are the abandon'd baths

The Baths of Leuk. This poem was conceived, and partly composed, in the valley going down from the foot of the Gemmi Pass towards the Rhone.

NOTES BY THE AUTHOR

The Scholar-Gipsy

'There was very lately a lad in the University of Oxford, who was by his poverty forced to leave his studies there; and at last to join himself to a company of vagabond gipsies. Among these extravagant people, by the insinuating subtilty of his carriage, he quickly got so much of their love and esteem as that they discovered to him their mystery. After he had been a pretty while exercised in the trade, there chanced to ride by a couple of scholars, who had formerly been of his acquaintance. They quickly spied out their old friend among the gipsies; and he gave them an account of the necessity which drove him to that kind of life, and told them that the people he went with were not such impostors as they were taken for, but that they had a traditional kind of learning among them, and could do wonders by the power of imagination, their fancy binding that of others: that himself had learned much of their art, and when he had compassed the whole secret, he intended, he said, to leave their company, and give the world an account of what he had learned.' – GLANVIL's *Vanity of Dogmatizing*, 1661.

NOTE 11, PAGE 217

Ah! where is he, who should have come

The author's brother, William Delafield Arnold, Director of Public Instruction in the Punjab, and author of *Oakfield, or Fellowship in the East*, died at Gibraltar on his way home from India, April the 9th, 1859.

NOTE 12, PAGE 218

So moonlit, saw me once of yore

See the poem, *A Summer Night*, p. 171.

NOTE 13, PAGE 218

My brother! and thine early lot

See Note 11.

NOTE 14, PAGE 222

Thyrsis

Throughout this poem there is reference to [another] piece, *The Scholar-Gipsy*.

NOTES BY THE AUTHOR

NOTE 15, PAGE 227

Young Daphnis with his silver voice doth sing

Daphnis, the ideal Sicilian shepherd of Greek pastoral poetry, was said to have followed into Phrygia his mistress Piplea, who had been carried off by robbers, and to have found her in the power of the king of Phrygia, Lityerses. Lityerses used to make strangers try a contest with him in reaping corn, and to put them to death if he overcame them. Hercules arrived in time to save Daphnis, took upon himself the reaping-contest with Lityerses, overcame him, and slew him. The Lityerses-song connected with this tradition was, like the Linus-song, one of the early plaintive strains of Greek popular poetry, and used to be sung by corn-reapers. Other traditions represented Daphnis as beloved by a nymph who exacted from him an oath to love no one else. He fell in love with a princess, and was struck blind by the jealous nymph. Mercury, who was his father, raised him to Heaven, and made a fountain spring up in the place from which he ascended. At this fountain the Sicilians offered yearly sacrifices. — See Servius, *Comment. in Virgil. Bucol.*, v. 20, and viii. 68.

NOTE 16, PAGE 229

Glion? – Ah, twenty years, it cuts

Probably all who know the Vevey end of the Lake of Geneva, will recollect Glion, the mountain-village above the castle of Chillon. Glion now has hotels, *pensions*, and villas; but twenty years ago it was hardly more than the huts of Avant opposite to it, – huts through which goes that beautiful path over the Col de Jaman, followed by so many foot-travellers on their way from Vevey to the Simmenthal and Thun.

[This note first appeared in 1868.]

NOTE 17, PAGE 230

The gentian-flower'd pass, its crown
With yellow spires aflame

The blossoms of the *Gentiana lutea*.

NOTE 18, PAGE 230

And walls where Byron came

Montbovon. See Byron's Journal, in his *Works*, vol. iii, p. 258. The river Saane becomes the Sarine below Montbovon.

INDEX OF FIRST LINES

MORE ABOUT PENGUINS, PELICANS AND PUFFINS

For further information about books available from Penguins please write to Dept EP, Penguin Books Ltd, Harmondsworth, Middlesex UB7 0DA.

In the U.S.A.: For a complete list of books available from Penguins in the United States write to Dept DG, Penguin Books, 299 Murray Hill Parkway, East Rutherford, New Jersey 07073.

In Canada: For a complete list of books available from Penguins in Canada write to Penguin Books Canada Ltd, 2801 John Street, Markham, Ontario L3R 1B4.

In Australia: For a complete list of books available from Penguins in Australia write to the Marketing Department, Penguin Books Australia Ltd, P.O. Box 257, Ringwood, Victoria 3134.

In New Zealand: For a complete list of books available from Penguins in New Zealand write to the Marketing Department, Penguin Books (N.Z.) Ltd, Private Bag, Takapuna, Auckland 9.

In India: For a complete list of books available from Penguins in India write to Penguin Overseas Ltd, 706 Eros Apartments, 56 Nehru Place, New Delhi 110019.

PLAYS IN PENGUINS

PENGUIN BOOKS OF POETRY

THE PENGUIN POETRY LIBRARY

These books should be available at all good bookshops or news-agents, but if you live in the UK or the Republic of Ireland and have difficulty in getting to a bookshop, they can be ordered by post. Please indicate the titles required and fill in the form below.

NAME _____ BLOCK CAPITALS

ADDRESS _____

_____

_____

Enclose a cheque or postal order payable to The Penguin Bookshop to cover the total price of books ordered, plus 50p for postage. Readers in the Republic of Ireland should send £IR equivalent to the sterling prices, plus 67p for postage. Send to: The Penguin Bookshop, 54/56 Bridlesmith Gate, Nottingham, NG1 2GP.

You can also order by phoning (0602) 599295, and quoting your Barclaycard or Access number.

Every effort is made to ensure the accuracy of the price and availability of books at the time of going to press, but it is sometimes necessary to increase prices and in these circumstances retail prices may be shown on the covers of books which may differ from the prices shown in this list or elsewhere. This list is not an offer to supply any book.

This order service is only available to residents in the UK and the Republic of Ireland.

● ● ●